THE
WATCHERS

A.M. SHINE writes in the Gothic horror tradition. Born in Galway, Ireland, he received his Master's Degree in History there before sharpening his quill and pursuing all things literary and macabre. His stories have won the Word Hut and Bookers Corner prizes and he is a member of the Irish Writers Centre. *The Watchers*, his debut novel, was critically acclaimed and has been made into a major motion picture.

Follow him on @AMShineWriter
www.amshinewriter.com

Also by A.M. Shine

The Watchers
The Creeper

THE
WATCHERS

A.M. SHINE

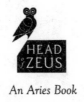

An Aries Book

First published in the UK in 2021 by Head of Zeus
This paperback edition published in the UK in 2024 by Head of Zeus,
part of Bloomsbury Publishing Plc

9 7 6 8

A catalogue record for this book is available from
the British Library.

ISBN (PB): 9781801102148
ISBN (E): 9781801102155

Typeset by Divaddict Publishing Solutions Ltd

Printed and bound in the U.S.A. by
Berryville Graphics Inc., Berryville, Virginia

Head of Zeus Ltd
5–8 Hardwick Street
London EC1R 4RG

WWW.HEADOFZEUS.COM

Prologue

John

The forest was dark on the brightest day. It was as though its ancient trees hid some terrible secret from the sun, and so weaved their branches together, casting a black gauze over the sky. The light broke through here and there in thin, hazy pillars but these were too rare to ever bring warmth. Any light was better than no light. It told John all that he needed to know, that there was still hope. There was every reason to keep on running. It was an unnatural place where the shadows never lifted, like a bleak lens forced over the eyes. He yearned for colour and light to guide his way, but amidst the trees there were neither. Hours had passed in that never-ending limbo, where John's every panicked breath was all that broke the silence. The end was still nowhere in sight. And those golden threads of light were beginning to fade.

He had left the shelter at daybreak, under the first cracks in the black above. John had rested for two days and nights, healing his muscles and conserving whatever he had left in his body to save all that he had left in life. So many failed attempts lay behind him. But he knew in his heart that he had been close. Just a few more feet. The man had drawn a compass in the earth, gauging its north as best he could from those rare fissures of sky. He had tested every direction, treating it like a clock, completing its cycle, combing the forest for some way out. But he could only run so far in order to make it back before nightfall. And it was never far enough. John retraced the markers he had left behind him, finding his way back to his wife's arms, sometimes with mere minutes of daylight to spare; always cutting it closer and closer.

In the time before, he used to bring presents home to his wife. Ciara always had a soft spot for surprises, no matter how silly, cheap or childish they might have been. There were the stuffed toys he picked up by the petrol station checkout. They now lived on the bed in their spare room, all glassy eyes set towards the window as Ciara thought they'd enjoy the view. Chocolates, flowers, even a punnet of plump strawberries bought off the side of the road; if John thought it would make his wife smile, then it was hers. And now, he returned to her, weary and defeated, and always empty-handed. He couldn't even give her false hope without the guilt of lying to her. They were never getting home. There was no way out. And he hadn't the heart to tell her.

John blamed himself. He never told Ciara this. He didn't think he had to. It was certainly nobody else's fault but his own, and he hardly had the strength to speak, never mind state the obvious. He had pushed the idea, even though he knew she would have preferred to stay home and laze about like she loved to on a Sunday, never stepping outside, as though for that one day in the week their new home was the whole world. She was like a child with her dream doll's house, still disbelieving that it was really hers. There wasn't a lone chair or lamp that she hadn't doted on. It was all she ever wanted, and just another thing she had lost.

Their last hot meal was an old-fashioned fry-up – John's one and only speciality – with fat slices of sourdough that looked crooked no matter how he cut them. He remembered it all so clearly. He had botched up the egg yolks again, not surprisingly. Ciara's fingers played a little drumroll on the table every time he stood up to the pan. The probability of good eggs hadn't improved since they met, but it added some excitement to their Sundays. He should have savoured every mouthful, but instead he ate as though breakfast was a daily given, never to be lost, as common as sunlight, fresh air and all those things taken for granted. He had been standing by the window over the kitchen sink, rinsing a mug long after it was clean, listening to its squeak under the warm water. The distant fields' long grasses were like eyelashes winking at him, shimmering under that summer blue.

That's when the notion of taking a Sunday drive seeded itself in his mind. John imagined it blooming into a perfect day; one that their shared memories would keep from ever wilting. If only he had known the horrors such seeds could grow.

Ciara was sunken in the corner of the couch, with her toes curled under her in those fleecy socks that were a Sunday staple. She was smiling like she used to when he peered around the door, humming to herself, flicking through the channels, most likely looking for a movie that he would enjoy. It was never about her. She would cuddle in under his arm, and he wouldn't know if her eyes were open or closed. That was their perfect Sunday, and for a long time it never changed. Not until John had to ruin everything.

'Come on,' he announced, slapping his hands, 'let's go on an adventure!'

She looked to him, lips lolling open, sharing that beautifully bemused expression she always did when he surprised her. Ciara's thumb ceased clicking. Her eyes glanced back at the television, almost sadly. She didn't want this. John knew that. Their day had found its natural rhythm like all those Sundays gone before it, and Ciara had mapped out the coming hours like a captain sailing a familiar sea. But she chose to play along, content to do whatever he wanted so long as they were together.

'Where will we go?' she asked, sitting forward, feigning the excitement that John eagerly lapped up like the real deal.

'Connemara,' he replied. 'It's so close to us, and we've only skirted around the main roads since we moved out here. Let's go deeper and see what we can find. Blue skies and hills, and sheep!'

'Sheep?'

'They're everywhere.' He laughed, casting his arms around him. 'There's nothing for miles but sheep.'

'Okay, handsome,' she said, peeling herself off the couch and plodding stiff-legged into his arms, 'I'll go wherever you want—' she stood up on her toes to kiss him '—and you had me at *sheep*.'

'There's nothing else out there,' he replied with a smile before planting a kiss on her forehead. 'You can pick out your favourite one and we'll bundle it in the back of the car.'

There, holding his wife in a home, not a prison of concrete and glass; that's the moment he could have saved them. John wished he had just held Ciara a little longer. If only he had asked her what she really wanted to do, not that he didn't already know. She had probably already picked out half a dozen movies for him. Ciara would read the blurbs aloud in her deepest theatrical voice and he would decide the winner. Maybe a better husband wouldn't have been so selfish. A day on the couch sure sounded good to him now.

John had to stop. He palmed the sweat from his face, gulping for air that seeped like mould into his lungs. The seasons held no sway over the woodland. An eternal coldness was trapped there, rising as mist by the deeper pits. It was a cemetery of trees whose black earth sank soft without need for rain, and the feeling of death and rot haunted it like the residue of some horrible dream. The stillness there was unnerving. John's clumsy steps were imitated from every angle, their dizzying echoes leading his senses astray. He had to keep his course. Ciara's life depended on him not losing his way.

But the forest's murky depths were wild and misleading. Like a maze of mirrors, it teased the eyes, goading John into doubting himself. Too many times he had stopped, comparing the path just travelled to what lay ahead, and marking no difference. He imagined a crow circling above the forest – if ever an animal was brave enough – watching John orbit the same claustrophobic tract of hell, lost like a rat in a maze.

He couldn't recall from what direction the car had come to stop at the forest's edge. Those serpentine roads had twisted and turned so often, moulting his bearings with every mile. If only he had followed the map like Ciara had wanted to. If only he had done a lot of things differently.

'It won't be an adventure if we know where we're going,' he had said, turning his head subtly to wink at her as she rooted through the glove compartment.

'Okay.' She'd giggled, sitting back like a child on a school bus, nervously excited about her first day. 'No maps! You had better make sure you remember how to get us home, okay?'

'Don't you worry, I promise to get you home in one piece.'

John had never broken a promise to his wife before. And at that moment in time, he thought he never would. They talked and laughed the entire way, admiring the sun-soaked world around them, following any road that took their fancy, opting in every case for the one less travelled, where the car bobbed side to side as though it sailed through a storm. Stone hills were marbled in light, and even the drabbest of meadow waved primaries like coloured ribbon. Soon there were no houses, no other cars, and not another sheep to be seen for miles. Eventually, even the birds grew scarcer. Wherever their adventure was taking them, it was a dead place that even the animals knew to avoid.

'Should we turn back?' Ciara had asked him, stifling a yawn.

'Let's just go on a little further,' he had replied, squeezing her thigh. 'There has to be something at the finish line.'

John had so many opportunities to prevent what was coming. But how could he have known? He had played out the memories of that drive so many times, like a movie reel on a loop. John pictured himself in the back seat, roaring at himself to stop, to turn around, to keep his wife safe from whatever the hell was in that woodland. But his past self couldn't hear him. The ignorant bastard just kept on driving.

After the car broke down, Ciara had wanted to wait it out. Somebody was bound to come that way eventually. But they had no phone battery and no clue as to where John had brought them. He had fidgeted with the engine, eyeing it up like a mechanic who genuinely knew what he was doing. But the truth was that he hadn't a clue. It was strange – even his wristwatch had stopped. Miles of lifeless road lay behind them, and without enough food or water, how long would they last? The nights were as dark as they were cold, and Ciara – despite her youth – was in no shape to make such a journey. John saw only one option, and she trusted him enough not to argue against it. They entered the woodland where the road faded to black earth and stone, and shadows sealed the way behind them like a trapdoor vanishing, never to be found again.

He had watched Ciara weaken over the months. Her tired eyes never opened for long, as though the air itself was an opiate, dulling and draining them. There was never enough food to feed all four mouths. Their appetites had swallowed themselves whole. Even the sensation of a blackberry slipping down the throat was nauseating. Water was divvied between them, leaving no thirst quenched. Ciara's skin, once so soft like white silk, became dry to the touch, and mottled with stains that she couldn't wipe clean. The toils of survival were ageing them with a cruel, unstoppable urgency.

A wiser man might have waited for the winter to pass. Its days were too short, and its dark nights too long. But the cold December had proven itself lethal. Sickness and injury were inevitable. Theirs was a slow death, and it broke his heart to watch his wife languish before his very eyes, wilting like a rose denied the sun.

He dreaded the thought of leaving Ciara alone with that woman. But she knew how to survive. She had long discarded the baggage of kindness and optimism, leaving only the essentials. These traits were Ciara's standards, and John sensed that the woman considered them a weakness. Somehow, his wife still smiled. Her green eyes still sparkled, with or without tears. At night, they would sit together. She would burrow into him and he would hold her close, caressing her hair until her breathing slowed to a restless sleep, just like they used to every Sunday; all those days cherished like a past never to be repeated.

The woodland was darkening, and still John forced his body through its snarled tangles of leaf and vine. His skin was torn. His palms bronzed from blood. There had to be a break soon. Those trees seemed to stretch around the world, growing faster than he could ever hope to outrun. Ciara would never have made it this far, John knew. He would happily trade his life for hers, if only fate would give him the option and stand true to its word. He kept on going. He wouldn't stop until those things found him, and of that there was no uncertain doubt. Deadwood cracked beneath his feet like brittle bones as he searched for any way out of that accursed place.

John had yet to see them. Even the woman who had been in the shelter when they happened upon it spun only vague riddles as to their appearance. She knew nothing, but her ignorance didn't disturb her like it did John. The woman was content to survive, to live a life with no future unlike the present, divested of the simplest joy and comfort.

She saw them all as burdens, the boy especially. John's gambit to find help was dismissed by her as suicide. Their pits are everywhere, she had said. Hidden across the forest floor and stretching far beyond it. And come nightfall, the door to their shelter was staying shut. They were the rules. That was how she had survived.

John fell to his knees; sapped of air and strength, head spinning, coloured freckles dancing across his vision, all the brighter in the last light of day as shadows flooded the forest, concealing the myriad roots that lined the earth like booby traps. His arms were crossed tight over his ribcage, trying to contain the pain that eviscerated every nervous fibre and tortured organ inside him. There was no end in sight. The darkness made quite sure of that. Any minute now, John imagined them swarming around their pits, waiting for the sun's fatal, final sliver to slip over the unseen horizon. What his mind conceived was influenced only by the sounds behind the mirror, where they watched them night after night for reasons unknown, as a child stares into a fishbowl, tapping its glass.

Suddenly, their shrieks filled the night. He was out of time. John had never heard them out in the open, far from the shelter whose concrete shell had kept them safe for all those months. He clawed his way forward, though now the darkness hid the way. Their voices were so close, so ear-splittingly loud that John expected them to fall upon him at any second. But how could that be? The shelter was a day's trek behind him. Had he become lost? Without daylight and a compass to hold his line, there was no knowing what wayward course had led him there, where the leaves now shivered from the thunder of their bodies, tracking his scent and all those footprints sunken into the black mud.

Those last nights, when John held his wife in his arms, he had dreamt of surprising her, not with more teddy bears. The spare bed was already teeming with them. He imagined Christmas together in their perfect home. If he could just find a way out, they could be back for her favourite time of year, and that heart-melting look of unbridled bemusement would return, and she would laugh and smile again, and stand on her toes to kiss him. And everything would be like it once was.

These were John's last thoughts as the watchers gathered around him.

DECEMBER

I

Mina

The dashboard darkened just before the engine died. Its red dials had been the only colour since nightfall. All else was black or white, or something in between; the ashen hue of moonlight. The headlamps didn't fade or flicker. The night swallowed the road ahead in one impatient gulp and the car sailed to a stop, its tyres scrunching over frosted stone. Then there was only that lightless silence and Mina straining to make sense of it.

'This is your fault,' she whispered to the parrot on the back seat; its cage was propped up between two coats. But Mina knew that the bird wasn't to blame.

'Just follow one of those country roads,' Peter had said in that husky smoker's voice that always made Mina consider quitting. 'They all lead the same way, and it won't take you more than a few hours, and the bird will give you no trouble. Tim told me that he only acts up when he's hungry.'

Peter had never driven in his life. He had drunk every

day for fifty years and still he was thirsty. He looked like a man who had seen it all. A sage and a seer who kept secrets others could only dream of. Maybe it was the eyes that squinted out from beneath those bushy eyebrows, or the silvered beard that glistened all the brighter when his mouth of dark, yellowing teeth was nattering away about nothing. The fact was that Peter had seen nothing except the bottom of a thousand pint glasses, and the drink had aged him terribly.

Mina had been sitting outside the pub before the black clouds rolled in from the bay, bringing the big rain. The cobbles were uneven, and puddles already spread like sores across every street. The rain never bothered her, and it certainly never came as any surprise. She could read the sky like a face and knew when it was welling up long before the tears came. This was a far cry from autumn's much-lauded epoch. Gone were the leaves – coiled and russet – that dragged the poet's pen to paper. This was the tail end of the year. These were the sombre, leafless days of December, and the first Christmas that Mina would spend without her mum. Never had a gloomy sky felt so fitting.

People-watching was her distraction of choice, and that's what led her back to the pub that afternoon. Of all her haunts, Quay Street was her dearest. Here there was coffee, ashtrays on tables, and always a barman in earshot to upgrade to something stronger. The street's upper reaches were festooned with bright bunting that changed colour with the festivals, always overnight and never with any witnesses. As picturesque as a postcard with its quaint shopfronts and restaurants, crowds were drawn there like gulls to the open ocean. The pub's furniture was set behind windbreakers that sometimes fell in a gale, but they kept Mina apart from the people, separating the artist from her subjects – those who, unlike her, probably had places to be or friends to meet. Mina kept reminding herself that she was doing all right on her own, and some day soon she was bound to start believing it.

Her coffee was cold, and bitter as it was black. Mina scanned both ends of the street, searching for that *one* perfect face. All the while the pencil fanned through her fingers, hovering over the page like a kestrel waiting to strike. Winter squalls complicated matters. People kept their heads down and never stood still. The cold days were worse as their scarves crept up from their necks, leaving only the eyes on show.

For months Mina had been collecting her *strangers*, as she called them. She only had to glance at a face to perceive its subtleties, to fasten it to her memory. And her sketchbook was full of them; page after page after rain-speckled, coffee-stained page. The paper was organic. Faces grew on it easily. And they diverted her thoughts just long enough to enjoy a moment's peace.

There was the middle-aged homeless man with the jolly, bearded face, and kind eyes. His button nose made his hairy cheeks seem all the larger, like a stray Persian cat. There wasn't a thread on top, but his eyebrows, too, were untamed. They curled skyward in a style that reminded Mina of French filigree. Whenever she passed him, he would say good morning or good afternoon or good evening, as though he was forever watching the sun. Sometimes she threw him a few coins. Other times she just smiled. It never seemed like he was begging. He would just sit there, waiting for his luck to change, or for the sun to sink out of sight; whichever came first.

Then there was the moustachioed older gent. His every feature was bruised from the drink, as though he couldn't sweat it out, and so it gathered beneath the skin, bubbling up on the nose and cheeks. His eyes were marinated in the stuff. When eventually he dies no one will wonder why, and the blemishes will fade from his skin like an assassin escaping into the shadows.

Next was *the android*, as Mina had come to call her. The face was flawless; sharp and symmetrical, with alabaster skin so smooth that it had to be synthetic. Every detail was deliberately selected to maximise her beauty, probably by a scientist in a white coat. She was uncommonly tall; a multi-purpose robot with the athletic prowess to complement the looks. Science fiction writers had fantasised about this woman for decades.

Three times Mina had drawn her, and on each page her face was the same. She had never seen someone so sad, or so versed in hiding it. Suppressing a smile isn't easy. The happiness always creeps out somehow. But sadness can be stashed under the skin like a dark secret. It doesn't need tears to make its presence felt, and this woman's face was devoid of even the slightest expression. Wherever she had come from and wherever she was going, she was flanked between a past and future that kept her lips from ever creasing into a smile.

Then the pages settled on *that* sketch – the self-portrait that Mina had drawn after one too many glasses. Beside a hungry ashtray and two bottles of wine she had stared at her reflection until it seemed to smile back at her. Ironic really, all things considered.

This was her realised by her own hand with just enough honesty and disdain to make it matter. Mina had considered ripping the page out the following morning, but maybe that's where she belonged, lost amidst a crowd of strangers. No better, no different, just another face judged in that moment on her expression alone. Immortalised in that sad, pathetic second when life's seams were starting to fray.

The eyes looked close to tears. Even the eyeliner couldn't hide it. All that black only accentuated the sadness. They didn't stare at Mina. Instead, they looked right through her with a disinterest bordering on rejection. The lips didn't work, like moulding clay left in the air for too long. Smiling had become uncomfortable. Even talking now felt like a chore. The nose was neat and dead straight. It was boring. The cheekbones were high, and her whole face was this hackneyed heart shape. Everything else was uninspired. Small ears, tidy chin. Even the teeth, though you couldn't see them, were straight and orderly.

The hair was jet black, and the jaggedly chopped bob seemed like a good idea at the time. So did the fringe, but now Mina wasn't so sure. No matter what she did to bluff some individuality, she might as well have been made on a factory line. Her beauty was the generic sort, and where was the beauty in that?

If she had seen this face on the street, she wouldn't have drawn it. She would have kept on looking. *Here we go again.* Mina took a deep breath, slammed the book shut, and slid it back into her bag. She hated when she got like this: all sullen and melodramatic, as her sister would say. Besides, the night before had been one of her better ones. Her black dress had kept everyone's concentration off their cards. The bills would be paid, and the rent would be met. Wasn't that enough to imitate a smile?

The first bombs of rain began to fall; slow and sloppy warning shots. The main strike was approaching and no siren was necessary to clear the streets. Mina returned inside, taking her cold coffee with her, and there was Peter by the bar, swaying like a broken mast after too many storms. It was still early enough in the day to make sense of him, but late enough that you might not want to. His face always lit up whenever Mina landed through the door of the pub. He was old and ugly. She was all the opposites.

'There's a collector of rare birds and parrots and whatnot up in Connemara,' he told her. 'And I've this parrot. Well actually, it's not mine. It's Tim's. But we're selling it together. It's called a golden conure, and he's worth a pretty penny. That's a *golden conure*,' he repeated slowly, emphasising every syllable.

Mina hadn't heard of Tim before that day. It was strange to think that Peter had friends stashed somewhere away from the pub. She threw a glance towards the barman, Anthony, who leaned on the Guinness tap, listening in with a smirk on his face. The man's thirty-odd years were splashed in silver across the sides of his black hair. He was classically good-looking, like an early James Bond portrait, but lacked the charisma to realise the likeness.

'What was the bird's name again?' he asked, goading Peter into saying it for what felt like the millionth time.

'*Gol-den-con-yure*,' he repeated, to which Anthony just

laughed and walked away, leaving Mina with a man who may have already drunk more than she had suspected.

A pint of Guinness waited to be topped off, waves of bistre rippling above the black. Cups and saucers chinked. Stools were dragged across the floor. Everything was wooden and warm, and no voice was too loud. Anthony worked by the coffee machine, hammering out the old and pressing in the new. The steam gurgled the milk, burning it nearly every time. The register rang open and snapped closed, and there was music, all weaved together into a comfort blanket of familiar sounds. The pub was a safe place. Timeless until the lights flashed, and the last orders drew down the taps.

The windows were fogged up. Voices and breaths, toasties and soup – this hot, wholesome, almost nauseating air was trapped in an airlock, and only when the door opened did it explode outside, much to the dismay of those who distrusted the draught. It stole lives once upon a time, and now it stole the heat.

'You want me to drive this bird to Connemara?' she asked, both hands cradled around the hot whiskey poised just below her nose.

'That's right. A day's drive, no more and no less, and you can keep two hundred of the euro. Mind you, that'll have to cover the petrol cost. If you don't want the job, then I'll ask someone else. But listen, Mina,' he whispered with toxic breath, leaning in closer, 'this is easy money, and you'd be doing myself a favour.'

Peter was more tuned in than people gave him credit for. Or it was possible that Mina was so scattered that they shared the same social static. Some weeks earlier she had posted an advert online for him. It was for a beat-up cello that looked as though he'd found it in a second-hand charity shop. But it had sold for five hundred euro, of which Peter had slipped Mina an easy hundred. A few more friends like him and she wouldn't have to treat every bill like the enveloped equivalent of Pandora's box.

'Where in Connemara would you be sending me?' she said. 'It's a big place.'

'I've a map,' he replied with a wink and nod. 'Your man, the buyer, he told me where he lives, and sure you can't get lost these days.'

'And when does he want this…?' Mina asked, forgetting.

'*Gol-den-con-yure*,' he said, even slower this time. 'I told him that he'd have it tomorrow.'

'Jesus.' Mina laughed. 'That was nice of you.'

The rain against the window was reason enough to let her decision linger. Mina had worn her leather jacket; the short one that barely reached down her back. Loose threads marked where the buttons used to cling, and its elbows and shoulders had faded to grey. A few badges were pinned around its lapels. Her sweater was woollen white with black stripes, so long that its sleeves stretched down to her fingers. At least she had the good mind not to wear a skirt. The jeans slipped snugly inside her ankle boots, scuffed from too many winters and not enough polish.

Mina had yet to touch the canvas in her studio. Its blankness had bothered her since she agreed to the job, like an unwanted pet constantly crying out for attention. Commissioned work paid well, but she hated it more than counting out her change to afford a cup of coffee. The client was in control, and it always felt like homework. As if there was a right and a wrong answer to art. The cards had been kind. She had won enough to tide her over for a while. But luck like that was rare. Two hundred euro was a lot. Besides, the drive might clear her head. Amazing it was how after all those hot whiskeys the delivery of the bird seemed like a perfectly good idea.

'I knew I could count on you,' Peter said as he signalled for another round to celebrate. 'Easiest money you'll ever make, and that's the truth.'

The alcohol-fuelled optimism of that evening felt like a false memory as Mina unfurled the map across the windshield. In hindsight, she probably should have inspected it sooner, but there had been plenty of signposts when the roads still held some tarmac. Its paper stank of Peter's wax jacket and was so tattered that it must have lived in his pocket since he bought it a decade earlier. Mina had to wrench her seat back just to wrap her head around what she was looking at. When eventually she found the dog-eared section where she was supposedly parked with two wheels in the ditch, she saw that Peter had drawn a circle in blue biro, seemingly at random. Its circumference swallowed up most of the page. But never mind where she was supposed to be going, Mina didn't even know where she was.

'For fuck's sake, Peter,' she whispered to herself. 'If ever a map was more useless.'

The roads had narrowed. Their uneven walls had long fallen to rubble, and a matted spine of grass brushed under the car as it trudged forward, its wheels plunging into pits of crackling ice. Any variety to keep the eyes entertained died with the sun, and soon a chill mist swept softly over the surrounding bogs. Mina searched the horizon eagerly for any signs of life – the light of a distant house or the last vestiges of some backwoods people, but there was nothing. Even those bastard sheep that ambled down from the hillsides had abandoned her. Every animal was burrowed out of sight, demoralised by a day too short to make a difference. Silent and uncertain was the winter, and in Connemara it was never so bleak.

Every station on the radio had fizzled to static, and so Mina listened instead to the car's weary rattle and the thrum of her fingers on the steering wheel, waiting patiently for an answer to the question she kept asking herself – *where the fuck am I?* Her headlamps had been the only light as far as the eye could see – like a fallen star on a dead planet – and for the first time in a long time her loneliness was starting to trouble her. She should have arrived at the buyer's house hours ago. Peter's map was splayed on the passenger's seat beside her. Now and again, she'd frown at it from the corner of her eye. Every *móinín* and crooked stretch of road seemed to lead her back to nowhere. And the headlights only revealed so much – the same scraggy strip of muck and stone.

'Any ideas?' she asked her passenger on the back seat. 'No? I didn't think so.'

Even a call from Jennifer would be a welcome break from the parrot's stale company. But conversations with her sister always left Mina exhausted. Jennifer would talk at length about her new husband and their new home, barely stopping to catch a breath. This was routinely followed by a few anecdotes from the weekend just gone. These involved hills or hiking, or anything that produced fifty photographs to share with the world. All filtered so that the sky resembled a cheap watercolour. *You had to be there,* Jennifer would then say. Mina could think of nothing worse.

Jennifer had rung two days earlier, after lunchtime and then again in the evening. Both times Mina had stared at her sister's name as it vibrated hostilely on the table; one hand reaching to answer and the other holding it back. The longer they went without talking, the guiltier she felt. The second missed call had left a voicemail behind it like a stain that Mina hadn't removed yet. Now seemed as good a time as any.

'You ready for this?' she said to the parrot as she unlocked her phone. 'This is my sister. You'll get to hear the shit that I've to deal with now.'

Not surprisingly, the voicemail began with a long sigh of frustration. 'Why don't you answer your phone? I'm only calling to see how you are. I don't understand why you want to make this so difficult. I get it, you're an *artist* and you need time to, whatever, do your art. But it's time to get your life on track, you know? You can't muddle on like this, selling the odd painting or, I don't know. Listen, I'm not going to call you again, okay? I'll leave it up to you. Mum wouldn't have wanted this, Meens.'

That's what Mina's mum had rechristened her. Jennifer began using the name after she had passed away, as if *Meens* was a responsibility passed down through the family, like a broken heirloom they couldn't fix. Mina's mum was the only one who held her together, and the cracks glistened all the brighter beside the light of Jennifer's perfect life. *Selling the odd painting?* She shouldn't have listened to that. Her sister's voice had only made a bad situation worse. *Eyes on the road. Don't think about it.* There had to be a light in the dark soon.

'Keep it together, Meens,' she said to herself. '*All paths lead somewhere,*' just like her mum used to remind her whenever life took an unexpected turn.

It was then that the dashboard's instruments disappeared, like a pilot's cockpit losing power over uncharted lands. In the blink of an eye the world was drained of light and sound. There was only the moon, like a bulb in muddy water. Mina's hand had jiggled with the keys in the ignition, and when that failed, she fumbled around for her phone. She held down its power button like a paramedic searching for a pulse, but still the darkness remained unbroken. Mina dipped her hands blindly into her bag and rummaged around for a lighter. Her fingers found keys, lipstick, a pack of playing cards, lipstick again, and then she felt it. *Click. Click.* She took a deep breath. Nobody could be this unlucky. *Click.* There was light. No more than a single, heroic flame. But it was enough to help Mina find her tobacco pouch without further foraging. She always kept one pre-rolled for emergencies. This was definitely such an occasion.

Her breathing seemed louder in the absence of all else. She pined for the engine's warm purr; the companionship of something as simple as sound. Mina's hands were trembling now. They wouldn't stay still, as though they belonged to somebody else; someone whose nerves had clearly got the better of them. She smoked quickly, with the cigarette suspended by her mouth, staring at nothing, because there was nothing to see. The bird thrashed its wings against the cage, making Mina jolt from her seat. How was everything suddenly so loud? The clang of its thin, iron bars was deafening.

'Take it easy,' she said, rolling the window down and waving the smoke outside with her hand. 'Jesus, you're worse than my sister.'

Mina took her thumb off the lighter. There was no telling how much gas remained, and she knew better than to waste any. The ember of the cigarette would have to light the way for now. The bird calmed itself as the cold air crept inside. Soon the only sound was Mina's pursed lips drawing in smoke, and the tired exhalation that followed. She sat with her arm stretched out the window, her head arched to the side so that she could see the stars. It was eerily quiet. She closed her eyes and thought of all the places that she would rather be – anywhere but the middle of nowhere.

She would wait until sunrise, and then she would decide what to do. Mina had driven for so long that there had to be someone nearby who could help. The daylight would reveal some distant cottage, or maybe a tribute as trifling as a signpost. There was always the chance that the car would miraculously start back to life. As financially harried as she was, she would happily retrace the way she had come and let Peter have his bird back, free of charge, and his fucking map.

'Well, this wasn't one of my better ideas,' she muttered. 'I guess I'll just add it to the list.'

Too attuned had Mina become to the din of her city apartment. There was always some busker warbling on the street below. The same songs, the same awkward chord changes. The pigeons tap-danced on the roof slates during the intervals, and by night the gulls glided inland to tear open the bins with their beaks like hooked swords. The silence now felt unnatural. But it was nothing like what was to come, when that shriek sounded through the night like a siren, pinning Mina back into her seat and dashing the cigarette from her fingers.

It was unlike anything she had ever heard; so savage and shrill. It wasn't human. It couldn't possibly have been. And she hadn't seen an animal for hours. Its voice was so clear that the stars themselves must have shivered from its force. Mina drew her arm back inside and screwed the window up.

'What the fuck was *that*?' she said, shrinking behind the steering wheel.

Mina locked all the doors, feeling suddenly exposed. If there *was* something out there, then she sure as shit couldn't see it. Her car was met on all sides by an impenetrable blackness, as though she had sunk to the ocean's deepest trench, where old things live without time or light, in secrecy and in darkness. She clambered into the back seat and shifted the parrot's cage over to the side. There she huddled under the coats in the hope that they would keep secret her presence in a place where she no longer felt safe.

'Don't make a sound,' she whispered, curling her legs up beneath her. 'Something's out there.'

There was no crack of ice, no soft crunch of frost. The windows eventually fogged and whitened from the night's breath but there wasn't a sound to be heard, however delicate or innocent. Even the parrot knew to hold its beak. There was only the memory of that scream stalking Mina's thoughts with pounding steps. Her arms were cradled around her shoulders, holding in whatever warmth they could, listening, and waiting for that unearthly voice to return.

2

A sliver of light crept in by Mina's feet. She pulled the coats loose and tossed them aside, kicking one of them into that forgotten space behind the passenger seat. Her bones unfolded like broken patio furniture as she stretched her legs between the two front seats. She had never felt so old in all her thirty-three years. The bird, with its head quizzically atilt, seemed almost surprised by Mina's unveiling. Its little pink feet shuffled on their perch. Peter wasn't wrong about the name at least. The *gol-den-con-yure's* feathers were gleaming in the morning light. Despite everything, it really was quite beautiful.

Frost spangled the windshield's centre. Mina could hear the ice cricking and cracking around her like brittle eggshell. She reached over to the passenger seat to retrieve her phone. It didn't matter who she called, just so long as it wasn't Jennifer. Mina had ignored her for far too long now to ask for help. The phone's plastic felt cold, as though rigor mortis had set into its battery. Not a good sign; dead, as expected. She let it drop behind the back seat where it sunk without a sound into a coat. Not the best start to a new day. Mina sat back and looked to the yellow one. 'What do you reckon; if I tie a note to your foot will you go and get help?'

The bird trilled and whistled, experimenting with the most ludicrous of melodies. It was too early in the morning for that kind of carry-on. *He only acts up when he's hungry,* Peter had said. Mina could relate to that. There was a bag of bird pellets in the boot of the car – a consolation gift for the buyer willing to drop a small fortune on a yellow bird that couldn't hold a note. Mina unlocked the door and placed a wary foot on the ground. One of them might at least have some breakfast.

She reached her arms into the sky, cracking her neck from side to side, moaning as every sore part of her seemed to relax, if only for a moment. Everything outside was sharp and cold, and stones still glistened with a light rime of frost. She came to stare with some surprise at the road ahead, where a low fog skulked through the shadows, avoiding the sunshine like a prisoner dodging a searchlight. The car had broken down not far from a forest, but far enough that the headlights hadn't revealed it before going blind. Trees were scarce in Connemara. A few wind-warped hawthorns maybe, but Mina never expected to find a wooded area of this size, in all its leafless misery. It was strange how the car came to stop where it did, at the edge of the treeline, as though the forest had denied her entry. The trees looked ancient, brittle and decayed like dead skin. Even with the sun breaking behind her, its depths looked dark as night.

Looking back the way she had come, there was nothing, not even a bird in the sky. The barren lands were uneven and ugly, rising into hills and dipping into hidden depths. The same muddied hue was everywhere, identical to the day before. Even the rocks with their discoloured splotches looked familiar. She had driven for so many hours, unable to see beyond her headlights. As it turns out she hadn't been missing anything.

The boot clicked open and lifted to the subtle crack of ice. Even the most sheepish sound seemed to have had its volume cranked up. The bag of bird food was beside the spare tyre and a half-empty bottle of water. God only knew how long it had been in there. But Mina knew a survival necessity when she saw one. The day was only beginning and there was no telling how long a walk lay ahead. There might not be another source of water for a hundred miles.

'Are you ready for this?' she said to the bird as it nibbled at the pellets she had slipped into its cage. Mina never did ask Peter how much to feed it. That was meant to be the buyer's concern. A handful looked right.

She stood by the open door, with one hand on the car roof, staring – absolutely unimpressed – at the forest. It looked so dismally uninviting beneath the blue sky, like a renaissance impression of heaven and hell. There was no point in walking the way she had come; that much was obvious. But as rocky as the road had been, it looked even worse going forward. It was as though some heavy machinery had simply ploughed a way through the trees. It was a mucky scar that nature had tried to cover up. Gangly weeds and fat nests of briars had stretched out from the wilds within, and nothing moved. Even the lanky, arid weeds were steady as hard stalks. There wasn't a sound. Mina scratched around her ear just to make sure she hadn't lost her hearing.

She eyed up the treetops breaking the sky like a jagged shore and fancied two possibilities. The first being that she was so utterly lost and apart from civilisation that she had happened upon a part of Ireland that no one had yet discovered, in which case hers was a hopeless cause. This was unlikely. But Mina had already proven herself to be the unluckiest woman in the west of Ireland, so it was by no means an impossibility. The second and more promising likelihood is that what she had found was in fact a little-known national park. One with actual living people who pruned the branches and sang to the gorse. Coachloads of tourists might come this way every day, and Mina would happily suffer their company if it meant she could get home and finally attack that canvas. *That* was easy money. *This* disaster was something different.

'Let's never come to the countryside again,' she said to the yellow one, hoisting its cage out of the car. It was more cumbersome than it was heavy. Mina dashed some pellets into it and left the rest in the boot. Her handbag was already packed tight, and that was before the water bottle went in. The phone's corpse could stay in the car – a four-wheeled mausoleum with tax and insurance discs. But the sketchbook and pencils were coming with her, and the tobacco, and other essentials that were worth an aching shoulder.

Mina locked the car, smiling to herself as she did so. Maybe a seasoned thief would have the know-how to get it moving again, and if so, they were welcome to it. She took her first stride towards the forest but some subconscious hand tugged on the reins. *Where do you think you're going, Meens?* It was *that* scream. Its memory was constant as the faint fog by her lips. Was leaving the safety of the car such a good idea? Her artist's imagination fancied a hundred horrible things that could have been responsible. Every horror movie she had ever seen and every Gothic tale she had ever read, they all paid their contribution. But this was the real world. Monsters didn't exist. Of this fact, at that point in time, Mina was certain.

With no food and so little water, waiting for help to find her wasn't an option, and so with the air fresh against her cheeks, Mina walked, following the only road she could, with a caged bird dangling from her left hand and a rolled cigarette in her right. If only her sister could see her now. Maybe the dead phone was a blessing in disguise. She might have called Jennifer in her panic the night before. As if being an artist didn't earn her enough flak. The little-known role of *parrot courier* promised more of the same.

She didn't have to take many steps before the gnarled trees gathered around her, swallowing the sky, making Mina feel all the lonelier, and turning the air that little bit colder. The path was uneven and, judging by the tufts of wilting grasses that broke its surface, it didn't enjoy much use. Roots tore through the earth, coiling their tendrils around each other like a bed of worms, making her watch every step. The ditches on either side were steep enough that had she driven through in the dark she may well have tipped her car on its head.

Mina hadn't eaten since leaving the city, and that was only a snack. Her appetite never woke up until the late afternoon.

Anything before then was a struggle, like force-feeding a baby with a full belly, minus the tears. She had nibbled at some pasta saved from the night before, managing maybe half a dozen forkfuls. It was one of her mum's recipes. Mina followed it down to the finest detail, but it still never tasted the same. Such was her hunger now she would have wiped the plate clean.

The parrot suddenly let out an almighty squawk. The sound of it seemed to tremor across the underbrush, travelling up the body of every tree before soaring into a sky scarred and latticed by their many branches. The fright of it nearly took the legs from under her.

'Jesus,' she said, lifting the cage to meet the bird in the eye. 'Do that again and I swear to God I'll...' She paused and the parrot almost seemed to grin at her.

As bad as Mina's circumstances may have been, surely her lot was better than the bird's. The poor thing had probably spent its entire life in that cage; gifted flight only to be clipped, imprisoned, and put on display. Still the parrot's little face beamed with excitement.

'Sorry,' Mina whispered, feeling almost guilty now. 'Just try to keep it down, okay?'

When she was a child, her parents had taken her to the zoo. The animals all looked so bored, so sad; repeating the same torpid routines as though their minds had cracked. The elephant was the worst. Its foot was tethered to a block with a fat chain, and it just swayed back and forth, staring into space. Mina had been convinced it was crying. Some memories become hauntings over time, and this was one of those days. *Nothing should have to live in captivity* – that was little Mina's take-home message from the zoo. And if it hadn't been for the money, she would have set the yellow one free there and then.

The forest stretched on for miles, drawing her deeper and deeper into that eerie, sylvan labyrinth. There had to be a break soon. But the trees were so tightly packed that there was no way of knowing. She couldn't even pinpoint the sun's whereabouts anymore. Hours had passed. Here and there Mina had seen burrows in the earth, but there were no animals. No nests up high or droppings down below. Nothing living seemed to call this place home. She became quite glad of the bird's company, even if her arm was straining now from carrying its cage.

'I think we're long overdue a break, don't you?' she said, placing it down on the earth so that she could massage some feeling into her shoulder. The pain was already working its way around to her back, like a snake coiling around her body.

The thirst had hit her an hour ago. A half bottle of water wasn't a lot, and so she swore that she would only take a drink when her mouth couldn't even muster up some spit. Now, ruddy-cheeked and out of breath, was that time. She would give the bird a capful soon but seeing as she was doing all the heavy lifting, the yellow one could wait a while.

As she leaned down to pick up its cage her eye caught something amidst the trees. Everything was grey or brown, or a smeared palette of both, and so the red glove was unmistakable. It seemed so out of place. This was the first indication that another living person had been there before her. The glove was entangled in some brambles, floating in the air like a fly trapped in a web.

'That's a good sign, isn't it?' she whispered. 'I mean, at least we're not the first to get so fucking lost.'

What faint light crept between the branches was fading fast. Mina hadn't found the cold discomforting until then, but she was tired now, and the aches had colonised every part of her. The night was coming. There was nowhere to escape it. The earth was stiff to the step, and a silvered mist was starting to seep through its pores. Though the trees had cast their dead parts around them, the wood was too damp to be used as kindling. Besides, even if it were dry as old bone there was no guarantee that the lighter would hold a flame to it.

It must have been around half past four, or closer to five o'clock, maybe. Peter was probably perched on his stool by the fireplace in the pub, awaiting her return with his share in *the easiest money she'll ever make*.

'How do I get myself into these situations?' she whispered through chattering teeth.

Mina could feel the cold across her nose and cheeks, and her hand holding the cage burned a sore red. The fingers throbbed as though she had caught them in a door. She had taken those hot whiskeys for granted. Even just to hold one now – to nurse it between her hands and breathe it in deep – that would be enough. Suffice to say, Peter now owed her more drinks than even a man of his seasoned constitution could handle. And an extra hundred would be docked from his share for all the trouble he had put her through. And if she lost a finger or a toe from frostbite, she was keeping every cent.

Just then, in the distance, jumping between the trees as she walked, there was a light. Mina stood perfectly still, arching her head, hardly believing her eyes. But there it was, constant and bright – a bulb. It hadn't been there a second ago.

'Well, would you look at that,' she said, holding up the bird's cage so it could see. 'Come on, it looks like we're not going to be sleeping outside after all.'

The last of the day's light was waning fast, and Mina could scarcely see the ground beneath her feet. The yellow one screamed wildly as she forced their way through a bank of brambles, stumbling out the other side and nearly dropping its cage. The bird's voice was deafening, and someone had heard it.

They appeared standing below the light. Their silhouette was all that Mina could make out through the ever-creeping darkness. It was a house. She couldn't tell much more than that. Luckily, whoever had heard the parrot's screech now saw Mina trudging towards them. She was already worrying about how the stranger would react to her.

'Run!' the woman shouted. 'Get inside, quickly!'

Mina couldn't understand what all the rush was about, nor did she care. She had half-imagined that they would draw a shotgun and chase her back into the briars. But she had no other choice. Without shelter she might not last the night.

'I'm coming,' she shouted, trying to catch her breath as she peeled her body away from whatever thorny monstrosity was holding her back.

Mina skittered across the undergrowth as fast as her tired legs could carry her, keeping on the tips of her toes as the heels of her ankle boots kept digging ruts in the earth. So focused was she on the light ahead that she could see little else, like a blinkered horse racing towards the finish line. The woman stood inside the doorway, holding it open. It looked as though she might close it at any second.

'Come on, come on!' she yelled. 'Faster!'

Mina didn't even think. She just did as she was told and ran inside. The woman slammed the door behind her and went about securing a slew of locks. The hall was in darkness save for the single bulb that hung from the ceiling.

The woman was older than Mina, maybe in her late forties, and she was much taller. The bulb hung just above her head. She was awfully gaunt; a body hewn of flesh and vigour. Her skin appeared freakishly thin and it stretched all the lighter across her high cheeks and chin, fine as an insect's wing. The woman had probably been so beautiful once upon a time, but her bright blue eyes were now sunken and framed by the deepest fatigue. All features were faded and limp, and no aspect of her seemed clean. Her hair was the palest blonde, as though the colour had been sucked out of it. It shone pearly white when the light caught it, and hung lifelessly past her shoulders, its ends crudely chopped and uneven, as if gnawed by a rat whilst she slept. Her body was all but lost beneath the dim, swaying light of the bulb. She was a scarecrow low on straw, picked apart and abandoned. Her fingers clutched the fraying edges of a downy shawl that draped down to her feet; as much a part of her as her face, her hair, and her hopelessness.

A sudden cacophony of shrieks poisoned the air – the same fearful strain from the night before. It was so loud and the voices so many that Mina fell back onto the floor, clutching the bird's cage as though the yellow one could somehow protect her. The screams came from just outside, from the darkness where only moments ago she had run towards the light. She looked to the many locks – some bolted, others mere chains – that stood between them and whatever had overrun the woodland.

'You're lucky to be alive,' the woman said, reaching out her hand. 'Quickly now, come with me. The light is already on.'

3

Mina was pulled to her feet by the coldest hand; its fingers were as bone, their grip like a vice around her wrist. The woman's thumbnail cut the skin where the veins run blue. Faint specks of dust flittered around the bulb, its restless light awakening shadows in every corner. Their footsteps and the cage's rattle echoed off the walls, scattering in all directions. Despite the cavernous air, the passage was tight, and the birdcage scratched against it as Mina lumbered forward, so exhausted now that she struggled to throw one foot in front of the other.

'Come on!' the woman screamed; her voice riled and shrill. Even the bird baulked back into the corner of its cage, too flustered to pare a sound from its beak. There was light at the corridor's end – vivid and unnatural – and they were hurtling towards it.

'Get inside, now!' she screeched; throwing Mina through the doorway and slamming it shut behind them.

A skinny hand reached out from the woman's shawl, securing the locks quickly and skilfully as though she had practised each one a thousand times. Mina, meanwhile, slid down the wall, still holding the cage in both arms, with the bird's wings flailing against her fingers. She stretched her aching legs out across the floor. *What is this place?* The light reflected from every angle. It burned like the summer sun, scoring colours into her mind. She shielded her eyes as best she could, but still it crept in. Her hands felt cold against her face; all fingers numb.

'That was too close,' she heard the woman say. 'That was stupid.'

'Where did she...?' a man's voice tried to ask before she cut him off. He spoke so low that Mina had hardly heard him over the parrot's screeching.

'I should have left her outside. We're supposed to be in here before the light even comes on. That's the rule. That's the way it has to be.'

The shrieks Mina heard had been so loud, so close, as though they had chased her to the door, snapping at her heels. Would the woman really have left her out there?

Mina's fingers fanned apart over her eyes. Her cheeks were flushed and warm. Her lips were chapped. They felt prosthetic, and probably looked even worse. Every part of her felt rusty, as if the cogs that kept her moving were starting to grind each other down.

The room was coming into focus. Details were beginning to differentiate and darken in the white. Mina could feel the blood pumping in and around her skull. Flat as the floor might have been, she had to press her back against the wall just to keep steady.

'Come on, Meens,' she whispered, 'you got this,' and through squinted eyes she could finally see.

The wall facing Mina was one immense mirror, duplicating all within the room and obscuring all that lay beyond it, in the darkest night, where the memory of those voices still haunted the woodland. She saw herself, fingers pressed to lips that had no feeling. Her fringe was smeared to her forehead. Her eyeliner had bled out. Filth swirled through the floor like marble, softened and shaped by too many tired attempts to clean it. The toes of her boots wore a sock of wet mud, slowly caking to solid. Her jeans were stippled in more of the same.

A low table – cut from the fat, dissevered bole of a tree – occupied the centre of the floor, out of place in a room of stone and glass. Mina drew her feet away. There were berries on the table – fat black ones and red pellets – arranged like a feral child's tea party. She was on the far side of starvation now. She couldn't have eaten, even if she tried. In the corner a few blankets and a discoloured quilt of no clear design were piled. It was, however, the only hint of colour in a room as dispiriting as the forest outside. A fluorescent light buzzed somewhere overhead. It reminded Mina of the noise her fridge made in the days before its motor burned out. Could they not dim it a little? Did it have to be so painfully bright, and so loud? It was like a hive of bees picking through the honeycomb of her brain. She couldn't think straight.

The woman came to kneel in front of Mina, both hands tugging the shawl tight around her body. The other voice she had heard wasn't that of a man, but a boy, possibly still in his late teens. He stood awkwardly by the mirror, arms crossed, hugging his body, staring at the parrot.

His raven-black hair was scruffy and long, starched from

grease, and in need of a good wash with soap and water. The only stubble on his face clung like gunpowder above his lip. The eyes were the palest blue, and bloodshot; painfully so. Their threaded capillaries trickled through the white, and they hadn't blinked. The face was narrow, and his mouth was always slightly ajar, revealing a few crooked teeth.

He wore a bomber jacket, zipped up to the neck. Every inch of him was filthy, most noticeably where he had rubbed his hands on his jeans whenever they touched anything he didn't like the feel of. He paced back and forth, throwing cagey glances towards his own reflection, until eventually he slinked over towards the hill of blankets, and there he sat, watching Mina.

'Is she okay?' he asked.

'Daniel, please,' the woman replied sharply. 'She's still in shock.'

She was even older up close. Mina zoned out, staring at the bruised bags under the woman's eyes and the deep creases that ran through her skin like cracks through clay. *Was this shock?* Mina's fingers were clenched around the bars of the birdcage again. They wouldn't release their grip. Maybe that's where the shock begins – at the tips of the fingers.

'What's your name?' the woman asked.

Mina didn't respond. The question sounded so far away. Her throat was dry; parched as sun-dried paper. She tried swallowing. She could feel and hear her neck tightening but couldn't draw a bead of moisture from her mouth.

'My name is Madeline,' the woman said.

'Danny,' the boy added, waving one of his hands timidly from the corner.

'Daniel, please,' she snapped. 'What's your name?' she repeated, placing her hands on Mina's shoulders. The left one ached from her touch.

'Mina,' she whispered, meeting her in the eye, seeing only the woman now. 'My name is Mina.'

'How did you get here?' Madeline asked.

Mina didn't know where *here* was. She thought of Peter's map and that vague, nameless area where he had marked her destination – where somebody still peered out from their window, waiting for their golden conure. How could she have gotten so lost?

'My car broke down, just outside the forest, and so I walked it.'

It was Daniel who reacted. He slapped both hands on his head in frustration and began circling the room like a shark. Madeline ignored him but made no attempt to mask her dislike of the boy; the furrows of her brow folding into a magnificent frown.

'I knew it,' he said. 'Everything breaks down there. My bike did the same. Phones, too, don't work here. Nothing works except the fucking lights.'

'You're not helping, Daniel,' Madeline said without turning her head. 'Well, *Mina*,' she said grudgingly, as though she didn't like the sound of it, 'you're probably wondering what's going on here.'

Mina nodded her head. The woman released her shoulders, satisfied that she now held her full attention.

'It must all seem very strange to you,' Madeline said, like a headmistress addressing a new pupil. 'Well, that's because it *is* all very strange – the light, this building, the things outside.'

43

'What *things* outside?' Mina repeated, peering over Madeline's shoulder, seeing only the reflection of her own face and the bulk of the woman's blanket.

'I don't know what they are. They only come above ground when it's dark. And when they do the only place we're safe from harm is in here.'

'They don't like the light,' Daniel put in.

'They don't like *daylight*,' Madeline said angrily. Everything the boy said seemed to creep under her skin. 'The artificial light has no effect on them. That's not what keeps them from breaking in. You should know this, Daniel. I've already told you. As long as they can see us, then they leave us alone. It's that simple.'

Mina looked to the boy in disbelief. Could she really accept what they were telling her? Should any sane person stand such words next to the truth and judge their likeness? There was no doubting Madeline's earnestness, or the agitation that kept the boy from standing still. The reality they presented was unbelievable; imaginings torn from the pages of a *penny dreadful*. And yet Mina knew that they both honestly believed it. For how long, she wondered, had they lived it?

'We stay in here when it's dark,' the boy said, sadly gazing towards the mirror. 'And we don't leave again until the sun comes up.'

'That's correct, Daniel,' Madeline said, nodding her head approvingly.

Mina was adrift in someone else's nightmare, too exhausted to shake herself awake.

'What do they look like?' she asked.

'Like us, I suppose,' Madeline replied calmly. 'But they're

not like us. They're leaner and they're longer, and I won't describe their faces to you. I couldn't, to be honest, even if I tried.'

Mina frowned at the woman like a child who suspected the adults were lying to her.

'Why don't you see for yourself?' Madeline said, unblinkingly, pointing towards the glass. 'Go on, have a look. I see no reason why you should take my word. I did only just save your life.'

Daniel's sore eyes widened. Somehow, he seemed to turn even paler. He looked to Mina and shook his head. *Don't do it,* he was telling her. But with Madeline standing between them he couldn't say a word.

'I can tell that you don't believe me,' Madeline said. 'So, what are you afraid of?'

'Madeline,' Daniel said, 'I don't...'

'Quiet, Daniel,' she snapped. 'We don't want her to think we're liars now, do we?'

Mina rose to her feet with legs so weary that her knees rattled together. Without the wall to support her she would never have gotten off the ground. The bird watched her intently, as though she was performing some wonderful feat for his entertainment alone. Simply standing up was miraculous enough. She walked tenderly towards her own reflection, fixing her hair and wiping something from her cheek, trying to make the other Mina more presentable. She came within an arm's reach of the glass, and still couldn't see beyond her mirror image. She would have to step closer. Mina hesitated.

'Go on,' Madeline said, 'what are you waiting for?'

Mina cupped her hands against the glass to block

out the light and brought her eyes in closer. The forest should have been illuminated. The light on the wall was so intense that it should have flooded outside, revealing the trees and anything that may have skulked between them, but there was nothing, just the dark reflection of her own eyes.

'I can't see anything,' she said.

'It's the glass,' Daniel explained. 'Whatever it's made of, the light doesn't pass through it.'

Mina tried to draw some sense out of the dark, but nothing inhabited that black void save for mystery and anticipation. Did Madeline really expect her to see something, or was she the butt of some cruel joke?

'You should step away from the window,' Daniel said quietly, almost a whisper.

'Why?' Mina asked, 'I can't see any...'

An ear-splitting scream sent Mina tumbling. Her legs relinquished their burden, and both palms slapped down on the floor. It had been right there, in her face, so close that she fancied she had felt it through the glass. She scurried backwards against the wall; the heels of her boots scraping across the concrete. Mina watched her own terrified reflection retreat. But what horrors had the mirrored pane kept secret? *What had stood on the other side of the glass?*

'Did you see it?' Madeline asked, her voice mischievous, but the face as motionless as a mask.

No, I didn't fucking see it, Mina thought; her nerves wrought into wiry knots. She sat, knees tucked, with her head in her hands, fighting back the brimming tears awaiting the signal to flood their banks. The shock alone had blacked out her senses. This was a hard reset. The last five minutes had undermined a lifetime of rational thinking. *Monsters don't exist. All of this isn't happening.*

'What's wrong with you?' Daniel said to the woman. 'You knew that would happen!'

Madeline didn't respond. Instead, she looked over to the room's corner where the mishmash of throws and blankets was stirring.

'Oh, Ciara,' she shouted over, 'did we wake you?'

'Leave her alone,' Daniel whispered, the words slipping out so quietly that Madeline didn't seem to hear them.

A tousled head of red hair poked out from the mound, like one disturbed from hibernation. She had been crying. Her face was drained of everything but tears. Their streams still traced her cheeks and swirled the emerald water through her eyes. For a wonderfully benighted moment she seemed to have no idea where she was. As if a dreamy fog still clouded her consciousness. She licked her lips and yawned like a cat that had slept all its nine lives and just woken up for supper.

Mina felt that familiar urge to grab the sketchbook from her bag. She needed this – some distraction from whatever monstrous complications now gathered outside the window. *Focus on the face,* she thought. *Lose yourself for a second –* anything to stop the shaking.

The woman had the greenest eyes that Mina had ever seen, and they were set in the kindest of faces, like jewels in a brooch. The mouth was small, but shaped with sumptuous lips, and the little teeth behind them were still white. She had the appearance of one so young, and yet her sadness was the most striking part of her; that was what Mina was drawn to. She knew what it felt like. You never pick up all the pieces when you shatter like that.

Another person was obviously the last sight that Ciara had expected to see. Her jaw hung open like a little girl who just woke up to catch Santa Claus filling her stocking. She looked to Daniel for answers. This didn't surprise Mina in the slightest. Madeline stood askance, like a bitter stepmother, angry with her for sleeping in so late.

'This is Mina,' Daniel said to her, his tone soft and comforting. 'Her car broke down and she walked into the forest. She just made it before the light came on.'

'*Mina*,' the woman repeated with a tired smile, 'that's a lovely name.'

Ciara's hair was wonderfully chaotic, like flames licking the cold air around her head. She ran both hands through it, and scratched the back of her neck, screwing up her eyes with satisfaction. Her face lit up when she saw the parrot. The smile was perfect. It was open and genuine, and Mina made a mental note to remember it.

'No way!' she said, standing up frantically amidst all the layers. 'You brought a parrot? It is a parrot, isn't it? I don't think I've ever seen one in real life.'

Ciara was wearing an oversized green jumper and a pair of jeans. Much like Daniel's clothes, they would have all profited from a wash and some fresh air. She had her sleeves stretched down over her hands, with her thumbs poking out of two well-worn holes. Mina had many like it.

'It's called a golden conure,' Mina replied, thinking of Peter. What she wouldn't have given to be sat beside him, drink in hand and briquettes on the fire, not a worry in the known world, and no *things* outside the window. A chill slipped down her spine. Could it all be true? Was she now trapped here like the rest of them?

'He's golden, all right,' Ciara said, kneeling to examine it more closely. 'Or wait, sorry, is it a boy or a girl?'

'It's a boy, I think,' Mina replied, distantly. *Is all this really happening?*

'He'll be dinner soon unless Daniel can catch us some food,' Madeline put in, her tall body now looming over them.

Ciara looked horrified by the prospect and turned her gaze to the floor. Daniel, also, just looked away. Mina wondered how long this bully had picked them apart, wearing them down to this sad, silent acceptance.

'When I leave this place my bird is coming with me,' Mina said. 'You'll just have to find a different dinner, Madeline.'

The woman considered her quietly, as if disappointed. In a room full of children, as she thought them to be, perhaps she had hoped that Mina, being older, would become a party to her interests.

'If you think you're leaving this place, then you're a bigger fool than the rest of them,' Madeline replied. No anger, no frown. This was spoken as a matter of fact.

Ciara was seen to fidget with her fingers. Daniel stood with his arms crossed again, his gloom focused on the parrot, still trying to figure out why anyone in their right mind would carry a caged bird into the woods with them.

'There's some food on the table,' Madeline said. 'It's all we have for now, but you should eat. There's some water...' Here she paused before drawing a hand to her mouth. 'I left it in the corridor by the front door. I left the water outside.'

'We can get it in the morning, Madeline,' Ciara said, feigning a smile. 'I'm sure we can survive a night without it.'

'It'll be gone by the morning, you stupid girl,' she replied. 'We needed that bottle. We need to drink. We can live off currants and nuts all we like, but we need water. I can't believe I forgot it.'

Mina rummaged through the bag still roped around her shoulder. Madeline's hawk-like eyes turned in an instant, eyeballing its contents. She edged slowly closer and closer, like a heron stalking its breakfast. It was no surprise that Mina's body was bent out of shape. Her bag was fit to burst at its seams.

'There you are,' she said, reaching the bottle towards Madeline. She wanted nothing more than to drink it herself, such was her thirst, but it seemed the right thing to do; a thank you, if nothing else, for taking her in.

'There isn't much left,' Mina said, 'but I'm sure it's enough to get us by until the morning.'

Madeline stepped gingerly forward. A long arm reached out from her blanket and took the bottle, like a wild animal snatching a morsel of food from a stranger's hand.

'Thank you, Mina,' Madeline said, and she placed the water in the centre of the table. 'Now, shall we sit down and dine together. Daniel has gathered us some food for dinner. Maybe afterwards we can talk about the bird traps again.'

Mina's thoughts were still fearfully transfixed on the voice that had come from behind the glass. *What could it have been?* The horror, so fresh and perplexing to her, didn't seem to affect the rest of them. They had each conceded to this wretched life, imprisoned in a single cell by the nightly hours, to be watched from the darkness by unseen eyes. But why didn't they flee? If daylight was their guardian, then they had ample hours to run for help.

'Mina,' Madeline said, as she knelt by the table, 'won't you join us? I speak for Daniel and Ciara when I say that it's nice to have someone new amongst us. It's good to sit together, to share in a meal. It proves that we are still civilised, despite everything.'

Madeline divided out the berries amongst them, giving each person an equal share. It was by no means enough, but all that they had. She seemed less like an evil stepmother now and, surprisingly, more like a mother. Albeit a strict one. As erratic as she was, Madeline had obviously applied some element of routine to their days. Mina wondered if they sat together every night. A dysfunctional family, bound not by blood, but by the want to survive. Maybe Madeline was the reason for them lasting as long as they had. However long that was. Mina was curious to know, but the time would come. The hot topic of why they weren't dead was not exactly dinnertime conversation. It was unusual to sit down and eat with others. But then, nothing about that day was borderline normal. Why should dinner be any different?

Mina lived alone. Instead of renting out the spare room as her sister suggested, she had flipped the mattress against the wall, and christened it her studio. Artistic enterprise and inspiration took priority over her cooking. That's partially why Mina dined out so much. The food was always more interesting than her half-hearted attempts. But more importantly, she could spy on the oblivious diners seated around her; candidates for the sketchbook – the enterprise. If she were familiar with the restaurant's layout she would request a table in a corner, out of sight, where she wouldn't be disturbed and yet had a view of those around her.

First dates were her favourite to watch. All those nervous ticks and tells that Mina looked for when playing cards – they all revealed themselves, untamed and exaggerated. The silence was never allowed to settle because that meant there was nothing to say. So, between the postured laughter and anecdotes carefully selected to sell their best parts they usually managed to hold a conversation until the bill arrived. Mina hated dinner dates. The pressure to keep the dialogue afloat always sank her appetite.

She accepted Madeline's invitation and took a blackberry from the table, pinching it between her thumb and forefinger. Daniel had nearly devoured his portion already. Ciara, on the other hand, was making them last, and seemed to be slowly sucking hers instead of chewing them. Madeline took each berry and currant one at a time; masticating it slowly, savouring it, swallowing it through, and then waited a moment before proceeding on to the next. Did the woman realise how odd she was? Her every action followed a system. It was as though she was on autopilot, like the animals in the zoo.

'Hopefully,' Daniel said to Mina, 'we'll have more food tomorrow. There's not much meat on the birds, but it's better than this. We'll just keep it out of sight from your friend over there.' He winked towards the parrot. 'We don't want him getting upset.'

Madeline nodded her head as she licked around her gums. 'Very good, Daniel. We can discuss the traps again while Mina is getting some rest, that is if Ciara would be so kind as to relinquish our only bed.'

'I'm sorry,' Ciara replied, looking anywhere but at Madeline. 'It's just been a hard time.'

'Yes, well,' she replied with an air of disinterest, 'none of us have it easy, do we? Hopefully with three of us awake they won't start shrieking when they lose sight of you, Mina. I suppose we'll know soon enough. Now go on. Lie down before Ciara steals the bed from under you. I have no doubt that you are tired and when we are tired, we must sleep.'

4

Madeline

The building was constructed of concrete blocks. Plastered, but not painted. Its walls were clouded with a black damp that spread from the ground up. The gabled roof was corrugated iron. Fat, furry mosses spread through its grooves, and no gutter fringed its edges. When it rained the water just spilled right off it, carving trenches of wet silt on both sides. There was one way in – the same door that Madeline locked before sundown.

It was divided into two rooms by a corridor that ran through its spine. This had no windows for light, only the bulb that dangled by its entrance, and was so narrow that only a single body could pass through it at a time. Hands and fingers had left their trails across its walls. The floors were cold, grey cement. In stark contrast to the soil and uneven trees that surrounded it, everything within was hard and square; immovable and manmade.

At the far end of the passage, on the left, was an empty doorframe that led into *the living room*. This housed three rectangular windows in the main wall, set high at five feet off the ground, all of which held no glass. Lacerations could be found on their frames and throughout the room in its entirety. On the floor, across the ceiling, and on every wall. New ones were easy for Madeline to spot each morning when the plaster burned like a fresh wound.

This room was known as the living room because of the square cavity and flue in its wall – the fireplace, just to the right of the doorway when one entered. It sometimes flooded during a downpour, but most of the time the trees bore the brunt of the rain. It was the building's only source of heat. It kept people alive during the colder months, hence the name.

So empty was this room that sounds echoed off its walls. Each word spoken merged into the next, until it was just noise; indecipherable layers. It was disorientating. No one raised their voice there. Some nights, when the watchers crept inside, their screams coursed through the building like a cancer, tainting every part of it. Nothing was ever left there overnight. When darkness fell it was off limits until the dawn, when there was peace, and the light clicked off.

On the floor and wall by the middle window there were bloodstains. No manner of Madeline's scrubbing could remove them. Blood on concrete was like red wine on white carpet – a reminder that bad things happen, and a warning that they could happen again. A few flecks could be found around the frame, beside a lonely, smeared thumbprint. If anybody stood by a window to get some fresh air, they instinctively avoided that one.

The room had no electricity. There was no comfort. This

was where they went during the day-lit hours to rest their eyes after the night before – when they were confined to *the coop*, as Madeline had humourlessly coined it. Where they gathered like moths whenever the light was on.

Above the fireplace, someone had written on the wall. They had used some scorched timber to scratch out their lesson, pared to a needle's point and bathed in hot, hypnotic flame. The letters were sharp and tortured, and reiterated so many times that they scored deep into the plaster. If written words could shout, these were screaming at anyone who would listen.

Stay in the light

Life was cold amidst the trees, where the sun fought to be seen, always overwhelmed by the branches that reached across the sky like a cage. Madeline lived and slept wrapped in her fleece blanket. It had become like a second skin, and she a shrinking skeleton beneath it. She had considered taking it down to the stream. It was musty from smoke, and the stains had collaborated to form their own pattern, and not one that Madeline particularly liked. Blood, dirt, and ash from the fire. But the air in the woodland was never dry in December. It was misty and it was damp. It could be days, weeks even, before she could wear it again, and she wasn't willing to make that sacrifice, not when her bones creaked the way they did. Every joint cracked out its unique key, arranging an almost musical score to the simplest movement. Spring was only months away, and she wasn't going anywhere. No one was. She would wash it then, when those rare beams of light did more than thaw ice and make the white parts black. They brought warmth and made the woodland a little less cruel.

Madeline had sent Daniel out that morning to forage and inspect the bird traps. It had been two days now without a catch. Their stomachs were running on fumes. Madeline had shown him time and time again how to set them. Those blank eyes of his assured her that the boy didn't have a clue. He was the most able-bodied amongst them, and the only one who could climb high enough. This was his responsibility and his alone, but he wanted nothing to do with it.

He was a child in Madeline's eyes, only nineteen, and so Daniel did what he was told. He had left his motorbike outside the coop overnight at her behest. The scrambler, as he called it, was never seen again. Madeline had hoped as much. It was a relic from the Eighties apparently, and he had said it had been in his family since before he was born. Daniel had pushed it all the way from the woodland's edge when it broke down, unable to part with it. They all came to stop there. There was one way to enter the forest, and that was on foot.

Ciara hadn't stirred for three days. Not since her husband took off to find help. Madeline's pity for her was cold and active like a twitching corpse. Ciara was naïve and she was fat. She had these wonderfully romantic notions about love and the world, and she seemed to genuinely believe that escape was possible. Now she was a widow at twenty-six. Her crying was constant; a leaking faucet beyond repair.

She had become a liability. A drain on what little they had, offering nothing but tears. Madeline wished that Ciara had gone in search of help, and that her husband had stayed.

At least he was strong. She could have made some use of him. But he was gone now. He was dead, and she remained, bundled under their blankets in the coop's corner, weeping to no one, wondering how everything could just disappear, leaving no proof that it ever existed.

Ciara looked young and still relatively healthy. In the right light her innocence was almost gaudy. Madeline envied her for that. Her youth and the beauty it bestowed; something she could never mimic. But on their diet and without sunlight this would fade fast, becoming a memory too painful to recall, like anything lost that was never cherished. She still had that softness around her face and body, the kind that children keep until the years chisel a shape out of them. Give it one winter, Madeline thought, if she can survive even that.

Ciara's hair was copper red and had grown just below her shoulders. The girl had spent every moment of every day smoothing it behind her ears; a nervous habit that, despite their circumstances, never failed to make her husband smile. Ciara was pale the day she arrived. Not a wilting grey pallor like Madeline's. Her skin was perfect porcelain, and her eyes were like emeralds, always glistening, always searching for happiness when there was none to be found; just another excuse to pity her.

She had the doting husband, the home, the life that she had always wanted – the unspoken checklist. During her first days she had taken to sharing everything about herself, even airing their plans for the future as if nothing had changed. Holidays and festivals, children's names and the schools where they would be spoken, like a record from a different time stuck on repeat. Madeline's disinterest was obvious, and soon the sound of Ciara's voice softened to silence.

She and her husband, John, had clung to each other for support, and now she was reaching out for someone who wasn't there, and Madeline knew never would be again. Ciara would come to realise this in time. As young as she was, she was still old enough to learn what hopelessness meant.

Madeline had ventured out at dawn. Thin tapers of morning light broke the canopy above, melting the frost in patches, leaving the rest crystal white. The spring was their sole source of water and requisite to their survival. It wasn't far. Madeline had cleared a path and could reach it within half an hour at a stable pace. Daniel had packed a two-litre bottle of water with him when he set off on his bike all those months ago; his one contribution. Maybe he wasn't so useless after all. Madeline had emptied out his backpack onto the floor the day he arrived and taken all that she wanted. The boy was too nervous to stop her, and too confused by his surroundings to collect his courage. He had never seen a room like it.

The coop was Madeline's responsibility. She alone held all the keys. She kept it locked when they were inside. Ciara and Daniel had been warned. If they weren't there come nightfall, then they weren't getting in, and so they rarely strayed too far. Madeline's threats were not to be taken lightly.

The coop's entire front, from the floor to the ceiling, was one colossal pane of glass that framed the surrounding woodland. Madeline tried to keep the window clean, wiping it down whenever they had water to spare. It made the myriad scratches on its exterior all the more noticeable. Everyone struggled at first. But that sense of being so exposed and vulnerable never went away. They just learned to live with it.

On the other wall was set a long electrical bulb that stretched between both gable ends. It was encased in what looked like glass, but it was unbreakable. Madeline hoped that the pane that stood between them and the forest was as strong. It was all that kept them safe. The light was blindingly bright and couldn't be looked at directly. No one had worked out yet how it was powered. It came on automatically at night, and turned off at dawn, when the first rays of light scourged the forest floor of darkness.

This is where they spent all their nights. In the far corner, tucked under the light, was their bed of blankets; a mismatched clump of faded fibres. Ciara had been buried under them for too long now. Usually, they weren't allowed to sleep when the light was on. They had to stay awake, otherwise the watchers would scream and howl, and hammer at the glass. How many attacks could it take before it shattered?

There was a table in the room's centre. It was a chunk of deadwood, crooked and wobbly, and so low that one had to kneel on the floor in order to eat off it. It was unsightly. But like Madeline, Ciara, and Daniel, it was part of the room.

In the coop they stored their supplies – edibles they had gathered during the day, fresh water from the spring, and anything that was or may have been of some use to them. They kept it clean. Madeline made sure of that. Unclean spaces bred infection, and they had no medicines to fight it.

Daniel and Ciara were in the coop when Madeline heard

the parrot's squawk. Birds never landed on the forest floor. They knew what was down there, and they valued their lives more than a few nuts. The air was always deathly quiet in the moments before the watchers crept out of their pits, as though the woodland held its breath, waiting for their screams to sear through the silence. She had seen the woman struggling towards her. Madeline was surprised by how fast she had moved. Truth was that had Mina fallen only once, the door would have slammed shut.

5

Daniel

The coop's light switched off. Daniel never knew the time, but when the mirrored pane turned to glass, it had to be morning. He lost so many hours staring at his own reflection that the version of him trapped in the mirror had become somebody else; another Daniel who, like the watchers, only appeared when night fell, and departed just before the dawn.

It was still dark, inside and out, and the air was cold as a tomb. The paling sky was leaking through the trees, revealing a forest still and lifeless, and crisp from a frost that would last through the day.

Madeline unlocked the door without hesitation. Some mornings she stood by it, waiting, as though, unlike Daniel, time was something she could measure. When the bulb was dull and dormant it was safe to leave the coop. The light never lied to them. But Daniel wasn't so eager to step out. It was, after all, not quite daylight. Not yet.

He often wondered how deep the burrows went. Did

they stand atop a vast catacomb of tunnels and hollowed-out chambers, stretching for miles in all directions? Did the watchers continue to dig, expanding their subterranean empire, edging ever closer with each claw of dirt towards civilisation?

Madeline had marked out the locations of those pits closest to their water trail. They didn't seem to bother her. She might as well have been side-stepping a puddle. Daniel imagined the watchers lingering close to the surface as the darkness dissipated, hoping for him to abandon the coop too soon and to step within reaching distance of them. How deep would they drag him? Would anyone hear his screams?

He always waited. It wasn't morning until Daniel saw daylight. Ciara would join him, in silence, by the window. The air felt empty without the light's constant hum. Sometimes he almost missed it. Without the warmth of the sun or the sound of birdsong it never seemed like morning, just a lighter shade of night.

Madeline inspected the building every day without fail. Sometimes she brought Daniel with her, showing him what to look for. As expected, the water was gone. Everything they valued should have been stored in the coop where it was safe; the only space that was essentially theirs. There were some fresh scratches on the living room's open frames that she pointed at until Daniel pretended to understand their significance. A few had come inside, Madeline had told him, but they hadn't caused any meaningful damage that she could identify. The walls and ceiling seemed unchanged to Daniel's eyes. The stench of their bodies still lingered; a noxious, unclean air of excreta and old flesh. A lit fire would smoke it out of the room. Aside from that one scream that sent Mina to the floor, the watchers had been surprisingly quiet. Madeline said that she was obviously a novel enough addition to keep them entertained for one night.

While Mina slept, Madeline had sat Daniel down again. Ciara, too, was told to listen in. Madeline's words had the sharpest edges, just like Daniel's father, and they dripped in bitterness, stinging long after they were spoken.

'You're certainly young and able enough to climb a few trees should our next meal depend on it,' she had said to Ciara. 'Besides, you're bound to lose some of that puppy fat eventually.'

Daniel had his head lowered, willing Madeline to stop; wishing that he had the courage to stand up to her. Maybe he was a coward after all. He had run away from his father and given half a chance he would run away from Madeline, too, taking Ciara with him. It didn't matter where they went, so long as it was far away, where nobody knew what a failure he was and how he couldn't catch some stupid birds, even when Ciara's stomach ached from hunger. Madeline explained how to set the traps again. How many times had she gone through those simple steps? Talking down to him as though she were house-training a dog. He always tried his best, but the birds were smarter than Madeline gave them credit for. They knew better than to fly too close to the woodland. They knew what was down there.

'Do you understand now, Daniel?' she had asked him, placing her hand tight on his shoulder, watching him flinch from her touch. 'If you don't ask me any questions, you'll never get any answers, and then you'll never learn. Do you want to starve to death? And Ciara, too?'

'I got it,' he replied. 'Don't worry. I'll do better next time. I promise.'

'Let's hope so.'

The winter nights were long and uneasy. There was nothing for anyone to do; nothing to distract them from their reality. Maybe, in that sense, the reflective glass was a blessing. Their doppelgangers stood guard tirelessly, calling for their attention whenever their thoughts drifted towards that which watched them from behind the mirror.

Daniel and Ciara had sat together with Mina's parrot perched between them, both drawn to this new pet to take care of when they themselves were barely holding on. Nothing Daniel could say would soothe her sorrow – the last gift her husband had given her – and so he said nothing, offering only a sad smile whenever their eyes met.

John had journeyed on foot as far as he could, always returning to the coop before *lights on*, to Ciara's side. He had explored all points of the compass, and each time came back dejected. The woodland was enormous, so wild and overgrown that to range the shortest distance took hours. His only choice was to not turn back, to keep on going, and hope that he could outrace the watchers' reach. It would be four days that morning since he left. Daniel harboured the hope that he was running still, and that he would someday return with an army behind him, burning every tree to cinders and pouring hot oil into all those pits.

Ciara was the big sister he never had; kind and sweet-tempered. He hated the way Madeline spoke to her. It twined his stomach, and made his heart beat so loud that he was worried she could hear it. But she was in charge. Madeline kept them safe and he had no choice but to follow her instructions. He cried occasionally when he least expected it. Those sudden bursts of tears, like a pipe exploding behind his eyes. He made sure nobody saw, but he guessed that Ciara knew. It was the same when his father used to hit him. Only after the bruise rose in a bump or when the blood was sealed with a plaster would the tears come, always where the old man wouldn't hear him. Crying wasn't allowed in that house. Neither was happiness.

Madeline held all the keys, and she had threatened to lock him outside if he didn't do as he was told. Scary as it was, he believed her. She wouldn't hesitate for a second. Daniel felt like an unwanted stray, running from house to house, looking for a home but finding only more of the same – cruelty and shame, and that gnawing suspicion that nobody would ever want him.

Mina seemed nice. She was beautiful too. Even though she was much older than he was. And she had actually stood up to Madeline. That was a first for any of them, but probably not the shrewdest move. Daniel had considered warning her about the possibility of being locked outside, but if Madeline found out, then he was as good as dead. It was exhausting, being scared all the time.

The earth in winter was solid as the cement. Would it be warmer underground if that's where he ended up? How long would he suffer before his body was bled dry and the watchers' screams eulogised his short, insignificant life? Hopefully, it would be quick. At least then he wouldn't be scared anymore.

Stepping outside was never easy, especially when that low fog brooded over the earth. It clung to Daniel's jeans, steeped through the denim and under his skin, squeezing the bones with its icy hands. He tugged the zip of his jacket up to his neck. The cold was already soaking into his lungs. His breath gathered around him like steam fresh from a spout. He hadn't lifted a foot off the cement yet and he was rubbing his hands together, trying to rekindle some feeling in his fingers. He had no choice but to go out. Madeline made sure of that.

'Are you checking the traps?' Ciara asked him from down the corridor.

'Yeah,' he replied, blowing air into his cupped hands. 'It's fucking freezing. Make sure you wrap up if you're going outside. I shouldn't be too long. Hopefully the old traps have caught something. I think I set them right, but I'm still getting the hang of it.'

'Madeline wants me to forage us up some food, and fill this,' she said, holding up the empty bottle. 'I think we should let Mina sleep awhile longer.'

'Good call,' Daniel replied. 'Get some rest yourself, too. I don't think either of us slept last night.'

'I think if Madeline catches me sleeping again, she'll lock me outside.' Ciara laughed, but Daniel couldn't fake a smile.

6

Mina

The coop was deserted when Mina woke up. Memories of the night before returned to her in broken fragments. For a brief, blissful moment before they assembled, she toyed with the thought that it had all been a dream. Then she heard the parrot fretting about in its cage like a child calling for attention, and the pieces fell into place. But the room wasn't as she remembered it.

The wall was now a window into the woodland. Gone were the reflections, and in their stead hung this lifeless painting, almost monochrome in its palette. The bird's golden feathers seemed all the brighter because of it. He trilled excitedly when Mina cast off the blankets and faced the cold.

'Good morning,' she said, stifling a yawn, and stretching some feeling back into her bones. The bedding's stale mustiness had soaked into her hair and clothes, and even her socks felt damp.

She held both hands over her face, fingers peeled apart

as she looked around the room. Mina remembered running towards the light, and those screams that were so quick to surround her. *It can't be real.* She rubbed her eyes, still stinging, and looked back to the window, seeing only the long scratches running through it. How long had she slept for? She had walked from dawn till dusk and must have passed out the moment she lay down. And where was everyone? It was so quiet. She shivered from the cold and brushed her hands together.

'Jesus,' she muttered, grinding her teeth, 'this place is fucking freezing.'

Mina smelt wood smoke. Through the doorframe, across from the coop, a fire had been raised. Its glow unfurled across the floor like warm carpet, inviting her to step inside. She held her hands over the flames and curled her cold toes up inside her boots, grateful for whoever was responsible.

'Well, isn't this lovely?' she whispered, examining the living room for the first time.

Dead leaves and dirt gathered in its corners, and the ground around her feet was pixelated with burns. The windows were high and held no glass. Even in the frail morning light she discerned the gashes around their frames. Mina took a step back from the fire when she saw the writing above it.

'*Stay in the light,*' she read aloud, just before the front door slammed.

Please, don't be Madeline, she thought with fingers crossed as the footsteps approached. It was too early in the day to be dealing with her. It was a habit of Mina's to avoid humankind until at least the evening time, when a glass of wine was the social norm.

'Oh,' Madeline said, stopping in the doorway, 'I see that you're up.'

'Yup,' Mina replied, not entirely sure how to act in the woman's company. The word *yup* escaped her lips before she could stop it. 'I was just admiring what you wrote on the wall.' Again, she regretted opening her mouth. *This is the reason why I don't talk to people.*

'*I* didn't write that,' she said, indifferent to Mina's play at humour. 'It was there when I got here, and they are words to be heeded, Mina, not admired. They saved my life like I saved yours.'

She moved up beside Mina, shuffling her feet so that they chafed across the cement. Madeline made no attempt to speak. Those long arms extended towards the warmth; mere skin and bone, so slender that they made her large hands look all the ghastlier. Mina tried not to stare at them but the eyes of an artist are easily led by curious things.

'Did you light the fire?' she asked, to which Madeline replied that she had, succinctly and without embellishment, as was to be expected.

Mina had so many questions wrestling on the tip of her tongue. Was now the time? The building itself was an architectural mystery, and Mina had yet to see a bathroom. That fact alone was as grim as Madeline's cryptic warnings of things in the dark. Things which, Mina reminded herself, she had yet to see. For all she knew this was some sadistic attempt at a reality show, with a nation of viewers in the comfort of their homes mocking the gullible girl with the parrot who believed it was all so real. How could she ever set foot in the pub again? What if Peter was in on the joke?

'I want to explain to you how this is going to work,

Mina,' Madeline said, snapping her back to the moment. 'An extra body can be a burden, as I'm sure you understand. We will need more food and more water. But if you make yourself useful, if you help rather than hinder, then our lives here can be less arduous. I only hope that you're cleverer than the other two.'

'They don't seem so bad,' she replied.

'Not so bad?' she echoed, her long neck twisting so that her eyes met Mina's. 'You do not survive here because you are friendly, idiotic and naïve. You survive if you are strict and abide by the rules. Being nice won't save your life, Mina. You'll understand this soon enough. You're lucky that you have me to guide you. When I found this place, I had no one. All I had was the writing on the wall.'

Now was Mina's chance. The conversation, if that's what this was, had wended its way precisely to where she had hoped. She noticed that Madeline's mouth had tensed, as though she was chewing over a thought that she refused to spit out. Mina had spent so much time studying people's faces that no detail – however slight – escaped her.

'How long have you been here?' she asked.

Madeline reached towards the pit and took out a long, spindly branch; scorched black and so damp that it survived when others had split. She poked around the embers, sending sparks flaring up into the air and flitting down like autumn leaves.

'What date is it today?' Madeline asked.

'It's the...' Mina paused to think '...twelfth of December.'

'And what year is it?'

'It's 2019,' Mina replied, somewhat surprised by the question.

'Of course it is,' Madeline said, throwing the branch back onto the fire. 'I've been here for two years and just over three months. Though, I must say, if I'm to be honest it feels much longer.'

Mina froze at the thought of it. She looked to Madeline's profile, skeletonised by the firelight, picturing how she might have been before the woodland became her world.

'Have you family, Mina?' she asked. 'Is there anyone who might come looking for you?'

Jennifer had probably tried to contact her again, even though she had said she wouldn't. Despite the umpteen distractions of her perfect life she always made the time to call, but seldom would Mina answer. Their conversations only served to highlight her shortcomings, and she was already more than aware of those. Weeks could pass without them speaking.

Mina's father had withdrawn from life, like a shadow receding in the rising sun. Since her mother passed away, he had taken to the drink. They had been saving for years. Now all those numbers that made up their joint account – the ones her mother never spent on herself – would fund the man's self-destruction, one bottle at a time, or else he would drink the well dry and die a thirsty wreck of a man beside it. She used to call him now and again, but more often than not he would cry over the phone, his tears washing through old scars, scalding them, too drunk to remember that they had even spoken.

Mina kept no close friends, only acquaintances. Bar staff and regulars – people you can walk away from without saying goodbye. The landlord would receive his rent by direct debit. It wasn't unlike her to hide away for extended spells to focus on her work. How long would pass before anyone realised that she was missing? Only Peter knew where she was going, and the general consensus deemed him a true-blue drunkard. No one believed a word he said, even when he enjoyed an hour or so of coherency.

'There's no one,' Mina said. 'No one is going to look for me.'

'It's for the best,' Madeline replied. 'Even if they knew your exact location, they would only make it as far as the woodland. You just about made it here before sundown. I often wonder how many don't make it at all. How many people have walked into the forest and never walked out?'

Mina heard the front door open. One of the longer chains rattled against its wood, and it closed ever so gently. Ciara could be heard humming to herself before she peered around the corner, her cheeks rosy from the cold. She carried a canvas bag, and the bottle that Mina had given to Madeline the night before had been replenished. Her hand was blue from holding it, probably not wanting to squash whatever berries she had found.

'Good morning,' she said, smiling. 'Madeline, you're a lifesaver. It's bitter out there today.'

Ciara hurried over to the fireplace, and Mina moved aside to let her into the heat. Madeline didn't budge an inch. She didn't even acknowledge that Ciara had spoken.

'We need wood,' she said, her hands retreating under her blanket.

'Can I just get warm first?' Ciara asked, spoken like a child requesting permission. 'It's so cold.'

'It'll be colder if you don't get the wood,' Madeline

replied. 'And if we're to cook the birds then we'll need a good fire, unless you want to eat yours raw?'

Mina looked to Ciara; subdued, her every part dithering from the cold. The faint firelight glossed her eyes, enriching their disbelief at Madeline's optimism. It was obvious that she worried about Daniel deeply and dreaded the reception that awaited him should he return empty-handed again. Ciara was his silent champion. And whether she believed in his abilities or not, Mina could tell that she would sooner stand by his failures than beside Madeline's long shadow.

'Okay,' she said, waving a hand almost through the flames, as though she was trying to take the longest one with her. 'I'll leave these bits and bobs in the coop and get going. We'll have the fire nice and big for when Danny gets home with the birds.'

Home, Ciara had said. The word sounded almost alien. Mina's home was in the city. A canvas stood in her studio, untouched. She had forgotten to turn off the storage heaters to save on the electricity before she left. They only worked in the living room. The dampness would already be staking its claim on the corners of the bathroom ceiling. That half-bottle of wine on top of the fridge would be corked by now. She had forked her bit of pasta into the bin and left the plate unwashed in the sink. The sauce would be plastered onto it. She would have to steep it in boiling water and washing-up liquid. That was her *home,* in all its chaotic glory.

'The days are too short to waste time,' Madeline said once Ciara was gone. 'Unless you tell them what to do, they won't accomplish anything. She would have sat here beside the fire, watching it slowly die in front of her, never thinking that maybe, just maybe, she could do something about it.'

'What was it like?' Mina asked.

'What was *what* like?'

'Being here on your own,' she added quietly, as a branch cracked, spitting sparks towards their feet.

Madeline pursed her lips again and stared at the last husk of wood fighting against the flames, overrun and defeated. All that time alone, hopelessly abandoned and forgotten. And yet she survived and had done so willingly.

'One mouth to feed and one body to keep warm,' she replied. 'My life was never so simple.'

'It must have been very lonely,' Mina said, 'having no one to talk to and no company during the night. I don't think I could do it.'

'You haven't seen them, Mina.'

'What do you mean?' she asked.

'If you could only see how many of them are out there, behind the glass, watching us,' Madeline replied. 'How could I ever be lonely here?'

7

Daniel

Daniel was sat cross-legged in front of the fire. He gently rocked back and forth, smiling to himself, like a child watching his favourite cartoon. Three branches had been pared down to slender spits and wedged between the walls that receded into the hearth. He was careful to turn each one, keeping the birds just out of the flame's reach. Three was more than he had hoped for. Even with Mina amongst them, it would be the best meal they'd had for weeks.

Madeline had been out when he returned from the traps. She seemed to be the only one with the free rein to do as she pleased. Mina was hovering by the fire when he practically slid into the doorway with the birds held aloft, beaming with a smile revealing every one of his crooked teeth.

He went about the business of plucking the feathers and prepping the spits. Daniel had told Mina that there were no animals in the woodland, and so birds were their only option. But it was as though they knew to avoid the place, and so Daniel climbed the highest trees he could find. And there he set his traps to entice the hungriest travellers from the sky. Madeline had shown him how to tie a noose around the bags, to which he would set some berries or nuts as a lure. Its weight would cause the string to tighten around the trap, sealing the bird inside.

'It's mostly luck,' he had said, skewering the first. 'I reckon the birds have to be really starving if they're going to risk dropping down close to this place.'

When Madeline stepped into the room she stopped abruptly, as though something there had changed in her absence but she couldn't place what it was. Maybe she had supposed that Daniel's traps would have failed, that the fire would be floundering, and that the onus would be on her to do what everyone else seemingly could not. Neither Daniel nor Mina spoke. Both held their breath, staring at the fleece-shrouded wraith that edged closer to the flames.

'Three, Daniel?' she had said, expressionless.

'Yes,' he replied, like a polite employee. 'And I've reset the traps in the same trees.'

There was no more that he could have done. This was the peak of Daniel's achievements, and still he worried that he hadn't reached high enough, as though Madeline expected him to touch the stars. He learned at a young age that disappointing people came naturally to him. Some kids had art. Others could keep a ball in the air. Daniel wasn't allowed to be good at anything, not so long as he lived under his father's roof. Any exams he passed in school were burnt as tinder. Those that he failed held circular stains where the old man's whiskey glass pinned them down, keeping them safe like collector's items. There were no victories, however small or insignificant, and after so many years of unbroken defeats, Daniel came to believing that that's all he was good for. His father certainly made sure to remind him that he wasn't good for anything else.

'Are you confident enough to cook these?' Madeline asked. 'Mina, perhaps you can lend a hand?' she added before Daniel could reply.

'Of course,' Mina replied.

'Good,' Madeline said, nodding her head. 'I suggest you start now. We have just over an hour. I'll make sure that all the locks are working and then we can prepare for dinner. Where's Ciara?'

'Just catching some sleep,' Daniel told her. 'I'll wake her when the food is ready.'

Madeline had frowned and left without saying another word. How did she ever keep track of the time? Daniel slotted the spits into place, carefully judging the height, and positioned the birds so that they would cook evenly. When all was done, he sat down in front of the fire and waited, staring at that which made him feel like an adult and an asset, finally.

8

Mina

Mina didn't interfere. Their dinner was far safer under Daniel's close supervision. When Mina's mum was receiving treatment, she wrote all her recipes down in a notebook; simplified and sprinkled with silly messages. They never tasted the same. It may have been her mum's recipe but it wasn't her mum's cooking. Even the *pasta alla norma* – a dish that a child could throw together – was missing something. That something was Mina's mum.

'Time to move,' Madeline called out. Mina couldn't believe it had been an hour.

The coop's bulb hadn't yet buzzed into being, and so the woodland was still slightly visible through the glass. The shadows had spread like an army of black ants, devouring the last morsels of light. Daniel set their food down on the table as Mina tiptoed towards the window.

'You won't see them,' Madeline said, drawing the door closed. 'They only come when the light is on. I've already told you this.'

Mina knelt, with both hands pressed against the glass. The woodland was darkening quickly, but her eyes were attuned to it. She would see them when they came.

'Come on,' she whispered. 'Where are you?'

In an instant Mina was staring at her reflection. Both palms pressed against those of her mirrored double. She backed away, drawing her hands over her eyes to ward off the light, and shuffled towards the sound of the parrot's panicked fluttering. She couldn't tell if its tantrum was brought about by the sudden brightness or by the sight of their next meal. Hopefully, the former would keep secret the latter.

The locks were put in place with surgical precision. Daniel crouched beside Ciara – still entombed under all those layers – and gently nudged the mound until her head emerged, all squinty-eyed and rumple-haired. Ciara's nostrils tightened as she caught the scent in the air, and she smiled.

'I caught three,' he whispered in her ear; Mina heard him, but Madeline was out of earshot, still triple-checking the door's many chains and bolts.

When the door was secured to her satisfaction, Madeline approached the table. She examined their feast like a finicky head chef. Mina had half-expected a smile from the woman but it never came. Too many winters had frozen all that bitterness in place.

'No one takes a drink until we have finished dining,' she said, meeting the eyes of everyone individually. 'There is precious little water for four of us, and I should imagine that the meal will make us quite thirsty.'

Mina, along with Ciara and Daniel, nodded her understanding. The smell of the food jump-started her stomach. She felt like an obedient Labrador, awaiting permission to devour its dinner.

'Now then,' Madeline announced as she squatted by the table, 'shall we?'

Everyone received their berry and nut portion first, and then the meat was shared out. Mina couldn't imagine the fallout had Daniel burnt it, but looking at it now – admiring the honeyed colour of its crisped skin and the tender flesh that tore, still slightly steaming, in their hands – it was perfect.

Madeline kept her head down, methodically dissecting every morsel. The others smiled amongst themselves, relishing the moment.

'It's just like Christmas,' Mina said, to which Madeline threw her a look of utter disapproval but passed no remark. Perhaps she was making a conscious effort not to spoil their dinner. Ciara seemed oblivious to the woman's glower.

'John loves Christmas,' she replied. 'Even the songs, if you can believe that? He starts playing them as early as November.'

Ciara blinked her tears away as best she could. They had come upon her so suddenly – the moment she mentioned her husband's name. Madeline stared at her indignantly from across the table, her meal potentially ruined by another's sadness.

'We should play a game after dinner,' Mina put in quickly, trying to steer Ciara away from those thoughts.

Madeline's spindly fingers ceased clawing meat from the bone. Ciara wiped her cheek, and after a few sharp sniffs it seemed that her curiosity had pushed through the crowd of her emotions.

'Does anyone play cards?' Mina asked, slapping both hands on the table. 'I always keep a deck in my bag. You know, just in case.'

'Just in case of *what*?' Madeline said. The sternness of her voice almost made Mina smile.

'In case I want to play cards, Madeline,' she replied, acting as though the answer was obvious.

Madeline returned to her food, unimpressed. The others had nearly finished their meals and were picking away at the last berries. The woman had a flair for making them feel ill at ease. She spoke so little – only to dispense orders or criticisms. Her silence was like a sleeping dragon. They had learned to not disturb it. Mina, however, was already rummaging through her bag.

'So, what do you reckon?' she asked her, dropping the deck playfully down on the table.

'A game would be good to keep us awake,' Madeline replied as she placed a bone down slowly and carefully, aligning it with those already in front of her. Every shred had been gnawed off it.

The light of the coop was stark in contrast to the casino's intimate, almost ember-like glow. The plush green of the poker table, the edgy silence broken only by the dealer's gloss and the plastic tap of chips by thoughtful hands. Mina was surprised by how much she missed it.

With the exception of the occasional commissioned piece, the casino provided her main source of income. There was only one in the city. At the weekend it attracted scores of temporary members, eager to gamble for a single night. These were mostly men who had imbibed enough to make gambling a misguided idea. They would melt into their seats like cheap candles, sending towers of chips trailing across the table.

Facial tells were reliable, especially when sired from one drink too many, as was so often the case in the late hours. They weren't so much letting slip a few clues as they were showing Mina their hand. The eyes alone could give someone's game away. Some of them blinked too much or too little. Others had an overactive tongue or lips that pouted like a fish when the cards were kind.

'Do you all know how to play?' she asked as she slid the cards out of the deck.

'*I* do,' Madeline replied, looking at the other two, assuming that a game as complex as poker was beyond them.

'I used to play a bit,' Daniel said, 'but never for money or anything like that.'

Ciara looked like a sheepish schoolgirl who hadn't done her homework. If only to deny Madeline the satisfaction of belittling her, Mina explained to them, collectively, how all the different hands worked. A quick refresher course, she had called it, just to make sure that they were all playing the same game.

Mina ripped two pages from her sketchbook and tore them into smaller pieces to use as money. The book was promptly returned to her bag. Mina wasn't sure why exactly, but she didn't want anyone, especially Madeline, to see her drawings.

'I'll deal,' Mina said, fixing her posture. 'Let's make someone rich.'

Madeline, to her left, discreetly slid her cards into her palm; straight-faced, as always. Daniel, kneeling across from Mina, grabbed his hand as though one of them might steal it. His eyebrows lifted and Mina knew that he liked what he saw. Finally, Ciara, sitting to her right, struggled to peel her cards off the table. Upon inspecting them she rolled her eyes and let out a sigh that made Daniel and Mina smile.

'Jesus,' she swore, shaking her head.

'You're supposed to keep it a secret.' Daniel laughed.

'Oh, shit,' she replied, holding her hand over her mouth in mock embarrassment. 'Well, you never know, maybe I'm trying to trick you.'

'Well, you're very convincing,' he said.

'It's on you, Madeline,' Mina announced.

Each of them had to put in one of their makeshift tokens if they wanted to play. Judging by Madeline's steely gaze and the way she guarded her cards, she wasn't playing strictly for the fun of it. This didn't surprise Mina in the least. Everyone looked to Madeline expectantly, waiting for her to commit and in that moment there was quiet, and there was a peace amongst them for what would be the last time.

All heads turned to the glass when they heard the scream; drawn out, tortured, and human. Mina would never forget it.

'John?' Ciara screamed.

Everyone looked to her, but no one knew what to say. He was out there, in the darkness. Her husband had come back to her, just as he had promised.

9

Madeline was the first to stand. Her skeleton unfolded in an instant and those spindly arms recoiled out of sight. But the woman's poise was not one of action. She stood rigid. Even her bones were quiet. This was survival. Mina knew enough of Madeline already to guess what she was thinking: they were only as strong as their weakest link. Madeline stepped back warily, eyeing up Ciara as though she now presented some threat to her. She held all the keys and the door was staying shut.

'John!' Ciara called out, hoping perhaps that her husband could hear, and that her voice would soothe his anguish.

She scrambled to her feet, sending cards flying about the floor. It was startling how swiftly – how viciously – everything changed. Mina still had her cards fanned open in her hand. The stolid faces of two queens peeked out from the back. She watched Madeline and Ciara in the mirror, like a televised fight on the big screen.

'What do you think you're doing?' Madeline said.

'John's alive!' Ciara cried, her tears of joy ousting those of grief.

Mina and Daniel rose to their feet slowly and reluctantly. They stood between Madeline and Ciara, in the divide. However long the three of them had survived before Mina's arrival, they had done so together, but that was about to change.

'That door,' Madeline stated slowly, 'does not open until the light turns off. Do I make myself clear? Have I not reiterated the rules enough?'

Another horrific cry came from beyond the mirrored pane. There was no telling how close John was to them. Sounds travelled fast and far, and in that concrete cell they rang all the louder. This man who had set out to save them was in untold pain, and yet Madeline's gaze was unflinching. To her, Ciara's husband was already dead.

'You can't leave him outside!' Ciara screamed in disbelief, storming towards the door.

The darkness outside and the light within conspired to keep the man's whereabouts a secret. His voice, strained and constant, seemed to stem from all directions, as though it echoed through the trees. Daniel's expression replicated Mina's. They dreaded to imagine what they were doing to him. John was living their worst nightmare.

'Let me out, Madeline,' Ciara shouted, standing face to face with the woman. 'Open that door!'

Mina knew Daniel wanted to support her. Ciara had become more than a friend to him. They shared their tribulations like two siblings born into hardship, gleaning strength from one another. Survival without her was inconceivable to him. And Daniel must have known that if she stepped outside, he would lose her forever.

Was loss now a mandatory part of Mina's life? She had grown quite fond of Ciara in the short time since they'd met. The only warmth in that room came from her hope and her humanity; strengths that Madeline didn't seem to understand. Even with her husband out there, alone, racing against the odds to save them, Ciara had welcomed Mina with a smile; like an antidote to the horror, and one that only she could administer. Mina never had a friend like that before.

'If I open the door,' Madeline replied calmly, 'then we're all dead. You know the rules, Ciara. When the light is on, the door stays closed.'

'My *husband* is out there!' she cried. 'He nearly made it back to us. We were too quick to close the door. If only we had been keeping watch, we would have seen him. We would have gotten to him.'

That could have been me, Mina thought. Without Madeline's help she would have shared the same fate.

'Your husband left four days ago,' Madeline said, her tall frame towering over Ciara. 'He did *not* come back to save you. He couldn't even save himself. *They* brought him back, and *they* want us to hear his suffering.'

'But,' Ciara replied, whispering now, 'why would they do that?'

'Because he tried to escape,' she replied. 'I am tired of wasting my breath on you. No one escapes this place. How many times do I have to tell you this? John was dead the moment he walked out that door thinking that they wouldn't find him. They *always* find you.'

Ciara held her face in her hands and wept to the sound of her husband's suffering. Mina inched over towards her as though walking on broken glass. Daniel followed. There was nothing either of them could say or do. Madeline was outnumbered, and so frail that Mina guessed she could take her on, with or without Daniel's help. But what would they have achieved? They could have wrested the keys from her hand and released the many locks that the woman inspected each and every day. They could have thrown open the door, defying Madeline and her rules. But what was out there? What had Madeline seen that made her guard the door like the very gates of hell?

'Is there nothing we can do?' Mina asked her.

'Not until morning,' she replied, already walking back towards the table, dismissing them entirely.

'I'm not leaving him out there,' Ciara said, wiping the tears from her eyes.

'That's not your decision to make,' Madeline replied without turning as she began to tidy up after their dinner.

'You can't stop me,' she said.

Madeline didn't respond. Ignoring Ciara was not going to calm her down. Mina knew that much. She placed a hand tenderly on her shoulder, trying in vain to console the woman. She was somewhere else. Her thoughts were out there, in the forest, with the man whose cries for help were weakening by the second. Mina knew that they couldn't leave the coop. As heartless as Madeline's approach to the situation may have been, so long as the door remained locked, they were safe.

'Please,' Daniel said, 'don't go out there. We can look for John as soon as the light turns off.'

Ciara stared at the boy, shocked that he could side with Madeline when she needed him most. He looked close to tears, as if he already hated himself for saying it. She then turned to Mina in the hope that she would support her.

'He's right,' she said. 'We can't go out there, Ciara. I wish we could, but we can't.'

'I can't believe you're both doing this to me,' she whispered.

Mina didn't know what to say. She had never experienced that blind, selfless devotion that would send Ciara to her dying husband's side if only so they could die together.

John's cries stopped abruptly. The silence struck Ciara's heart like a spear and she sobbed at the sight of her lone reflection, condemned to never stand by her husband's side again. Mina and Daniel couldn't take their eyes off her. It was like witnessing a terrible accident; one they had caused. Their cowardice had affected another. Mina imagined the watchers fighting over John's scraps. A leg here and an arm there, each part of him dragged into a different pit. Her imagination dealt only in horror now.

Ciara collapsed into bed and buried herself out of sight. *This* was hopelessness. Mina looked at Madeline who sighed as though she knew that it would find the girl eventually and secretly dreaded the inconvenience of it all. Ciara's husband had died for them, and it had all been for nothing. Mina knew that the storm of Ciara's tears would someday calm, and in their ocean she would see all of their faces; the ones who let her husband die.

'We'll find John first thing in the morning,' Daniel called out to her. 'I promise.'

He should have known better than to make promises like

that. Mina suspected that if Madeline could have thrown Ciara outside and been rid of her, she would have. It was obvious that she saw her as an encumbrance. But then why didn't she? Was the threat so immediate, so at their door, that she wouldn't risk prising it open for a short second to let her out? What if they were right outside, in the corridor, listening to their every word, waiting for *that* moment of weakness?

Madeline wasn't concerned for Ciara. She was looking out for her own safety. And so long as Mina followed her lead, then maybe she was safe too.

'How did you know?' Mina asked her.

'How did I know *what*?'

'That those things out there brought John back,' she said. 'That they want us to hear him dying.'

Madeline indulged in that little habit of hers, pursing her lips before she spoke. The woman wasn't aware of it. Mina searched through her memories, throwing past moments from the shelves of her mind, laying bare all the occasions when Madeline had answered one of her many questions, and the times that her mouth performed those subliminal stunts. Mina understood what they meant now.

'I don't know anything, Mina,' she replied. 'My guess is as good as yours.'

Though Madeline had tried to conceal it, Mina knew then that so much she had told her was a lie.

JANUARY

IO

Mina

The storm lasted for two days and nights. The gale howled loudest through the living room's bare frames, throwing nature's wreckage into its corners, and spinning dry ash in whirlwinds across the floor. Branches split and fell. Some hung on by the flailed sinew of ivy and through tangled knots of thorns. The rain was relentless, breaking around the trees in waves, making their old wood creak like a fleet of sinking ships.

On the third morning it moved on and the sun made a brief appearance, making all that damp glitter like cut crystal. Drops of rain still trickled from the broken, leafless gutters above, and it would be a long time before the forest was dry. The calm was unnerving. It felt deceitful. Winter's white had melted into a gritty black. It made the simplest chore that bit more difficult as feet sank and slid, and every leaf and body of wizened bracken soaked clothes through to the skin.

It was the thirteenth of January. A month had passed

since Mina left the city. She had kept careful record of the days. Otherwise, there would have been no Christmas, no New Year's Eve – those days still guarded by memories, fond or otherwise. In the forest they were like any other. All days were the same. Dates were insignificant numbers. Life in the forest was one of routine and struggle. No memories worth keeping were made there, and the future's horizon was lost to the trees.

No one left the coop during the storm. Accidents and injury were too great a risk and Madeline wouldn't allow it. They had agreed to ration what they had and wait it out. The rain was deafening. Its bullets barraged the iron roof without ever reloading and the days were unnaturally dark. Somehow life was even more miserable, and each other's company all the more claustrophobic. As soon as the light clicked off, Mina was out the door. Within moments everyone else had done the same.

'Well, I'm not going to walk through you now, am I?' she said to the cluster of stinging nettles. Each leaf was a flooded little boat waiting to capsize. She could still recall the childhood trauma. Every trip to the countryside, especially those summers in Menlo Village, the nettles were everywhere. No one was safe. Mina was all too fond of sashaying through the high grass, feeling their blades slide through her fingers. She was an easy target and a repeat casualty. The skin would rise up like red bubble wrap, and the itch would burn and then it would burn some more. Dock leaves were the cure, her mother had told her. But even now, as a so-called adult, Mina wouldn't be able to pick one out of a line-up of leaves.

She was already sodden. Her toes squelched in her boots.

Mina had taken a page out of Madeline's book of woodland fashion and now when she ventured out, she always wrapped a blanket around her body. Madeline should have the fire built and burning by the time she got home. *Home* – even Mina caught herself saying it occasionally. She would commit the socially unspeakable and dry her wet socks by its warmth. The heel had already frayed to nothing on the left one. The right wasn't too far behind it. She tried not to think of all the fresh, folded clothes neglected in her apartment, and of the countless socks paired up in balls in the bottom drawer of her dresser.

She had to wade through the bushes to keep her course. Her shawl felt heavier with every bead of moisture that it absorbed, but the air was milder. She was thankful for that. Her breath no longer hung around her lips like exhaled smoke. Mina missed that habit most of all. Gone were the halcyon days of hand-rolled cigarettes. She had stretched the remains of her tobacco pouch as far as she could. But it had been nearly a week now without one, and Mina's hands had started to fidget. She missed the yellow stains on her fingers and the cough that always warmed her throat.

'There you are,' she whispered when her eyes found the burrow.

Mina had two bags with her that afternoon. One was her own, containing everything that was only hers. She had taken to picking at its fake, black leather out of boredom. She never let it out of her sight. Madeline had watched it like a hawk, trying to catch a glimpse of whatever she was hiding in there, not that any of it was particularly interesting. But Mina reaped some pleasure from keeping its contents secret. Madeline kept her fair share. The other was a canvas bag that she used to carry the bottle, and to store any edibles that she found along the way. Such was the life of a forager. Her sister would be proud.

She slid her sketchbook out, careful to keep it safe from any stray droplets; those that seemed to sprout from a hundred hidden sprinklers high above. The burrow was more or less where she had expected to find it. The detour around the nettles had thrown her course off slightly, but she was confident that it lined up with the rest. The hole in the earth was unusually wide and mostly undisturbed, or else the rain had smoothed out the soil, removing any tracks. Its location was duly jotted onto the page.

Madeline had warned them that the burrows were all over the forest, randomly dug into the earth, and so it was in their best interest to stay on the path she had made for them. But that wasn't the case. Mina suspected that Madeline had known this all along. There was a pattern. Mina just didn't understand it yet. Ciara and Daniel may have been content to eat up the woman's lies, but it was Mina's intention to spit them back.

Every day, Mina made the trip to the spring. She had volunteered to do so. Before her arrival, Daniel and Ciara had taken turns to replenish their water supply. They both saw it as a chore. Daniel worried so much about the burrows that they genuinely upset his sleep. And Ciara made every errand seem like a burden, which coincidentally was exactly what Madeline thought of her. Any break from that environment, however short, was a gift.

The walk was a chance to enjoy some peace and solitude, once so underappreciated. Madeline stressed to her that collecting the water shouldn't take more than an hour.

Mina made sure to draw out her time, if only to prove the woman wrong. She would sit by the spring and listen to the trickle of water whispering between the rocks. She always rinsed her hands and face, and doused fresh water through her hair, squeaking like a field mouse from the cold. Simple rituals like this were important. They kept her clean. And, more importantly, they kept her sane. The days were too bitter to strip but if she were feeling brave, she would slip off her blanket and leather jacket, and splash some water under her jumper and around her body. It was a kindness, she believed, that the sight of her naked self should remain a mystery. Mina dreaded to imagine how she looked.

Her arms had thinned. The veins glowed beneath their pale skin, and her hands – like Madeline's – looked larger. She couldn't stop staring at them, horrified by how they had aged in such a short time. Keeping them clean became a hobby of sorts, and another reason why she had volunteered to visit the spring each day. Her nails may have broken but they were never dirty.

When Mina hugged her body, she could count her ribs. It was as though a layer had been shaved off her. Gone was the flesh, its welcome softness. Her bones now felt exposed, like a delicate exoskeleton that would shatter if she took a bad tumble, her limbs scattering all around her. She was all jagged lines and sharp edges – a sketch from a Gothic novel; the thing that creeps through the night with all the silence of a spider.

Mina despised the coop's mirrored glass, not because of what it hid, but for what it revealed. Every night during those long, lit hours she would study her own reflection. She imagined it ageing before her very eyes or fancied that it wasn't her at all. It was some Dickensian vision – a ghostly warning to never enter the woodland. A warning that the spirit forgot to pass on, thus precluding the miracle that could have been.

Her hair was tangled and clumped together like a helmet. The fringe had inched down to her eyes, visible only if she acknowledged it. She pinned it back with one of her rare, remaining hairpins when she went about her jobs.

The eyes suffered the worst. The coop's light was a constant strain. There were days when they felt like the heaviest piece of her, holding more weight than all her bones combined. They were always tired; never fully opening like a new-born puppy. Mina could feel the folds gathering on both sides. The creases would eventually break like the veins of a leaf from her eyes to her ears. She had tried to rest them, to not squint against the light, but it was impossible. It was too painful.

The fading beauty in the mirror was forged from Mina's fears and the squalor that was everywhere, as though it had soaked into her skin, poisoning her self-esteem. The eyes always find what they search for, and she sought out the blemishes and the ugliness. Daniel would blush beet red whenever she caught him watching her from across the room. Mina couldn't understand what he saw.

Ciara hadn't forgiven them for what they had done. Not that a full pardon was ever expected. They were, each of them, responsible for her husband's abandonment. Ciara had forgotten *why* they did it, recalling the act without the reason. Every grudge, if it is to stand the test of time, relies on the certainty of a selective memory. The woman had hardly spoken since that night. Though it was Madeline who had held the keys and guarded the door, it was Daniel who bore the brunt of Ciara's resentment. His betrayal had cut her the deepest.

He tiptoed around her, treating Ciara like a cracked china doll, desperately trying with every kind act and utterance to win back her trust, to cement over the fractures. She was having none of it. He had the saddest smile that Mina had ever seen.

'Maybe he's still alive,' he had said to Ciara days after that night.

Mina knew that the boy's heart was in the right place. But that was no excuse. He just had a knack for always saying the wrong thing. There were days when he couldn't bring himself to look anyone in the eye, and then there were those moments when he would stare at Madeline, his intentions towards her guarded and deranged.

Madeline was unchanged. She spoke strictly of matters regarding their survival. Her face was dull as a death mask. It was unnerving. Only the eyes ever moved. It was as though she knew that Mina was studying her.

The tensity between Madeline, Ciara, and Daniel was palpable, like a gas leak you could taste in the air. They went about their jobs and survived as best they could, together. But Madeline had been right. Daniel and Ciara were weak. There was no gauging what they were capable of should their emotions get the best of them.

Only the bird seemed to adjust to their new lives with ease. It looked healthy enough and was tirelessly upbeat. It slept during the days, and its bright face beamed at everyone throughout the night, thrilled to always have company. The yellow one only lost its cool when Madeline stepped too close to it. Her unpopularity had, or so it seemed, spread across species.

Mina made her way back to the coop. The clouds cracked, and faint pillars of sunlight slipped through the branches above. Wet stones waxed like mirrors, and leaves brimming with water shimmered all around. The bottle had been filled, and her foraging had added a ball of weight to the canvas bag.

The same thoughts and theories tracked her every careful step, keeping her company, always buzzing around her head like a swarm of summer midges. Undeterred by Madeline's restated belief that their escape was impossible, Mina knew there had to be a way. John's attempt was ill-conceived. The man had made a run for it; simple, rash, and ultimately suicidal. He didn't understand the lay of the land or what he was running from. And the forest was so dense. It was unlikely that he had covered much ground before nightfall.

Would he have been so brave had he actually seen what was out there? Mina had studied the gashes around their burrows, and she had heard their screams. But she had yet to see them. That, she decided, had to change. She had to test Madeline's version of the truth. She said that the things weren't human, that they were leaner and longer. But if they weren't human, then what were they? And if they didn't build that cryptic prison deep in the forest, then who did?

'You took your time,' Madeline said when Mina stepped into the living room.

She had cleared the storm's debris from the floor. And was now trying to stoke some life into the fire using what little wood they had stored before the rain came, which wasn't a lot. The deadwood outside was too damp to be of any use. Mina chose to ignore the thorny welcome. Besides, she always *took her time*.

'I'll leave the water and the bit of food inside,' she said. 'Were the traps checked?'

'Nothing,' Madeline replied. 'The storm destroyed them. We should have taken them down.'

If only we had watched the weather forecast, Mina thought, but knew better than to say it. At least Madeline couldn't blame Daniel this time. However, testament to the woman's inventiveness, she was sure to ferret out some other reason for berating the boy.

Ciara was in the coop, shaking the blankets out, grimacing like a housewife disenchanted with it all. Mina had suggested taking one of them down to the spring each day for a wash. They could have dried them slowly by the fire over the course of a few days. Madeline vetoed the motion, saying that they should wait until winter had passed. She genuinely had no intention of ever leaving that place.

'Do you want some nuts, Ciara?' Mina asked.

'I will once I'm done here, thank you,' she replied in that monotone that was now her voice. Every response sounded almost automated.

Daytime in the coop was surreal as the night. Mina had grown so used to her own reflection that when the glass was transparent, she almost missed that ugly other self, as though she was one half of a complete person.

'I'm glad the storm has finally passed,' she said. 'Mind you, outside is in some state after it. You want to watch your step if you're going out.'

Ciara just grunted some sound that could have meant either *thank you, Mina,* or *Mina, would you kindly shut the fuck up.*

'What's everyone been up to?' Mina asked, leaning against the wall, showing that she wasn't going anywhere anytime soon.

'Madeline brought Daniel into the woods again,' Ciara replied, but not until after she had exhaled all the air out of her lungs in frustration.

'What do they do out there?'

'I don't know,' Ciara replied. 'I don't care. She's probably showing him how to make more traps, or maybe they were collecting wood. It doesn't matter. Madeline said we won't have any real food for at least another day.'

Mina noticed that Ciara's shoes and the calves of her jeans were tarred with wet dirt. She had already been outside, and unlike Madeline's movements there was no mystery as to where she wandered. It was a ritual of hers to search the area of the woods where she believed John had been taken. Truth was that there was no knowing where the man had died. His cries had come from everywhere. Ciara had yet to find any trace of him, or if she had then she had kept it to herself. Mina knew better than to ask. Even Daniel wasn't so blunt as to broach that question.

'Where's Danny now?' Mina asked.

'Setting the traps, I guess,' Ciara replied, utterly disinterested.

'But I thought you said that he did that earlier with Madeline?' Mina asked.

Ciara paused to assess what she was saying. She clearly wasn't even paying attention to herself.

'I don't know,' she replied, frustrated now. 'Either way I heard Madeline telling him to go and set them up. So, I suppose they were doing something else. Does it matter, Mina? Why don't you just go and ask her?'

Absolutely useless, Mina thought, looking at the girl who used to be so cheery – the kind-hearted antithesis to Madeline's dispassion. Ciara's hair, and around her neck and chin, looked filthy. Her hands, too. After all that had happened to her, what was a little dirt? She was just another tree in the storm, weathered and broken.

Hygiene had become an obsession of Madeline's after Christmas when Daniel caught a chill. That's why the coop's cleanliness had become a priority. Madeline wasn't taking any chances in case his runny nose was a symptom of something worse. She wouldn't even talk to the boy or let him take a sup from their bottle. He had to drink the water from his cupped palms, spilling most of it on the floor, only further waxing her irritation.

The cold was the killer. If the damp soaked into you, if it chilled your bones and you let it linger, then you were inviting trouble. That's what Madeline had told them. That was why she built a fire every day. They were tired and malnourished, but there was warmth when they needed it, and it was their fault if they got sick.

Mina heard the door slam. Then, in the corridor that heightened every sound, there was silence. Madeline must have ventured outside again. She wasn't in the habit of letting them know where she was going, and Mina knew there was no point in asking her. No matter where Madeline went, she was always back before the bulb clicked on.

There was scarce natural light in the living room but the

fire had reacted warmly to Madeline's efforts, and its orange glow now flooded across the floor, splashing giddy shadows on the walls. Without the wisp of a breeze to steal away its heat, the air there was a novel reprieve from what Mina had been used to. Her hair was still damp, and her boots were as wet inside as they were out. She was glad that Madeline hadn't noticed how cold she had gotten during her trip to the spring. There would have been some stern words and a cautionary wag of her bony finger.

Mina spread her blanket down in front of the fireplace, flittering off any clingy twigs, and she sat, cherishing a heat that was always hottest against the eyes. Each sock was peeled from her feet. The tear in the left one was worse than before. Mina tried to rub some feeling back into her toes. Thanks to Madeline's fire they would soon wiggle more freely. A few sparks leapt from the pit, but so clammy was the blanket that they dissolved in an instant, dead on arrival.

Mina trained her ear towards the coop. There wasn't a sound. Ciara had probably collapsed back into bed. It was as though her built-in battery never fully charged. Maybe that's why she rarely spoke anymore. Not that the rest of them were overly loquacious. They all lived in such close proximity and yet seldom interacted. But this had its advantages, such as this moment. There was no one to disturb her, and she would hear the door if anybody were coming. Peace *and* warmth. Mina could hardly believe her luck.

She took out her sketchbook, wiped it clean with some secret sense of ceremony and leaned towards the fire so that its paper was laminated in light, enriching all that white with the warmest tones. Its pages housed the myriad faces that she had come to regard as friends. They were links to her past life, to happiness, and to the city that went on without her. She often wondered if anyone ever asked where she had gone. Peter was probably still ranting on about how she had scarpered off with his money, telling anyone who would listen. Not that many would. Maybe he missed her for that reason.

Mina's memory was photographic. But the photos faded over time. The details were dulled, obscured by a static that no mental tuning could clear. She had tried to draw Jennifer but couldn't do her justice. Though the resemblance was uncanny – identical to the layman's eye – it wasn't the Jennifer she remembered. The intimacy between the artist and the subject was absent. Mina's sister had never felt so distant nor so lost. A large X had been scrawled over the imposter's face.

She had sketched the only faces available to her. Gone were the days when she would scour the street for that perfect *one*. Beggars can't be choosers, as her mum used to say, and Mina would sooner draw a dozen pictures of the parrot than do a self-portrait.

The coop's residents each looked so different on paper. Mina's past subjects, for the most part, had been strangers, and there was an element of invention in realising their personalities without interfering. But after a month of their company – close and compulsory – they were no longer strangers to Mina. She saw through the transparency of the physical and interpreted instead the truth and those distinctions that defined them.

Daniel's face was older, even in the short time she had

known him. It reminded Mina of the fantasy novels she had read as a teenager, and more specifically of the immortal ones. Those who by curse or choosing could not age and yet the years they garnered became an unmistakable part of them. They were especially noticeable in and around the eyes, and Daniel's were the coldest blue. On paper he was dauntless. Behind those gritted, mismatched teeth there was courage; the strongest kind, braced by suffering. The face was handsome. It could be trusted. He may not have been a man, as Madeline so often reminded him. But he was certainly not a boy. Not anymore.

Ciara's beauty had changed since the first night they met. Her kindness and the capacity to conceive and expect kindness from others, this purity had emanated through her. The eyes gleamed and the pale skin shone. She was, through her innocence, fragile, and had been targeted by Madeline for this very reason. But Ciara's sadness had given her strength. Her rage was the red, hot steel and her tears were the waters that quenched it. She stood by her principles like a knight given to die by her sword. She guarded the truth and the memory of her betrayal. Ciara's was a tragic kind of beauty now because there was simply no kindness left.

Madeline, whose ragged features and scowl would give children nightmares, had changed, too, in Mina's eyes. She was the great misunderstood. The dark clouds that drowned out the sun. The locked door that kept them as prisoners. She was the most unlikable woman Mina had ever met. But being liked was never a concern for Madeline.

She occupied more pages than the rest. Her exanimate features reminded Mina of *the android* who lived in the same sketchbook. She had taken to studying Madeline, layering her face with many lifetimes of experience, only to reduce it all to nothing – restoring the youth and the beauty that the woodland had divested from her. There were still glimmers of her younger self. It was the Madeline that didn't surrender when a million others would have; that rebellious decision to survive when the world couldn't give her a reason. Somewhere, inside her, there was a stubborn teenager who hated everything, but accepted that that's all there was.

Mina turned over to the sketchbook's back page, to the map of the woodland that was slowly expanding. Their home – *she had to stop saying that* – was drawn in its centre. As the days went by and more burrows were discovered, its location on the page became more significant. The pits extended from the building in lines, straight and plotted. If the remaining lineaments were consistent with the ones that Mina had recorded, they formed a circle, like the rings on a tree, with the coop directly in its centre.

They were aligned too perfectly to have been made by chance, and hinted at an underground network, a system of passages constructed with purpose and precision. Mina had linked these burrows together. Tracing, with the lightest hand, a pattern; a spider's web that, like a witless housefly, she hadn't seen until it was too late. To think of that day when she blundered into the forest still gave her chills. Had she stopped to take another rest, even for one minute, she would never have made it, and nobody would ever have known what had happened to her.

Mina gave her sock a gentle squeeze. She wasn't wearing them anytime soon. But there was still an hour, maybe more, before nightfall. It was impossible to tell. For all she knew the light could switch on at any second. Should the worst come to be, she would roll them dry in her hands and be barefoot for a spell. Madeline would throw her a look of annoyance, as was her wont, but Mina knew that she wouldn't voice it. The woman didn't need words to get her message across. That frown did all the talking for her.

Just then, the front door opened and slammed shut with deafening force. Mina hid away her sketchbook and grabbed the second sock from in front of the fire. She could hear anxious, strained breathing that could only be Daniel's. She knew in an instant that something terrible had happened.

'I made it,' she heard him gasp. 'Oh God, what am I doing?'

II

Daniel

Daniel ran through the forest. Like a wild animal released he didn't look back. Not once. Toils of ivy snagged his legs. With his hands he fended off barbs of thorns and the wet stems that whipped across his face. He knew the way, but his haste had scattered his bearings. His was a compass spinning in dizzying circles. The trees seemed to shift through the earth, blocking his path, throwing their bodies in front of him as though they had been gifted life and worked their branches like limbs to ensnare him. It was a maze; a darkening, ill-lit labyrinth where decay and dying things ruled supreme. Madeline was still calling his name. She was chasing him, but in that moment – driven by sheer fear – he was faster.

His breathing was loud and erratic. He muttered senseless sounds that even he couldn't understand. Panic had gripped Daniel hard with the intent to break him, but instead it threw him forward. He had veered from the route he knew. Despite everything that stood in his way, still he kept one eye on the ground. Some burrows were wide enough to catch at a glance, but others he wouldn't see until it was too late; until he slipped from the light and fell within *their* reach. He fought back his tears, but their coming was inevitable.

Daniel hadn't planned this. His movements – so swift, so instinctive – had surprised even himself. It was a moment of madness; an impetuous act that he was already regretting. Madeline had dropped the keys as she tinkered with one of the traps. He was looking away, but he had heard their soft jangle on the ground. She didn't rush to pick them up. She never suspected that Daniel would grab them and make a run for it. Up until it happened, he wouldn't have expected it either.

His foot collided with the root of a tree, sending him sprawling forward. The pain shot through his ankle like an arrowhead. Though he winced, and his whole body sunk into that wet blackness, his hand still clutched the keys. There was no turning back now. He had outrun Madeline's voice, but she was still following him. Daniel just had to get back to the coop before she did. Otherwise, his efforts would all be for nothing.

She was just like his father. Nothing Daniel ever did was good enough. He had been told he was useless so many times that he had started to believe it. No words were ever kind. Everything he did was watched by eyes that wanted him to fail.

He just wanted a home, somewhere safe, where he could be himself without some dirty hand always pushing or slapping him. He would never set a foot in his father's house again. Filth and neglect had orbited the old man's chair facing the television. Nothing there was ever clean or worked the way it should have. The air smelt of stale beer and cigarette ash. Be it the windows or the oven or the cracked bathroom sink, everything – including Daniel – was broken, and his father had no interest in fixing any of it.

He squeezed the keys in his fist so hard it hurt. The old man was probably glad when he left, or else he simply didn't care. One swing – that's all Daniel wanted; just enough pain to make his father remember him.

Daniel was getting closer. He had run for so long that the coop had to be nearby. A fresh dread grew inside of him. Had he taken a wrong turn? What if Madeline was already there, waiting for him?

He was always afraid and he was always ashamed. His father had never loved him. He never even liked him. And when his mother died there was no reason to hide the fact. Daniel had left in the hope of finding a better life, and instead he had found Madeline. He couldn't take it anymore. It had to end. That's why he stole the keys. That's why he ran.

The coop came into sight, like a ray of sunshine on the darkest day. Nothing ever played out the way he wanted it to. He had learned to meet disappointment like an old friend. But Daniel was going to make it. He hadn't lost his way, and to think that Madeline could have overtaken him was absurd. He clenched the keys harder; his knuckles whitening around them. When he reached its door, he hurled it shut behind him. 'I made it,' he gasped. 'Oh God, what am I doing?' He raced down the corridor. There he saw Mina, sitting on her blanket, drying her socks.

'Danny?' she said, wide-eyed and curious. 'What's going on?'

12

Mina

Daniel was struggling to catch his breath. He leaned in, one hand on the doorframe, trying to keep his body upright, but he was wilting. The other held Madeline's keys.

'Come on, Mina,' he panted. 'Get into the coop.'

'Why?' she asked. 'The light isn't on yet.'

'It doesn't matter,' he said. 'Where's Ciara? Is she in there now?'

'She's asleep. Well, I think she is,' Mina replied, rising to her feet, still holding her socks. 'Danny, what's going on? Where's Madeline?'

'I'm locking her out,' he said, dangling the keys in the half-light of the doorway. 'Come on, hurry. She'll be here any second.'

Daniel was a nervous wreck on the best of days. But Mina had never seen him like this.

'Danny,' she said quietly. 'You have to calm down, okay? We're not locking Madeline outside. Something's happened, hasn't it? So, tell me what's wrong.'

'Quickly, Mina,' he shouted, backing into the corridor. 'Get inside!'

'Danny,' she repeated, more sternly, 'we're not fucking locking her outside. Have you lost it or something?'

The front door was thrown open and Daniel disappeared into the coop, closing its door behind him. Mina heard him fumbling with its locks. Madeline came storming down the corridor and began beating her heavy hands against it. Mina's intuition had been correct. Something terrible *had* happened.

'Daniel,' Madeline screeched, 'you open this door at once!'

She hadn't even looked to the living room, and had no idea that Mina was standing there.

'Madeline,' she said, to which she turned. 'What's going on?'

'Daniel's taken my keys,' she replied. 'He's not thinking straight. Maybe you can talk some sense into him.'

'How long do we have before the light comes on?' she asked.

'Ten minutes,' Madeline replied, 'maybe less.'

If the woman was worried, she had a gift for hiding it. Mina had never stood on that side of the coop's door when it was locked. It was darker than she was used to. The bulb that had once dangled in the corridor had been smashed during the storm. No light graced the empty window frames. Everything, with the exception of the fire and its surrounding influence, was black and impermeable. Ten minutes was being optimistic. Mina was surprised that the light hadn't clicked on already.

'What have you done?' she asked.

'What have *I* done?' Madeline replied, pacing towards her. '*I* haven't done anything. I keep those keys safe for this very reason, Mina. The two of them, they've been conspiring against us, waiting for their chance.'

Had there been any mutinous whispers between Daniel and Ciara, Mina would have known. The two so rarely spoke to each other that any synergy – even that of a secretive sort – couldn't have passed unnoticed. And besides, if their plan had been to discard Madeline to the darkness, why wouldn't they have taken her with them? What had Mina done to deserve being banished to the night?

Madeline stood aside and gestured Mina towards the door. The woman's face smouldered like a stone gargoyle in the firelight. There was no doubt in Mina's mind that this was all Madeline's doing. She had probably been too hard on the boy. That was her way after all. Her words crashed against him relentlessly, eroding Daniel away, day by day. Maybe the last piece of him – the sensitive, caring chunk that was his best – finally broke off and floated away.

'Daniel,' Mina called out, drawing her head close to the door. 'Daniel, I know that you're upset. But we don't have much time. If you would open the door, we can talk about this, and we can work out whatever it is that's wrong, okay? Whatever Madeline's done, she'll apologise for it, and we'll all sit down and see if we can make this better. How does that sound?'

Mina waited. She looked back to Madeline's silhouette in the doorway, fringed with amber light, unmoving.

'Daniel,' Mina repeated, 'can you hear…'

'She's not coming in,' he interjected.

Daniel was far too upset to tackle with reasoning. Even if

he did regret locking them out, the thought of what Madeline would do to him now was enough to keep that door from ever opening. Mina couldn't think straight. Every thought was overshadowed by the image of a clock counting down to the end. They should already have been inside.

'Ciara,' Mina shouted. 'Can you hear me, Ciara?'

No reply came, just the crackling of the fire in the next room and the shuffling of Madeline's feet as she edged closer. Mina wasn't surprised by Ciara's silence. Out of the two of them, Daniel was their only chance. In the weeks since John's abandonment, Ciara's hatred for them hadn't dissipated. It was possible that all of this was her idea, and that Daniel was her patsy, coaxed into exacting her revenge.

'What do we do?' Mina whispered to Madeline.

'There's nothing we can do,' she replied.

The light clicked on. It illuminated the door's frame with the thinnest white outline. Their time was up.

'Daniel!' Mina shouted. 'Open this fucking door.'

'Shush,' Madeline whispered sharply. 'Don't make a sound. Follow me.'

The woman's body disappeared down the darkness of the corridor. Then there came the slightest succession of clicks and slides as she placed the front door's locks in place. Even without any light to guide her hands, she knew them each intimately. Mina crept towards her, losing all sight of herself as she withdrew from the light.

Her fears throve on the darkness. It pained her to put each foot forward, stepping into that black void, vulnerable to the horrors gathering around them. She wanted to call out to Madeline for some reassurance that she was not alone, but the slightest sound would have drawn the watchers to them. Then she felt those bony hands feeling along her arm. Madeline laced her fingers through Mina's. With the gentlest tug she drew her down to the floor by the locked door, and there they huddled together, both staring towards the corridor's end and the orange glow that brushed across it.

It never entered Mina's mind that Daniel would leave them outside. He was so weak and manageable. To think that he could submit them both to this fate, it didn't seem real.

'Don't scream,' Madeline whispered, so close to her ear that she could feel every sound. 'Close your eyes and ignore everything you hear.' Here her hand tensed tighter around Mina's. 'It'll be okay.'

Mina regretted all the times she had been so hard on Madeline; so quick to criticise. There was good reason for the way she was. But her survivalist's agenda wasn't selfish. She had taken care of everyone and asked for nothing in return. Not even their kindness.

'Okay, I'll try,' Mina whispered, so low that she wasn't sure if she had spoken.

The woodland was stricken with the watchers' chorus. It sent tremors through the walls. Mina could feel them reverberating against her skull. Their voices were louder than ever, and they were everywhere. The door would hold. It always did. But what did that matter when there were three open frames in the next room? She thought of the markings on them, imagining a claw so sharp that it could slice through stone. Mina wouldn't scream. She wouldn't let Madeline down.

She visualised her apartment exactly as she had left it.

Mina wasn't sitting on the hard cement with the cold stealing across her bare feet. She was in her kitchen with its faded countertops, on the top floor. The afternoon sun hung outside the open window like a child's balloon tied to the longest piece of string. There was warmth in the air and the smell of summer – hot cobbles, and herbs from the market. The vegetables were already prepped on that colossal chopping board that Jennifer had given her for Christmas. There were splotches of wine in one of its corners. They never came out, no matter how hard she scrubbed it. The tortillas were at a low heat in the oven. Mina wasn't shivering in the dark. She was in the sun, cooking the simplest lunch with her only ingredients, working her way through a bottle of *Rioja*.

Deadwood cracked outside the door, wrenching Mina back to reality. All had fallen calm after the storm, and yet now there was movement; bodies crawling on all fours, relishing in the night that was theirs, and only theirs, for they had killed all else. The coop had been so quiet. Its glass was thick, and the walls were strong. In the darkness of that corridor, Mina heard everything. The watchers were closing in around them.

Survival relied on them being in the coop so that they could be seen. *Stay in the light* – it was that simple. How would the watchers react when they realised that two of their pets were missing? And what would they do when eventually they found them?

The hollowness of the living room amplified every sound. If anything had entered, Mina would have known. She could hear the wood splitting in the fire. Sparks cracked like gunfire. She listened to her heart, pleading with it to soften lest the things should be drawn to her. Then she heard it – that sinister, rasping snarl, and the sound of claws gripping into the window's frame. There it perched, peering into the room, searching.

What followed was the dull clap of skin on stone. Mina's fingers were still intertwined with Madeline's. The watcher scuttled across the floor, sniffing furiously. There was nothing remotely *human* about it. This *thing* was a restless animal, driven neither by conscious thought nor soul's desire. It craved only soft, living flesh, and it thirsted only for blood.

Mina watched the firelight from the darkness. It flared across the wall and against the coop's locked door. Every evening, before the view of the forest was displaced by their reflections, she had hoped to catch a glimpse of these things that held them captive. They were leaner and they were longer. That's all she knew because that's all she had been told. Madeline once said to her that it was a blessing having never seen them. Mina pursed her eyes shut.

The watcher approached the other side of the wall. Its clawed feet notched into the floor. Mina could hear every foul, guttural breath, and imagined hot saliva pouring through its teeth, scalding the cement like acid. Was it staring at her through the concrete? Few blocks stood between them. Their talons could probably pick them apart like polystyrene. What if it had caught their scent? Neither Mina nor Madeline dared to move, to breathe, to think too loud in case the thing could hear their thoughts.

The watcher scurried across the room. Its shadow spilled onto the wall. It was standing at the doorway. Mina buried her face in Madeline's shoulder. She had kept her safe all this time. Maybe she still could.

Mina recognised the jangle of her handbag's buckles. She had left it beside her boots, in front of the fire. Not that it mattered anymore. That thing was drawing its filth all over it. She heard its fake leather tear like sheer silk. All her worldly belongings clattered to the floor. Pencils rolled, and pages swished open. Mina's sketches – her strangers, her friends – were gone. Somewhere there was a page with her face on it; the portrait that captured all that silly sadness that now seemed so irrelevant.

Madeline drew her closer, preparing for the inevitable. Could she feel Mina's heartbeat and the hope draining from her soul? The shadow on the wall was seen to expand. The watcher was approaching the corridor. Its feet thundered on the floor, getting closer and closer.

It wasn't supposed to be like this. Mina had promised her mum that she was going to be happy, that she was going to live her life. *I can see you in the sunny south of France, a famous artist with a vineyard all to your own cheek,* she had told her. Mina had laughed through the tears. Her mum always made her smile, even in the last days when she was nearly too weak to talk.

A sudden symphony of screams filled the forest. The shadow by the doorway stalled, listening, its head twisting from side to side, deciphering the call of its kind. Madeline and Mina's absence was the cause. The watchers had gathered by the glass, searching for their missing pets. And now their unhallowed shrieks marked the beginning of the hunt. They would scour the forest, disbanding in all directions, chasing their prey with a speed that was in itself terrifying. They would not rest until they had found them.

The shadow by the corridor's end disappeared in the blink an of eye. Mina heard its claws chafe swiftly on the frame and it was gone, answering its summons. Their screams filtered into the surrounding woodland, growing more distant with each agonising second. The watchers were communicating, dispersing in a perfect circle, leaving no stone uncovered, no pit unchecked, flashing between trees and across their highest branches. From the living room there wasn't a sound. The hearth was a soundless bed of burning embers.

It would take but a single watcher to return and to discover their hideaway. One voice could recall the rest, and they would descend upon them from all sides. The shadows were theirs, and the shadows were everywhere.

Madeline peeled away. She climbed to her feet, as quietly and cautiously as her tired bones would allow. Mina came to rest against the wall like a broken mannequin, too petrified to follow her. She watched Madeline's silhouette walk the length of the corridor with the lightest steps. It was darker now. The fire was all but dead.

'Daniel,' she said softly, 'please open this door. I am sorry. If you do not wish to let me in, then I ask only that you save Mina. She doesn't deserve this.'

There was silence as Madeline and Mina waited for their fates to be decided. And then the first lock clicked out of place, and then the next, until the coop's bright light dispelled the corridor of darkness.

13

'I can tell you what I know,' Madeline said. 'But I don't have all of the answers.'

Mina peeled back her hair with trembling hands. Elbows came to rest on knees as she sat on the floor, spine curved against the wall. They were in the coop. They were safe. She drew the bird's cage between her legs. The parrot tottered on its perch, full of the joys, its lilac beak almost turned into a smile.

'It's okay,' Mina whispered, 'I'm back.'

Her hands settled somewhere on her head, holding in whatever sanity remained, like egg creeping through a broken shell. Memories and fears exploded like fireworks in the black behind her eyes. The floor seemed to falter left and then right, swaying like the wildest ocean. Every breath was long and laboured as a bellows worked by hard, unforgiving hands. She was shaking but that was standard. If pressed she couldn't think of a time when she wasn't. It was always cold, or it was always terrifying, and that was the way of things.

The coop's light had hit her like a hard tonic, potent and disorientating. It was all that she wanted – the safety of the all-embracing white. But now it left her blinded and confused in a room where two bodies paced in one corner and Madeline stood in the other. It was Mina who had spoken first. None of the others knew what to say. The boy was inconsolable. The girl was bitter. Their leader, now usurped, was as poker-faced as ever.

She didn't tackle Madeline like she had planned, with her open sketchbook in hand showing the study of the burrows, parading like a petulant child all the mistruths that she had been fed alongside berries and gritty, sticky nuts. In that room – that horrible, lonely room where a hundred eyes could watch their every move – Madeline was her only friend. Daniel and Ciara may have opened that door, but they had also held it shut. When Mina spoke, she did so only to Madeline, and she asked the only question that really mattered – *what are they?*

'When I came here, to this place,' Madeline said, looking to no one in particular, 'I didn't expect to find them.'

Mina's head rose, eyes squinting. She had suspected for so long that Madeline knew more than she was letting on, and now that the truth was within her grasp – the answers to all those unspoken questions – she could barely keep her chin up. Was it even important anymore? Was surviving enough without knowing what was trying to kill you? Maybe that's just life.

This was the calm. These were the moments – sacred and silent – before the watchers returned from their search.

'You came here on purpose?' Mina asked her. 'Why?'

'I came here because of what I had read,' Madeline

replied, 'but I never believed for a moment that it was true.' Here she became uneasy and shifted her gangly frame against the wall.

Daniel and Ciara had retreated to the coop's far corner. He had dug himself into the bed and watched Madeline like a child awaiting punishment. Ciara stood near him, close enough for solidarity's sake, but only a few short steps from abandoning the boy outright. She was the one who had opened the door, and it was she who now held the keys. One month too late to make a difference for her own sake.

'What do you mean?' Ciara asked, her voice stern and older. 'You knew about these things?'

'No, I didn't know that they actually existed,' Madeline replied, glancing warily towards their reflections in the mirror. 'They'll be back soon once they realise where we are.'

'What *did* you know exactly?' Ciara pressed; it was like squeezing juice from dried fruit.

'I knew that people had gone missing here,' she said. 'There are records going back centuries. And superstitions – I suppose, you could call them – passed down, delivering the same message. They all warn against ever entering this place.'

Mina and Ciara exchanged a look of bemusement. Every answer they coaxed out of her was just another question in disguise.

'How do you know all of this?' Ciara asked.

'History,' Madeline replied solemnly. 'I was a historian. A lifetime ago, it seems.'

Again, silence. Mina couldn't fathom why the woman was so guarded, like a bat with her wings folded tight against the world. She noticed Ciara's hand tensing around the keys, her eyes flashing with a curiosity that wouldn't rest. Not until she had wrung Madeline dry of every ounce of information. That was, after all, the unspoken deal – admittance for knowledge.

'You had better start talking,' she said to her, 'or so help me I'll throw you back outside.'

Mina was torn. Her allegiance swung between them like a pendulum. Madeline had shown her such kindness that night, and she would stand by her should Ciara act on her threat, but she also needed to know the truth. Didn't they all deserve at least that?

'If that's what you want?' Madeline replied, sliding her body down the wall and settling beside Mina. 'I'll tell you what I know.'

Ciara abandoned the little boy in the corner and came to sit on the table, facing Madeline. Was there ever a moment when there wasn't some division between them? It didn't matter why Daniel had locked them out. So long as Madeline opened up, he was on his own.

'The earliest record of it I could find was in a journal,' she began. 'It's unlikely that anyone examined the source before it was shelved in the university's basement. The handwriting and language alone would be enough to deter most scholars. It dated back to the thirteenth century, by which time the Anglo-Norman forces had seized most of Ireland. Connemara had little to offer them. It was wild, open country with no established defences. But still they sent scouting parties there. That was, after all, the Empire's way. Greed and expansion, even when the prize was no more than bogland. I can't imagine they expected to find anything too removed from the ordinary. Some indigenous resistance, perhaps, but such skirmishes were more an inconvenience than a genuine threat to these men. Soldiers, all of them – trained, seasoned, and well equipped. They could handle themselves.'

'The journal belonged to a soldier?' Ciara asked, leaning forward like a teacher's pet keen to ask the obvious questions.

'No, the author was of Norman stock, but he was only planted here as a foreign dash to dilute the local scene. He was a blacksmith. And so would have had dealings with the military. He socialised with some of them, and that's how he came into contact with the soldier who had travelled west with a full party and returned with only one other.'

'But wait,' Ciara interjected, 'if something horrible happened to these men, then surely there would be more written about it?'

'This expedition was a failure and an embarrassment. Posterity celebrates success, and these men were denounced as cowards. Ciara, you really shouldn't be so naïve at your age.'

'What happened to the scouting party?' Mina asked, guiding the history lesson back on track, mildly irked by the interruptions.

'For days they traversed the country, happening on scattered nests of dwellings. Neither shared the same language and no arms were raised. These were harmless people and for the most part ignorant of the invaders' ever-expanding occupation. But the soldiers went deeper. There's no knowing where their journey took them, but it inevitably brought them here.'

'And they went into the forest?' Ciara asked, much to Mina's frustration.

'If any homegrown opposition hid in the area, it was likely that they would use the woodland for cover. Seeing as there are no other forests in the area, the soldiers entered with justifiable caution. Some stayed back to guard the perimeter, and as darkness was fast approaching, they also went about setting up a camp for the night. Our survivor knew something was wrong, or so he told the blacksmith. The horses were anxious and wouldn't settle. And it was so quiet. No birds, no beasts. And soon there would be no light as the bloodied dusk congealed on the western hills.'

'The horses knew what was in there?' Ciara butted in, again.

'I should imagine so,' she replied. 'Their smell alone would have been enough to cause the animals distress.'

'They do smell awful, don't they?' Ciara agreed.

'Christ,' Mina whispered under her breath. 'Can we just let Madeline talk, please?'

Ciara crossed her arms and leaned back; the first faint rays of a smile dampened in an instant. Madeline's hand squeezed Mina's knee. She was either pleased that she had spoken out or else she was warning her not to trifle with the emotional mess who held all the keys. Regardless, she picked up where she had left off.

'The author of the journal wrote down everything the soldier had told him. Suffice to say, recounting the events upset him greatly. Maybe he was searching for just one person who would believe him.

'At nightfall he heard the sounds that we know all too well. Any unfettered horses bolted immediately. One man was dragged across the earth as the animal kicked off with his hands knotted around its reins. Then there came the panic-stricken cries of his retinue. Each one silenced. Their death throes cut short. The soldier didn't hesitate. Along with another man who had lingered on open land, preparing the camp, they rode until their horses collapsed. The others – the ones who didn't flee immediately – died like the rest. Their screams were the last sound he remembered, and then it was just blackness, and the horse's hypnotic gallop through the whistling wind.'

'What happened to the two men after that?' Ciara asked timidly.

'The blacksmith heard only rumours. There was talk that the military covered it up. It was possible that the men were executed for abandoning their party, or maybe they took their own lives. It doesn't matter. Record of their experience survived.'

'And there are others?' Mina asked. 'Records, I mean.'

'Yes, a few. The most recent one that I know of was discovered by a colleague of mine. He was writing a paper on insane asylums in the nineteenth century and delved into the records of the institute in Ballinasloe. There was one case in particular he brought to me. A patient who raved incessantly about a forest, claiming that there was an evil there that had taken his brother. He used to imitate the watchers' screams.

'It was during the famine. The men were starved, desperate, and they knew better than to enter. They would have heard the stories surrounding it, and I don't doubt that they believed them.'

'How do you know it's the same forest?' Ciara asked.

'Because there are no forests of this size in Connemara or, at least, none that appear on any map, be they old or new. This place we each found was meant to be hidden. And I think we know why.'

The watchers' clarion call quit their search. The horde was returning; their untold claws and teeth primed to punish – to make an example of those who had deceived them.

Daniel buried himself under the blankets. Was he hiding from them or the watchers? If he had had his way, Mina knew that she would still be out there with Madeline, dreading their last moments. He had proven himself to be the weakest of them, and that weakness had almost gotten them killed. His blankets shivered as boughs were heard to crack and split. The watchers thundered towards the coop like an avalanche. The golden one flailed about its cage, feeling the force of its wings, yearning desperately to be free, to fly far away from that place.

'Thank you,' Madeline said to Ciara as the screams grew closer, and soon speaking was pointless. Their voices couldn't be heard.

The night had never been so riotous nor so defined by absolute terror. Bodies hammered against the glass, sending distorted reflections quivering wildly against their will. The mirror was never still. It shook and it creaked as though it would, at any second, shatter. The watchers had flooded into the living room, too, and now, for the first time, they beat against the door, causing all those locks to rattle.

On the cold floor, Mina held her hands tight to her ears. Every thought and afflictive imagining invoked only visions of blood and pain. Her tormentors assumed a legion of guises for she had yet to behold their true, terrifying form. Her fears focused on the claws – the markings and scars that were everywhere and would soon be upon her body. Skin and bone torn like a child's doll. Discarded or devoured, death was always the outcome – the inescapable end that they each shared.

Ciara had nudged in beside Mina. Their fingers entwined instinctively. Her hand, unlike Madeline's, was soft. It was warm. Ciara's façade of earlier had fallen away. She was again that timid little girl who had peeped, sleepy-eyed from her bed, smiling as though this moment would never come.

The watchers' assault was relentless. There was no telling which would break first, the glass or the door; castle gates besieged and soon to be conquered. They could do no more than wait and hope. With Mina and Ciara huddled on the floor, and Daniel hidden out of sight, only Madeline had the will to act. Her survivalist's sense had gotten her that far and she wasn't ready to give up. She was their tall, fading protector. Her outward appearance was one of frailty. Yet every hardened crease and cleft through Madeline's skin was another etching on her being; another day, another week, they all gathered and kept sacred her struggle. She reached out to Ciara with an open hand. Nobody knew the locks like Madeline, and the keys were passed to her without a second's hesitation.

Mina had watched her like an infant too young to help. But if this was their last stand, the last drop when all else was spent, then she would sooner die standing by Madeline's side than cowering on the floor.

The door was shuddering, all locks strained to their limits. Madeline pressed her weight into it. Those monstrous hands spread wide, all bones rising under the skin. Mina wanted to join in her effort, but what strength did she have to offer? She looked to Ciara, still petrified on the floor, staring as if in a trance at the table in the room's centre, so solid that it remained static when all around it seemed to shake. Only then did its worth dawn on her. That ugly hunk of wood could wedge the door in place. Its weight was more valuable than all their strength combined.

Mina tried to pull it out of place, body arched, fingers cracking dirt from its crust, but it wouldn't shift. She gestured over to Madeline for help, but the woman was hesitant; unwilling to pitch in. She was seen to frown with disapproval like a housewife who didn't want any aspect of her home altered. 'Come on,' Mina shouted, but the watchers' attack overruled her voice. Did Madeline not understand what she was doing? It was Ciara who ran first to Mina's aid, and only then did Madeline join in, having conceded that this was happening with or without her help.

These things had massacred a unit of armed soldiers. Against steel and skill, they arose victorious. Mina knew the hopelessness of their situation, encircled on all sides, waiting for the glass to blast into pieces. Her eardrums faltered against a beat that they couldn't keep pace with. None of them were soldiers. But they *were* survivors.

She looked to Ciara and Madeline, cheeks flushed and gasping for breath. 'Okay, on three,' she mouthed, nodding her head. 'One, two,' and together they dragged the table across the floor, leaving a rail-track of white on its cement. When it was jammed in tight against the door Mina turned and stopped suddenly, as if some invisible barrier had fallen before her.

Where the table had once been, in the centre of the room, there was now an indentation in the floor, perfectly square. Its outline was aligned in filth, and by the white light all eyes were drawn to it – this oddity concealed until that moment. The wood wasn't the cause of the depression. Heavy as it may have been, it certainly couldn't sink into solid cement.

Mina fell to her knees and drew her ear alongside the floor. She hammered her knuckles on the cement, and then again, searching for some explanation. She would tap, and she would listen. Every aching part of her was shaking.

Amidst the screams and the madness, she had to draw her mouth against Madeline's ear so that she could hear her.

'It's hollow,' she said. 'There's something under there.'

14

Peace came with the dawn. The earliest inklings of light were smoky and weak. They trickled like ash through the darkness, scattered by the wind's tender sough. The grey wept from the top down; white where the daylight dipped its toe. The night seemed reluctant to leave.

The building had been overrun. In all of Madeline's time there, she'd said she had never experienced anything like it. For the longest night imaginable they had endured the watchers' bound and determined barrage against them, and in the swiftest second, they were gone, leaving a silence suspect and unsettling. The light turned off, revealing an eyesore of scored trees and severed branches. The ruins of their labour. But Mina's focus didn't extend that far. All that she could see were the claw marks cleaved into the pane's every inch. It was a miracle that it had remained intact.

Even over their shrieks, the scraping of their talons had still been heard. A hundred nails on a single chalkboard, scratching out their horrific strain. The watchers had thrown every vicious part of themselves at the glass.

Madeline always maintained that it was the watchers' wish to merely terrify and toy with them, that they were safe so long as they lived by the coop's light. But that night changed everything. The rules had been broken and punishment was necessary. It was only a matter of hours before the watchers returned. They had nowhere to hide, and nowhere to run to.

Leaden rays of light were flooding in pools across the forest floor and trickling like silvered sap down trees. Their amputated branches were piled around them. The other side of the door had been hacked into a bloodied board of splinters, its wood coarse and whittled. To draw a hand along it would maul the skin like a cheese-grater. Madeline examined it closely but didn't comment. Some things are best left unsaid. The glass wouldn't last another night, and neither would the door.

The rest of the building was no different; defiled, and undeserving of the word *home*. Never before had so many of them entered. Their stench was nauseating, and Madeline had to hold the blanket to her face as if it were the only way to keep her stomach from retching. They must have fought their way into the narrow corridor, funnelling forward, clambering over each other's naked bodies. The gashes from their claws glistened in the dim morning light. Even in the darkest corners they burned like a brand hot from glowing coals. Mina thought of all the hours, days, and months Madeline had spent tidying that room, making it habitable and warm. It was all for nothing. In a single night, the watchers had made it theirs. Mina would never sit by the fire again, no matter the cold.

Madeline found Mina's keys in a corner of the living room, lost amidst the madness, under the filth and twigs dragged inside by the horde. She handed them to her without remark. Mina thought about throwing them away but that would be to relinquish whatever little hope remained, and so she put them in her pocket. They were all that she had left.

Time was not on their side. Should the attack recommence the following night, then they had one day to accept their fate, or to devise a means to escape it.

Mina met Daniel in the eye, still hunkered in bed, watching her. He looked as if he wanted to approach them, to align his life with theirs, to offer whatever help he could and to act as if nothing had happened. But he was the odd one out now. It was all his doing. It was because of him that the watchers had turned on them.

'What do you think is down there?' Mina asked.

The three of them stood around the hollow, all eyes glued to the floor. It was a dip in the concrete. A structural flaw, perhaps. But the fact of it being there – in the centre of *that* room – meant that it could be something so much more.

'That's where the watchers go during the day,' Ciara whispered. 'We can't go down there.'

'If they were underneath us, we would have heard them,' Madeline said, frowning at the floor as though it were a familiar face that she couldn't quite place. 'The concrete amplifies their screams. Whatever is down there, I don't think that it's part of their tunnel system.'

Mina curled her toes against the cement's cold grit. She had all but forgotten that she was barefoot. Other matters – the life-and-death variety – had distracted from her discomfort. Her socks had been in her hands when Madeline chased Daniel to the coop's door. She must have left them outside in the corridor. Everything that was hers – the remnants of her old life – were gone. The boots, like her bag, had been shredded into non-existence. The sketchbook, too, was gone, and with it her many strangers and the study of the burrows.

Mina crouched down and rapped her knuckles against the floor, both on the indent and the immediate space surrounding it. There was no mistaking the difference – the hollow echo of its centre. The coop's cement throughout the room was solid and had been poured on deep, but not there. The square was certainly large enough to fit through, assuming that that was its purpose.

'Whatever's down there,' Mina said, 'it can't be any worse than what's up here when that light clicks on.'

'Agreed,' Madeline replied. 'Daniel, come over here, will you?'

The boy was startled by the sound of his own name. Hours had elapsed since anyone had spoken to him. He approached Madeline hopelessly, as though a noose dangled from the ceiling, measured just for him.

'Now, Daniel,' she said, meeting him in the eye but with no fixed emotion, 'we're not breaking through the floor with our bare hands, are we? I need you to find us something hard and heavy. The more jagged the stone, the better. Do you understand?'

The thought of leaving the coop seemed to jump-start Daniel's heart. But if he were to earn their forgiveness, Mina knew he would do all that was asked of him. Now was not the time to be afraid.

'I understand,' he replied, nodding his head nervously. 'I'll find you a good one, don't you worry.' And with that he was out the door, his jacket zipped up to his neck, not giving his fears a chance to comprehend what he was doing.

'Ciara,' Madeline continued, 'we still need water. Can you collect some from the spring as quickly as you can?'

'Sure, no problem,' she replied. 'What about food?'

'There's no point in checking the traps,' Madeline said. 'No bird is going to fly close to the forest after last night, and they were most likely destroyed when they fanned out in search of us. Collect any edibles that you see, but the water is our priority.'

Madeline was the only one amongst them who knew what had to be done. Maybe Ciara and Daniel finally understood that. If survival were still a possibility, it was Madeline – and Madeline alone – who could save them.

'On it,' Ciara replied before skipping over to the corner to grab a blanket. She draped it around her shoulders, securing it around her neck. It was far too long and gathered in folds on the floor.

'It's definitely a size too big,' Mina said to her.

'I'm not going anywhere fancy,' Ciara replied, smiling.

Was this the same girl who had snapped like a Jack Russell at anyone who looked at her? The loss of John had cracked her mould. Despair had recast Ciara as someone all but unrecognisable to her old, optimistic self. But just there, in that second, her face reminded Mina of the girl that she used to be.

'Thank you for saving us,' Mina said. 'When you didn't answer me, I just assumed that...'

'I couldn't leave you out there,' Ciara interjected. 'I know why you did it,' she said to Madeline. 'I know why you didn't open the door that night, and it's okay. I've forgiven you for that.'

She left without another word, leaving Mina and Madeline standing over the anomaly in the floor like two witches prepping a ritual. If there was a conversation there – about John and that night – blooming in the faint morning sun, then now wasn't its time.

Mina still couldn't work Madeline out. There were too many sides to the puzzle. Did they now share a friendship? Had the night's gauntlet of emotion brought them together? Everything and everyone else seemed to have changed, and yet Madeline remained the same. Mina just saw her differently now. She resembled more so the woman who had lived within the pages of her sketchbook; the bravery and the beauty that was always there but stood just off-stage, behind the curtain that was Madeline's way with people; ill-tempered and cold even when spitting orders from beside a hot fire.

'Do you know about the patterns?' Mina asked her, to which the woman's head lifted. 'I think that their burrows are arranged in a pattern.'

Madeline looked at her, waiting for more. 'A pattern?' she echoed. 'What do you mean?'

'I can probably draw it better than I can explain it,' she replied.

Mina shared with her all that she knew. Drawing with her finger on the floor she explained the layout once hidden in her sketchbook, offering up the intelligence that she had planned to trade for Madeline's own secrets, back when they were rivals, surviving side by side, but always trying to edge one step ahead of each other. It was bizarre to think that it was the watchers and the events of the night before that had brought them closer together.

'So, you see,' she began to explain, 'it seems as though the coop is in the centre and these burrows have been dug around it. And they aren't just randomly placed, like you said they were. There's a set distance between them. I'd say it's like a pattern, but I can't be sure of that.'

Madeline just stared at her. It was impossible to tell if she believed anything Mina was telling her or if she already knew it all.

'So,' she continued, all faith in her findings dwindling under Madeline's gaze, 'it's possible, maybe, that this place was built smack bang in the centre of their underground system *or*,' she said, raising her index finger, 'I think the watchers built their tunnels around it. Maybe they all just wanted to have a good look at us *or...*' and this thought had just crossed her mind '...what if they were trying to get into whatever is beneath us?'

Madeline's deadpan expression didn't alter. Mina felt like a conspiracy theorist in a tinfoil hat.

'I don't know,' Madeline said abruptly, almost dismissively. 'But if we are *smack bang* in the centre of it all, as you so eloquently put it, then we've nothing to lose by going down there. We might even get some answers or, even better, somewhere to last out the night.'

Mina nodded her head, still unsure as to the credibility of her theories. Madeline seemed indifferent to them.

'I can tell you, Mina,' she continued, 'but keep it to yourself. There's no guessing which they will break through first, the window or the door. But the truth is that if we're trapped in the coop when that light clicks on, we're all as good as dead.'

'Maybe they will have calmed down after last night,' Mina said.

'Maybe,' she replied, 'but I doubt it. I don't think they need us anymore. They've watched us for long enough.'

'Why *do* they watch us?' Mina asked.

Madeline hesitated, her lips parting only to close without a sound. A sudden sadness seemed to overcome her. It was as though she wanted to answer but thought it kinder not to.

'Please,' Mina pressed. 'I need to know.'

'How is your knowledge of *fairy folklore*?' she asked. It was clear from her voice that she didn't approve of calling it that.

'Let me see,' Mina replied, biting her lip, thinking. 'I know about the banshee. People used to say that you could hear her crying outside your home before a death in the family. And I know that there are stories about fairy mounds, but that's all the little people and leprechaun stuff.'

'Pots of gold at the end of the rainbow, yes?' Madeline put in.

'Exactly,' Mina replied. 'That's hardly true, is it?'

'It was believed that the fairies were banished underground,' Madeline said, ignoring the question, 'and there were places, like this forest, that people knew better than to enter for fear of disturbing them.'

'You're serious about the fairies?' Mina asked.

'Well, based on our situation we can assume they used the word *fairy* very loosely,' she replied. 'There was one, how shall I put it, *type* of fairy that appears a lot in the old stories.'

'And which one is that?'

'Changelings,' Madeline said. 'These tales usually involved a fairy replacing a child, assuming its identical likeness so that even the mother couldn't tell the two apart.'

'And what *fairies* are we dealing with?' Mina asked.

'You still haven't seen them yet, have you?'

'No, thank God,' Mina replied. 'I kept my eyes shut last night, like you asked me to.'

'Their appearance changes,' Madeline said. 'In their natural form they're perfectly horrible; all gangly limbs and claws. There was one night when I lingered too long by the door. I had only been here a few days. I saw them. They all looked identical. It was the most terrifying thing I had ever seen.'

'Why?' Mina asked. 'What did they look like?'

'They all looked like me, Mina. Every last one of them looked like me.'

15

Ciara

Twigs and rotten branches crunched beneath Ciara's feet. She flinched with every step, as though the ground itself could shatter, dropping her into a lightless hell where all her fears converged, plotting new ways to torment her. The well-trodden path she had known was lost, and she fought through its ruins like a worm listening for the crow's searching patter, expecting in each moment to be picked out of place and devoured. All around her the trees braved their wounds. Sap bled from where the watchers' claws had torn deep into the very heart of them, lashing out at anything within their reach, driven by a rage that had yet to be calmed, and one that would return with the dying of the day.

The spring water had never felt so far. Ciara hadn't visited it for weeks. Not since Mina had assumed sole custody of the job. She was sure that she knew the way but now she had her doubts. The woodland had changed overnight. It was, however, the loneliness that troubled her most – that feeling that even her own shadow had abandoned her. There was no one to believe in her, no one to offer a smile when she needed it the most. Her eyes sparkled like gemstones in the morning light.

'Oh, John,' she whispered, 'just when we thought it couldn't get any worse.'

Ciara spoke to her husband often, gleaning from his memory the will to keep going. He would have wanted that. His last act was for her – his fateful attempt to seek help. To give up was to go against the man's dying wish, and a world full of watchers couldn't make her do that.

'We'll be home soon,' Ciara said, as she stopped to catch her breath, the damp air clawing through her throat. 'We'll be free of this place, just the two of us. Just like always.'

The last month of Ciara's life haunted her memory like a moment. There were no days. And there were no nights. She became indifferent to the coop's light. And her daily combs for some trace of John repeated like some purgatorial torture. Ciara's was a soul dissevered, searching for its missing half.

The others carried out the mechanical motions of survival, aware of what they had done but seemingly unaffected by it all the same. Every struggle needs a purpose. John was hers. And they had rallied to Madeline's side to take that away from her, abandoning the best of them to those things, just to save themselves. His cries for help remained like a ringing in her ear, loudest when she watched them going about their jobs; those who never knew what it was to love and lose someone, and to know that person's loss could have been prevented.

Ciara had nurtured Daniel like a puppy, only to have

him snap at her when she needed him most. He was more Madeline's pet than hers now. Cruel masters breed only cruelty, and the boy had learned from the worst. Mina could have taken those keys if she had wanted to. Ciara came to realise that she cared only for herself; always rambling around the woodland on her own and studying them under the coop's light as though she were a watcher in disguise. None of them could be trusted. If only Ciara had known this sooner. She would never have let John go.

But something changed in her that night when Daniel stole the keys. Ciara was still too numb to emotionally connect with what was happening, acting more spectator than participant. She had watched the boy slide his back down to the floor, trembling, covering his face in shame as though Mina and Madeline were stood at the window, shaking their heads in disappointment. If Ciara was pleased, then she had forgotten how to smile. The dark fog of depression had obscured all other identifiable feelings. It was deserved, surely, that they should share John's fate. Executioners with their heads on the very block that they once stood over, wielding their own selfishness like an axe. These thoughts trespassed in Ciara's mind like strangers, uninvited and unwelcome, and utterly unrecognisable.

She had looked to the mirror, squinting in disbelief at who she had become. Mina's voice outside the coop was a million miles away, her words registering only as sound, like a soft rain that would fade away at any moment. Ciara was listening instead to someone else. She had pictured John standing behind her, hands on her shoulders. There was a framed photograph above the fireplace just like it. Maybe that was the memory she had borrowed. What would John say to those who had let him die? Ciara knew that he would have forgiven them. He would have thanked them for keeping her safe. As agonising as the man's final moments had been, it was nothing compared to the horror had he seen her running towards him.

Ciara toiled through the forest, stepping warily over its many branches and meandering roots. The light was a welcome novelty, but its presence was felt only because the canopy above had been so distraught by the watchers' movements the night before. Like a tsunami of bodies, they had crashed through it, their strength and number obliterating all that stood in their way. Nature's colour palette was unchanged – blacks and browns, and woolly mosses that still retained a faint floss of green.

Amidst this pallor – where the daylight fell in sickly patches – something caught Ciara's eye. Had she not been paying such close attention to her every step then she may well have walked it into the soil, losing it forever without ever knowing it had existed. She took it in her hand and held it to the light. It was a white cable, manmade, like a piece of electrical wiring. John always took care of all the DIY stuff. One of its ends was cut, and some coloured threads frayed out from inside it. On the other end was attached a small black plastic cube, with what looked like a mirror on one side, no larger than a fingernail. Ciara glanced around her, searching for some clue as to where it had come from. It could only have fallen from one place – the branches above. She quickened her pace and made her way back to the coop.

During her walk, she fidgeted tirelessly with her discovery, examining it from every angle, caressing every inch of it, as though it were a magic lamp and within lived a genie that held all the answers. Ciara had hoped that she could present it to the group with some explanation as to what it was, but the implications of the thing – if there were any – were lost on her. What if it was nothing? What if Madeline should mock her for bringing back something so insignificant? Like a dog that found a stick in a forest, hoping to impress its master. If only John was there. He would have known what it was. Ciara closed her fist hard like a knot, hiding what she had found. Whatever it was, it was hers.

16

Daniel

Daniel had dashed around the forest in a panic. For every second spent outside the coop he was like a sailor thrown from his vessel. His fears and weaknesses barraged him in waves, and he struggled to breathe. There was shattered wood everywhere, and stones uplifted, but no rocks large enough to crack the cement. His shoes slid through the slimy blackness that was probably soil. He didn't like to look at it. It had no colour, really; just the sickly sheen that dripped from the leafless branches above.

Whatever was happening and whatever new hell-gate they were about to enter, Daniel didn't care. He would do as he was told. He would follow Madeline's lead because whether he liked to admit it or not, she was in charge. She could be trusted to keep them safe.

Flashbacks of the day before played out like an out-of-body experience. It *was* him, running terrified like a fox with a hound snapping at his heels, fuelled by blind instinct and no other thought than to go faster, with no thought given to tomorrow. He couldn't take it anymore, being trapped night after night with *her*. Daniel couldn't take a drink of water without worrying that he might spill a drop, and that Madeline would make another example of him in front of the others. Even in those moments when he was alone, he still couldn't keep his hands from shaking. Sometimes he cried so hard that he couldn't breathe.

It was as though his past follies were fated to repeat themselves over and over, punctuating and defining his pathetic existence with the same mistakes. His father had confiscated the keys to his motorbike; symbolic of the jailer who ruled his life. The old man took sick satisfaction in denying him even the simplest pleasure, not unlike Madeline. Daniel knew the beating that his father would bring down on him for taking them without his permission. And so, when he squeezed them in his hand, he had no choice but to follow through with it; to ride and never look back. Snatching Madeline's keys was an instinctive act, like a muscle memory that had worked once before, and Daniel's desperation had whispered in his ear that it might work again.

Would he have let Madeline back in had Ciara not peeled open his fist and taken the keys from him? He didn't know. Mina shouldn't have been left outside. But once that door was locked, the damage was done, and he couldn't see any means to fix it without inviting Madeline's rage upon him. Mina would come to hate him just like everybody else.

Daniel stared down at the stone, sizing it up, imagining its coldness against his hands. 'Okay,' he whispered. 'This is going to hurt.' He edged it forward with the tiniest steps, ignoring the pain and the irreparable damage he was no doubt bringing upon himself. Its unwieldy heft bent his body out of shape, like a fishing rod pulled to fracture. But this was it. This was the hammer that would crack the ground. Sweat seeped through his pores and pooled in his armpits. Every squelch of soil and every wheeze that burst from his throat brought him that little bit closer, slowly and sorely. Each ounce of pain that was his to suffer was another pardon for what he had done.

17

Mina

'We can't tell them,' Madeline said. 'They're not like you and me. They wouldn't understand. Since they each came here, neither of them has sought out the truth. They honestly don't seem to care. One is too young, the other too stupid. Keeping them both alive has been a chore.'

'But what difference does the truth make?' Mina asked. 'Despite what you know, do you have any intention of ever escaping this place?'

'I did,' she replied, 'and there are days when I still do. But you get one shot at it, Mina. We can't outrun them, even in the summertime. I've toyed with many ideas. I even tested them, and the results were all the same.'

'What do you mean you *tested* them?' Mina asked.

'I thought that maybe I could hide from them. If I travelled as much ground as I could before nightfall, and then dug a hole in the earth, concealing myself for the long night under a cover of soil with just enough air to breathe, then I would have a day ahead of them. I could have made the journey slowly, but always out of sight, and only with daylight on my side.

'With this idea in mind I buried a dead bird as far from the coop as I could reach. I buried it so deep, Mina. No one would ever find it, and no predator could ever catch scent of it. But the next day, when I returned, the earth had been carved asunder. They had found it.'

'So, we're fucked then?' Mina said, looking through the window's lattice of etches and to the trees that stood sentry over their lives; a prison of wood, with wardens that could sniff out the smallest jailbird.

'Maybe not,' Madeline replied, looking at the floor. 'All the time I've been here, searching for a way out. I never thought – not in my wildest dreams – that it could be beneath me.'

'What do you think is down there?' Mina asked.

'Somewhere safe to wait out the night, even if that's all there is.'

If the watchers had existed for centuries, and record of mankind's encounters with them enjoyed such ease of access, then of course another had sought them out. But how – with their threat so constant – could they possibly exploit the precious day-lit hours to build within the woodland?

'We're not dying here,' Mina whispered, and before she could say any more the front door creaked open.

Her eyes met with Madeline's when they heard the boy's tired, pained breathing echoing through the corridor. Mina hoped that he had found what Madeline wanted. Despite everything, she still wanted him to succeed, to find his place in a puzzle where none of them really fit. The boulder rolled into sight first, and then Daniel followed behind it, his spine so hooked that he strained to stand upright when he looked to them, searching desperately for their approval.

'That should do the job,' Madeline said to him, stepping against the wall, guiding Mina alongside her with the gentlest touch of her hand.

Daniel was spent – worn down to the bone. Mina saw how the pain reached like a rope around his neck, pulled taut, dragging him down. The promise of rest had forced him to that point, to the supposed end, but his role was far from over. Madeline's spiteful eyes guided him towards the room's centre. He wiped the sweat from his brow and secured his hands around the stone's cold sides.

Mina stood beside Madeline, surprised by how she had come to be there, nestled in the wings of a woman whom she couldn't make up her mind to trust or not. A lot had changed in twenty-four hours. Life in the woodland was, if anything, unpredictable. She wanted to help Daniel, even if her strength would do little to allay the boy's burden. But no, Madeline's hand slowly closed around her shoulder and though not tensed, its presence held her in place. Mina knew it was cruel to stand back and watch Daniel suffer, but in that moment, in Madeline's debt and seemingly under her control, she did just that.

The boy's pale skin burned red. Sweat soaked his forehead and gathered like a gutter above his lip. He lifted the stone as high as his aching arms could manage, and let it drop each time like an anvil on the weakness in the floor – this oddity in a world that couldn't get any stranger. There was the dull thud and the ringing chime, like a single-note song. Every time it disturbed the air the cracks grew larger, like a frozen lake breaking beneath their feet. It wouldn't take long. Mina was glad of this, for Daniel's sake.

The sound of stone cracking down on cement reminded Mina of home – her *real* home; of that summer when the city council tore up the street right during tourist season. Outside her window they had strewn about their orange cones, and for five days straight they had hammered, and they had drilled until she almost forgot what silence sounded like.

The cavity grew deeper. Daniel's every exertion was almost violent. His war alone was with the floor. It was as though this little victory – after so many defeats – was all that mattered.

'We should help him,' Mina whispered in Madeline's ear. 'He's going to hurt himself.'

'It's the least he deserves,' she replied.

The boulder sank into the cement like an anchor finding its niche amidst the deep, and they all heard it – the clash of stone against steel. The floor had given way. Daniel collapsed beside it, his every muscle wrung of life, his veins pulsating with a pain that would last a lifetime. But it didn't matter. His job was done. He had earned his place amongst them.

Madeline didn't hesitate. She was standing over their discovery before Daniel's shoulders had even felt the floor. Mina wasn't so eager. There was no knowing what was down there.

'Mina, come and look at this,' Madeline said, her voice carrying no hint of delight or depression.

Embedded in the floor was a black steel hatch, square in shape, with a silvered handle; the kind you pull and twist like an airlock. Madeline knelt beside it and picked aside the shards of cement. She wiped the dark metal clean with the palm of her hand.

'What is it?' Daniel asked, still spread across the floor, staring at the ceiling.

'Daniel, please,' Madeline snapped, drawing her eyes over their discovery.

She tapped it with her knuckle. The echo of steel occupied the room, hanging in the air like a thought. *Was this what they had hoped for?*

'It's a door,' Mina said.

There was no discussion about it. Madeline's leadership was far from democratic and her curiosity wouldn't wait for a vote. With Daniel enfeebled on the floor and Ciara still procuring water from the spring, there was only Mina left to present some opposition. But she said nothing. Why waste her voice on someone who wouldn't listen?

Madeline's bony hand reached for the handle. Mina thought of the watchers' tunnel system surrounding the coop, every passage leading to this one spot – the centre of it all. She imagined them, silently gathered behind the black steel, waiting for it to open.

'Are you sure about this?' she whispered.

'What other choice do we have, Mina?'

The mechanism clicked and the hatch was seen to lift ever so slightly. Mina held her breath. The desire to see what lay within was outweighed only by the dread of what it might be. The lid rose as though it was fresh from a factory line. There was no creak of rust or squeal of damp. Mina wouldn't have been surprised if there had still been a price tag on it.

Daniel rolled away when he realised what was happening. Even with all the strength squeezed out of him, still he found the energy to be afraid. Madeline was sniffing around the opening like a foxhound. After an especially long and almost savoury intake of air, she looked to Mina.

'They aren't down there,' she said. 'I don't think they've ever been down there, judging by the smell.'

'What *does* it smell like?' Mina asked.

'Metal,' Madeline replied, thoughtfully. 'And leather and...' she took another deep breath '...linen.'

There was no light below, just darkness; unbroken and undisturbed. Mina peered blindly into its depths, primed to fall back lest her fears be realised. She couldn't smell anything. She could see even less.

'Hello!' she shouted, and her voice dropped down the steel throat; no echo, no response. The dark was empty. The rungs of a ladder were aligned to one side. The little daylight that crept through the coop revealed the uppermost two, and no more. On the plus side, nothing had yet climbed *up* the ladder. But the next step was obvious. There was only one way to know what was down there.

Mina imagined her sister shaking her head disapprovingly. *This is a bad idea, Meens,* she could hear her saying. How many times had Jennifer repeated that famous line? It had become the slogan for all of Mina's decisions. Studying art in college was a bad idea. So, too, was smoking and drinking, and being single. Just being Mina seemed to be the worst idea imaginable. Luckily, Jennifer couldn't see her now.

'This is a bad idea, Meens,' she whispered to herself.

Daniel had retreated even further away, as if Madeline

might throw him down the hole to test its depths. Maybe he hoped that the coop could withstand another night, that the watchers wouldn't find him under all those blankets. Judging by the cracks that splayed across the window like glowing veins, what little hope remained was hardly worth mentioning.

'I'm sure it's quite safe,' Madeline said.

The woman's questionable opinion was irrelevant at this stage. It was time for Mina to take the lead, to balance the scales and show Madeline what she was capable of. She shifted her body towards the opening and came to sit with both legs dangling into the darkness.

'I suppose *quite* safe will have to do,' she said, before lowering herself into the hatch.

With each rung descended, another part of her vanished, as though her body was submerging in oil. Mina worked her way slowly downwards, praying that the silence would hold, all the while waiting for so delicate a thing to shatter. Would Madeline have shut the trapdoor if she were to scream? Would she have done the same if the roles had been reversed?

She took one last look at Daniel before going deeper. The sum of his years had never seemed so meagre. He sat, hunched forward, trying to keep his trembling down to a minimum as the adults went about their business. Had he been given the choice they would have left it shut. In that woodland, nothing good ever came from beneath the earth.

The parrot watched Mina descend warily from the safety of its cage. It no longer whistled like it used to, back when everything was new to its eyes and when the hum of their voices caused its little feet to dance. Though already a prisoner, caged and sold, it too had shrunk beneath the coop's light. It had grown bored of the day-to-day – of the same sights and sounds. But that would all change in a few short hours. The window would smash into a million mirrored pieces, or maybe the door would break in first. Either way, the room they all knew so well wouldn't feel like *home* anymore.

Mina softened her breathing. She could taste the stale air slipping through her teeth. Each rung of the ladder was met with care, her bare feet searching expectantly for solid ground. The sensation was disorientating; the darkness, the deafening silence, and the feeling of falling no matter how hard she held on. The air below was different. It was warm. Then she felt it. Her toes touched the floor. In the black nothingness beneath the coop there was *something*.

Mina hugged her body, squeezing arms and pinching flesh if only to reassure herself that amidst that soundless abyss she still existed. A bright tile of light hung above her head. Through it she saw the coop's ceiling, impossibly far away.

She was alone. Nothing – not even the watchers – could be that quiet. Mina turned her body, shuffling her feet on the spot where they had landed; too judicious to dip a toe into the unknown. With her eyes open she was blind. She occupied a black hole that swallowed life, light, and deluded the senses, stripping them of function. But there *was* something down there – a light, small and red, like an unblinking eye watching her from the far end of the room.

'Mina?' Madeline called out.

Her face now occupied the square above, peering down.

Mina's attention was transfixed by the red circle, like a distant planet seen for the first time.

'I'm okay,' she replied, startled by the volume of her own voice. 'There's something here. It's a light, I think.'

With her arms outstretched, fanning the empty air, Mina approached it. Sweet reason screamed at her to stop. Trying to survive and taking risks were two opposites that didn't attract. But what was there to lose? With each step the red dot grew larger, until it fell within her reach. Mina had no memory of ever beholding a colour so intense.

'What do you mean there's a light?' Madeline asked.

Mina pressed her finger into the red eye, and felt it sink and click into place. This wasn't what Madeline would have done; she who abided by every precaution and took no chance however pleading. There was an eerie second of silence as the red switched to green. Then a low hum occupied the air. It was comforting, like a cat's purr, and the room was bathed in soft light.

'What is it?' Daniel asked from above; his voice faint and distant.

'Light,' Madeline replied. 'Mina's turned a light on.'

The room was long and narrow, and no more than eight feet in height. Horizontal corrugations ran across its steel walls, so clean they shone. The light on the ceiling was similar in shape to the one in the coop, but its honeyed glow didn't sting the eyes. Rather it generated a sense of ease and security. All theories were tamed and tethered. Mina just took it all in, bit by bit, morsel by morsel. The same way Madeline ate every meal.

The green button was set into a metal casement that occupied the entirety of the room's end, from wall to wall.

Thick wires extended from it and wormed through the ceiling. Every incision through its steel was perfectly cut; professionally executed and probably at great cost. Mina suspected that it was, perhaps, a power source. The same one that supported the coop's cycle of darkness and light.

To the right of the generator, running along the wall to the midpoint of the room, were four tiers of shelves. All bolts and metal, and all rigidly locked in place. Even underground, an earthquake couldn't shake the stock from their shelves. Organised in neat towers were cans upon cans of food – sliced fruit, beans, meat, soup, and sweetened rice. Fat plastic bottles of water lined the floor. Mina gauged by the empty space on the lowest shelf that less than a quarter of the supply had been consumed. Someone's sojourn underground had obviously not lasted quite as long as they had intended. Only a single vat of water had been emptied. One other had been opened. The first proper meal in weeks was hers to enjoy, and still the mystery of the room held Mina in its hands. Why would someone go through all this trouble?

The ladder hung down in the room's centre, quitting ten inches or so from the floor. Mina's first impression was that of a submarine. It had been so long since she had seen the sea. If it ever had a colour, then she had no memory of it.

At the far end of the room, in the right corner, there was a bed. Unlike the unruly range of blankets that Ciara so casually collapsed into, this had a raised steel frame and a mattress. Its black linen was arranged and looked relatively clean.

Beside the bed was a desk, large enough to hold its two keyboards, dust-free and symmetrically arranged side by side. Between them was carefully set a compass and an opened deck of playing cards.

'Well, that's something,' Mina whispered. 'It looks like I'm not the only one.'

Whoever had lived there was a stickler for tidiness, or maybe it was the boredom. Two large desk monitors carried no trace of dust, and on the wall, reaching as high as the ceiling, were attached eight more screens, less streamlined than the others; chunky as though borrowed from a different time, when size meant quality. Their black, mirrored faces each showed Mina's reflection; standing lost, like a child trespassing where she didn't belong.

'What do you see?' Madeline called down. 'Mina, what's down there?'

'It's a shipping container, I think,' she replied.

None of it made any sense. The room was spotlessly clean. Someone had lived here. They had slept and eaten beneath the coop, in a steel box, modified, powered, and built with a purpose. Not even the watchers' claws could penetrate it. This was a safe house.

'What are you both doing?' Mina heard Ciara ask; she must have just returned from the spring.

'It's another room,' Danny replied. 'It was all dark, but Mina found the light.'

'What's down there?' she asked.

'I don't know,' he replied, 'but I think we're going to find out.'

Mina's bones sank into the chair's leather. She had forgotten what comfort felt like. Her hands glided over the keyboard without touching it. The fingers still knew their way. She could hear someone descending the ladder.

'Take a look at this place,' she said, swivelling her chair to face Madeline, the first to reach the floor. 'I've never seen anything like it.'

Madeline didn't respond. She looked uneasy as she stood aside to make space for the others. Ciara and Daniel eventually gathered around the ladder, unable to believe their surroundings. All they needed was somewhere safe, where the watchers couldn't get to them. What they had found surpassed even their most hopeful imaginings.

'Look at all the food,' Ciara screamed, rousing from Madeline an anger that her frown couldn't conceal. Mina guessed what she was thinking. The safe house was designed for a single occupant. That much was obvious from the bed. The food reserve was ample, yes. But how long could it stretch between four mouths?

Daniel, meanwhile, held on to the ladder. His mouth still hung agape as he looked around, dumbfounded. Madeline considered him with the same disdain, expecting nothing more from him than his trademark vacancy. The boy was useless in her eyes, and yet she knew that he would eat his share.

Madeline walked the room in silence, considering its many aspects, just as Mina had done. After so prolonged a spell spent inside the coop, any other space was going to throw them off-kilter. Everything about the room was purpose-built and installed before the container had been welded shut on all sides. How would someone even transport such a cargo into the woodland?

Mina relinquished the chair to Madeline when she approached the desk. Sometimes she felt so young in the woman's company, always in her way. Madeline sat without so much as a thank you, as though it was her office and they were distracting from her business. Mina didn't care. Too puzzled was she by the dead, black screens affixed to the wall. Why would someone need so many?

Ciara and Daniel were both fondling the canned food and talking excitedly amongst themselves. Mina had never seen them like this – genuinely happy. Their fears were, if only for a little while, forgotten. Madeline ignored them. To her they were probably like animals. Their next meal was all they thought about.

'I wonder if it still works,' Mina said, leaning in beside her.

She tapped the space bar on one of the keyboards and beneath the desk another steel box began to moan, awoken from its slumber. One of the monitors was flooded with reams of text – letters and numbers gone in a glimpse – and then the black lightened to blue.

'I guess that answers that question,' Mina said.

Madeline shifted uncomfortably in her chair. The bones of her face were highlighted by the monitor's light. The on-screen desktop was all but empty. The familiar trashcan was in its top corner and there was a single file in the screen's centre. It carried no title. Mina recognised it as a media file, possibly a video or voice recording.

Mina activated the other keyboard, and the second monitor followed the same routine. With its power returned, however, it presented them not with a desktop, but with software that she hadn't seen before. The screen was divided into eight blank squares, and beneath each one was the same date and time – *oo/oo/oo – oo:oo* – and the same message. *Feed lost*. Mina's eyes strayed to the eight monitors on the wall.

'They're surveillance cameras,' she said. 'It looks like whoever lived down here was watching the watchers.'

'Surveillance cameras,' Madeline repeated.

'Yeah,' Mina said, staring at the eight screens, imagining the horrors that once flashed across them. 'They probably installed them around the building or in the trees.'

'There aren't any such things in the forest,' Madeline replied. 'I would have seen them.'

'Maybe there used to be,' Mina said. 'You said it yourself, nothing escapes them.'

'Maybe,' she replied. 'Is that all this is?'

'Perhaps this will tell us more,' Mina said, pointing towards the blue screen and the lone file suspended in its centre.

Was this the answer they had been searching for? Daniel and Ciara had stopped nattering in the background. Curiosity had somehow distracted their appetites.

'What is it, Mina?' Madeline asked, and her voice had never sounded so uncertain.

'Let's find out, shall we?'

She opened the file, and the video began to play.

18

His eyes squinted back at them, raw against the monitor's light that fell flat on his cheeks. His beard was a nest, blindly trimmed, with stray tufts reaching out from its sides. The bald head was rounded as the moon, and just as pale. The camera recording him was functional, but of poor quality. Everything was too bright or too dark, with no textures to define either. His shoulders were slumped, and around his chest hung open a woollen cardigan. The room behind him appeared unchanged from where they now stood, staring at this stranger – the one responsible for it all.

'Well,' he began, his voice gravelly and low, as though he hadn't spoken for some time, 'if you're watching this, then I'm probably dead.'

Here the man stared not at the camera's lens, but somewhere else, almost distracted. With a large left hand that slipped into focus he squeezed the clump of hair around his chin and exhaled sadly as one facing a fate unwanted and yet inescapable. He obviously hadn't planned what he was going to say, or maybe – now that he was recording – he wasn't sure if he should say anything at all.

'No one knows about this,' he continued, 'what I've done and why I did it. Everyone who helped me, well, they're all dead.'

Again, he hesitated, pausing to reassess what he was doing. His eyes looked anywhere but at the camera or the monitor, as though he couldn't even face his own reflection.

'Fuck it,' he said, sitting back, 'I've nothing to lose. Not anymore.

'Many men are dead because of me. I needed to build *this*, you see,' he said, glancing around him. 'I promised them more money than they would ever see in their lifetimes because I knew they wouldn't live to receive it. Jesus, how many were there?' he whispered, rubbing his sore eyes. 'It took a few teams. Some of the men had families. Some were just boys looking for summer work. It had to be the summertime. I needed the long evenings.

'All the vehicles broke down outside the forest. Getting this container here was the hardest part. It took a few attempts. Each time I hid in here and left them all outside in the dark. I listened to them being slaughtered – these men I had lied to and brought to this godforsaken place.'

Mina looked to Madeline. The woman's face was stolid; a bust that betrayed nothing of her feelings or fears. Both of her hands rested on her lap. Their fingers were interlaced, as the hands of the dead are set for the long slumber. There was no way of telling what she was thinking.

'They built it exactly as I asked of them,' the man said, 'and worked so fast that it was almost as though they knew what was coming, racing against the clock. Each team picked up where the last one left off. They shared the same job and the same fate.

'So much of it was for nothing,' he said thoughtfully, his eyes looking up towards the eight monitors. 'They took all the cameras out. I don't know how they found them. All eight of them were hidden in the trees, in the fucking bark. Even I couldn't see them and I knew where they were. Anyway, it doesn't matter now. I don't suppose any of it does.

'I've destroyed all of my research. Every page burned. Every file deleted. All of it, gone. This recording will be all that remains.

'My name is Professor David Kilmartin,' he said, fixing his posture. 'I am, or I was, a lecturer at Galway's National University. I can only presume that you know there's something out there, in the forest, though I doubt you've seen them. The glass has two settings. It's controlled from in here, where it's safe, by a switch near the generator. It still works as I record this despite the damage they've done.

'I needed them to see me – to study me so that I might study them. But I knew that I would fear the very sight of them. That's why the glass can be changed to act as a mirror. Some nights I could face them. But these were rare. I had hoped that they would eventually accept my presence amongst them, albeit behind the safety of the glass, with the door locked and bolted. But they haven't. Given the chance they would kill me like all the rest.'

Here the man sat back in his chair, pondering what next to say. Again, his hand fidgeted with his beard, pinching at its wiry ends. His eyes darkened to black pits as the screen's light drifted out of reach. To think that they now occupied the same space; that Madeline now sat in the same chair. There was no telling how much time had passed since he made that recording, but nothing had changed.

'I still can't confidently tell you what they are. They are the stuff of legend and superstition, and yet they are real. Every tale passed down through the ages carries some grain of truth, I suppose. We couldn't co-exist with them. They have powers beyond our own. Science tells us that such feats are impossible. But science knows nothing of these things. That's why they were banished. Heaven knows how many lives were lost in doing so. And that is why I came to study them. That's why, after centuries of no communication between our two species, I took it upon myself to meet them face-on.

'Dear God, what have I done?' he said, leaning forward, holding his head in his hands. 'I wanted them to change form. I needed them to do it so that I could understand how it was possible. And so, I let them study me.

'Some were more accomplished than others. In their faces I saw my own likeness, almost indistinguishable. But there was no emotion. No capacity to express feeling and so no true means to mimic our kind without noticeable flaw. The less skilled amongst them presented me with some of the most hideous sights I could ever, in many lifetimes, conceive. I saw my face twisted, malformed and monstrous, watching me from amidst the trees, like some malicious clone eager to steal my place on this earth. But it's the bodies that haunt my days and nights. Despite their best efforts their frames remain too thin and disproportionate. Even when wearing the mask of man, still they are monsters to the eye.

'I needed them to attempt new guises other than my own, but I didn't think to bring any more photographs with me. I forgot many things. What I wouldn't give for a gun with a single bullet. Just one is all I need.

'I had but one photograph. The only one I ever carry with me – that of my wife. The woman I lost three years ago now. I wasn't thinking straight. I never imagined the effect it would have on me, to see her again, but not her. A horde of imposters, desecrating my memories of her, turning the woman I loved into my greatest fear.

'And I spoke to them. I told them so much and each night they listened. It's terrifying how quickly they learn. I shared with them my studies and the history of the world that they were denied. What was I thinking? I wasn't. I wasn't fucking thinking.'

Mina looked to Ciara and Daniel, pressed together for support, standing behind Madeline whose jaw was now tensed. Had the man's words inspired in the woman a sense of sadness or of anger? Looking at him, now close to tears as he laid bare his life's ruin, Mina wasn't certain of her own feelings either.

'Don't run,' he said, recouping his composure. 'They will catch you. Don't think that this woodland is their prison. They can reach the lands beyond it. Your legs will only take you so far, and that's not far enough.

'You have one chance to escape. It is no longer of any use to me. I cannot travel fast enough on foot. I slipped in the woodland. I wasn't paying attention. It's my ankle. I've shattered it, and so I'm stuck here. But you can make it.'

Mina, Ciara, and Daniel leaned forward in unison. Even Madeline, ever so collected, arched back in her chair, willing the man to speak – to gift them hope across the passage of time and death.

'To the south of here,' he continued, 'there's a river. It's narrow but its waters run. With a steady pace you could make it there in…' here he paused to think '…seven, maybe eight hours. Don't let up. You must run for as long as you can. You will find a boat there, upturned and covered with a black tarpaulin. It will take you the rest of the way. I can't guarantee that you will make it but it's your only shot. If you ever want to escape this place, then you must go south. I have left a compass on the desk in front of you. I regret to say that I won't need it. Not anymore.

'You need the daylight to keep them underground for as long as possible. Summer is your best chance. But if your supplies are low, then maybe you can make it if you leave at first light and don't look back. Watch your step,' he added, looking down at his foot, 'if you're a damn fool like I was, you'll never make it out of here alive.

'I've lost everything. To top it all off, I think my mind is failing me – the one thing I have left. There are moments when I feel as though there is another. I know they can't come above ground during the day, but what if they can? What if even one of them has found a way? Some days I can't shake the feeling that I'm being watched. It's ludicrous, I know, but I've heard branches break. I've seen *something*. I don't know. Maybe I've finally lost it.'

Kilmartin's hand reached for something on the desk. When it rose into view it was holding a photograph. Mina could only discern its blank underside.

'I hope that in reaching out to them that I haven't doomed us all. What if they had forgotten how to mimic us? What if my presence here has merely reminded them?

'Should you make it out of here, I need you to go to my office at the university in Galway. You must destroy everything that is mine. If someone were to examine my research, they might follow the trail that led me here. More may die because of me, and I can't – I won't – let that happen. Promise me that you will never speak about this place to anyone, please. Save yourselves and see to it that the world forgets again. These things are wicked. They toy with you. It's like they enjoy it.'

The man sat back in his chair with the photograph of his wife held in both hands. Its corners were worn from his touch. Had he said enough? He had told them nothing about his research. But then, that wasn't the purpose behind the recording. Kilmartin wanted all knowledge of the watchers wiped from the face of the earth. But why offer them safe passage, knowing that their deaths would best keep his secret safe?

'Run,' he said. 'Run because there is nothing here but pain and death. This is their home and we don't belong. Forgive me for what I have done. Go to the university. Destroy everything.'

Kilmartin's hand was seen to reach towards the keyboard, and for a moment he stared directly into the camera. The tears in his eyes shimmered against the screen. And then he was gone. His final message had been delivered. Escape was possible.

19

A shaft of light dropped through the hatchway, causing the ladder to gleam like some heavenly passage, as though paradise was but a short climb away. The reality was never so disparate. Night had fallen, and without the sun as their shepherd they were four lambs surrounded, and the wolves were ravenous. The moment they had dreaded was upon them.

No one had realised the time. Even Madeline – she with the ever-functioning hidden clock – was caught unaware. The hatch should have already been shut. What use was the safe house's discovery if they left its door open?

'One of you,' Madeline snapped, looking to Ciara and Daniel. 'Go, quickly!'

'I'll get it,' Mina put in, already racing towards the ladder.

She wondered how Ciara and Daniel would fare on their own. They seemed to act only when asked to do so; manual gears that grinded when put into action. The likelihood of their survival without Madeline's supervision was faint at best, like flowers in a long frost. *My God,* Mina thought, *I'm starting to sound like her.*

The door to the coop was still unlocked. Ciara hadn't even closed it behind her when she returned. Not that it really mattered anymore. It was too late. There was nothing up there that they needed, except maybe a few blankets, but their mustiness was probably best abandoned. And then Mina heard the parrot's sad little cry in the room above. How could she have forgotten about him?

'Don't you dare,' Madeline shouted at her when she realised what was happening.

'I'm not leaving him up there,' Mina replied, bounding up the ladder and hauling her body into the coop.

She heard Madeline leap from her chair, sending it crashing back against the desk, shaking the keyboards out of symmetry. Ciara and Daniel would be standing to the side, neither helping nor hindering. They were life's bystanders, their lives apart from the events around them.

'Mina,' Madeline screamed, 'so help me, I'll lock you out.'

The light was disorientating. Mina made the mistake of looking directly at it when she climbed from the opening. Her raw eyes darted towards the door with its chains dangling loose and feckless. She was stricken by that familiar vulnerable feeling. Death always stalked them. And with the door ajar, Ciara had practically invited it inside. The bird was by the wall, beaming at her from its perch. He was the only thing worth saving and the one thing that she had forgotten. She didn't even stop to listen, to hear for some sound of their approach. If the bulb was on, then the watchers were coming in their droves, and they were coming fast.

Mina heard Madeline's body lurch up the ladder, moving at a pace so swift that it was unsettling. Was she actually going to seal the hatch?

Mina's fingers linked through the birdcage, pulling it up and into her arms. Memories of that day in December flashed across her mind – the innocence, the panic, and the call to run when her tired limbs screamed out to fall. It was the parrot's screeching that had caught Madeline's ear that night. Without the yellow one she would never have made it.

Mina stole a fleeting glance at her reflection – at the imposter mimicking her every frantic movement. Much like Kilmartin's monsters, it copied her down to the finest detail and it remained a horror to behold. Her memory took a snapshot; the kind of photograph one hides in the back sleeve of an album and removes only in private. For weeks she had observed her slow and steady decline. Should the mirror shatter, as she expected, then there was no telling when she would see again what she had become.

How would she have drawn *this* face if she had seen it on the street? The dark folds around her eyes couldn't be washed away. They were dry as dead leaves glued into a scrapbook; flaky and red from scratching them in her sleep. Her lips, once so full and shimmering from a fresh ply of gloss, had shrivelled up like a pair of slugs sprinkled with a heavy dose of salt. All skin was limpid; stark against the raven hair that she would shave off given half a chance. It had grown knotted and heavy, and just another burden weighing on her mind. Her scalp was always itchy. She imagined every horrible insect she knew crawling through it, nibbling into her skin and laying their eggs.

Would anyone recognise her when she returned to the city? She would side-step the truth because the lie was kinder. Her car had broken down. That much was true to some extent. She had found shelter in the woodland, in a house of glass and stone, and that's where she had been all that time. *But why didn't you look for help?* This was the inevitable question, and one that she couldn't answer. She had injured herself, just like Kilmartin had done. No more questions.

How would she slot back into the world she had lost? What if she no longer fit? She liked to think that someone – even Peter – had asked after her and missed her company. But the ties to these people were tenuous at best and non-existent at worst. Maybe no one cared. She was just the sad, quiet girl who always left without saying goodbye.

Madeline had almost reached the hatch when Mina thrust the yellow one towards her, giving the woman no time to react and certainly no time to slam the lid down.

'Take him,' Mina shouted, forcing Madeline back down from where she came.

Mina clambered in and dropped the door over her head, letting her full weight hold it down, both feet scrambling to find a rung for support. An encouraging click was heard when she twisted its lever. *Was it closed? Did that sound mean they were safe?*

'What if they know how to open it?' she shouted down to Madeline who had since dropped down to the floor, discarding the yellow one as though it didn't belong amongst them.

'Kilmartin wouldn't have gone through all this trouble if they could just open the door above his head,' she replied angrily.

Mina climbed down the ladder, slowly and reluctantly. Her chin was held high as she stared at the hatch, waiting for it to lift and for the coop's light to flood down from above, declaring their destruction.

'Come on, Mina,' Madeline said. 'Try as they will, they're not going to get us down here. The door locks from the inside.'

Madeline returned to *her* chair. With her back turned to them she sat, her fingers' calloused tips tapping the desk at a tempo to match their hearts. Mina, Ciara, and Daniel came to stand around one another. No words were spoken. They weren't necessary. Each one extended a hand towards the ladder, holding its cold steel for support as though they shared a subway train to oblivion. If death was coming that night, then it would come from above and there was nothing they could do about it. *The hatch's mechanism had locked, hadn't it?*

Surveillance cameras weren't needed to see the carnage that swept into the coop. Their fears, their minds, and the creeping madness that such horrors inspire were enough to imagine the scene above. The watchers' grim refrain returned, but the steel was strong. They sounded further away than was possible. It instilled in Mina a feeling of safety, like a taste she couldn't place – a sensation forgotten. Huddled beneath the hatch that divided them from certain death, all three of them smiled. They would see daylight again. Madeline's wide shoulders didn't budge. Her neck didn't turn.

'Who's hungry?' Ciara said, playfully nibbling her lip in a smile.

Mina instinctively looked to Madeline, like a child

unsure of the rules. She couldn't help it. In all her life she never needed permission to do as she pleased. Why should Madeline be in charge? They were all in the same situation, and they all had a say in how they handled it. And still they dithered, all eager to eat, and yet deterred by Madeline's silence and her unspoken sway over their lives. She must have been starving too.

'Would you like to join us, Madeline?' Mina asked.

No response. It's not as though she hadn't heard.

'Madeline?' she pressed, casting a confused look at Ciara and Daniel.

'You eat,' she replied. 'I'll eat after. I want to watch the recording again in case I missed something.'

That was sanction enough. Ciara was snatching cans from the shelf immediately. Daniel bounded in beside her. Mina's fascination with Madeline had yet to serve its sentence. There were moments when the woman was like them. But they were few and far between. If life after the coop was to prove testing for anyone, Madeline would struggle the most. Even in a society of four she was an odd entity.

'Go on,' she said, sensing Mina's gaze without turning, 'I'll join you shortly.'

'Whatever you want, Madeline,' she replied, feeling almost jealous of the woman's self-control.

The ping and peel of steel, and the aromas that blasted into that tiny room were euphoric. Every can they opened was another cause for laughter. This was happiness – the sweet smell of fruit, the texture of soup, the feeling of soft meat between their teeth; so much food that it clung to their gums, and they let it linger because it wasn't about the morsel. This was a meal.

Daniel dragged a plastic vat of water between his legs, hugging it like an old friend. It must have held ten litres. How many trips to the spring was that? How many days traipsing back and forth around the watchers' pits?

They ate like animals – all hands and teeth, grinning as they made absolute messes of themselves. No manners, no apologies, with every reason to gorge their fill. They were alive and sometimes that's celebration enough. They ate so loudly as to drown out Kilmartin's voice. His food was all that concerned them.

When the recording had finished, Madeline turned in her chair. She didn't look upon them as Mina had expected, with disgust and disapproval. The woman seemed pleased that they had ransacked their food supply like clumsy, starving thieves.

'We leave tomorrow,' she said, rising to her feet as though an order had been given and they were to fall into file.

'Leave tomorrow?' Ciara asked through a mouthful. 'But we've so much food and water here.'

'I can see that,' Madeline replied. 'And that's why tonight we eat and drink, and we build up our strength for the journey ahead.'

'But didn't the video say to wait until the summer?' Daniel asked. 'There's more daylight and we'll have more time.'

'*The video*,' she said, visibly annoyed, 'has given us a way out of here. We are, each of us, healthy. We carry no injuries. Who knows what will happen in the coming days, and unlike Kilmartin there are four of us. Unless none of you noticed there is a single bucket in the corner for a toilet and the building above us has been overrun. Sickness is inevitable. Do you understand? We will never be stronger than we are in this very moment.'

'Shouldn't we wait a few days?' Mina put in. 'Just to recoup our strength. And we do have so much food here.'

Daniel nodded eagerly, as though Madeline had dragged him within sight of the gallows and only Mina could save his neck. She'd seen him break down before and knew that every silent alarm was sounding in his head, calling his fears to attention. Given the choice he would probably have rationed out their supplies until Kilmartin's bunker became his tomb.

'No, Mina,' Madeline replied. 'Now is the time. I am leaving tomorrow at first light. There is one boat and one way out of here. If any of you want to join me, then you're more than welcome. But we're only as fast as the slowest person, and I don't intend on stopping once we leave. Do I make myself clear?'

No one answered. No one knew what to say. Daniel looked nervously at Ciara whose full mouth had ceased to chew. As gladdening as the thought of escape may have been, the reality of going through with it had finally occurred to them.

'Good,' Madeline said, content that her words had been digested. 'Now, Daniel, if you would kindly pass me the water. I think I will join you for dinner.'

The watchers' disruption above suddenly seemed louder. There was no telling how many of them were up there, exerting every ounce of hate in their efforts to tear that hatch apart. Mina examined the can of peach slices in her hand, with its ring pull warped out of shape, and its lid bent upwards. To the creatures in the coop the shipping container was the can, and Mina was the meal; the fruit whose juices would splash red across corrugated walls.

Her death would come easily for the watchers. It might even disappoint them. Her bones – so brittle, so sore and light – would break like the breadsticks in her favourite Italian restaurant where they always poured generously from the bottle, and where the windows carried no scratches. She had been so sure that she would never see it again. The table for one could still be hers.

She watched Madeline inspect the rows of cans. So meticulous was her selection, Mina wondered if the woman was even peckish. After such prolonged starvation, her appetite would probably never recover again. It was just another thing that the forest had taken from her, never to return.

Even on its driest day the woodland was a maze of obstacles, all vying to slow them down. Kilmartin's compass would guide them but keeping their course as the crow flies was out of the question. If they weren't in that boat and on that river by sundown, then it would all be for nothing.

Mina knew that the odds were stacked against them. But hope isn't founded on certainties. It's the belief that the bad ending might not happen. She kept her head down, not wanting her doubts to rub off on the others, listening in to hear how they were dealing with Madeline's impatient play for freedom. Daniel was watching Ciara from the corner of his eye. She was so still, staring at the ground like a riddle she couldn't solve. Mina suspected the worst, that her mind had been abducted by dark, unsettling imaginings, of all that she had lost and all that they now stood to gamble.

'What will you do?' Daniel asked her.

'What?' Ciara replied, spooked by another's voice amidst her sadness.

It was as though Daniel knew she needed saving. Despite what Madeline thought, his kindness wasn't a weakness. It was his greatest strength.

'I mean,' he said, 'what will you do when you get out of here?'

'I don't know,' she replied. 'I suppose I'll go home, but I don't really want to. I'm more scared of going home than I am of this place, I think.' She forced a little laugh. 'It will be so empty. At least here I have you. I have company. As horrible as it is here, I'll never forget it. I don't want to. This is the last place that John and I were together.'

'Maybe you could stay with someone?' Daniel said.

'I could stay with my parents, I suppose,' she replied. 'But they'll have so many questions, and I can't talk about it, Danny. I can't. And they don't need to know about any of this. I love them too much to tell them the truth.'

Mina knew that Ciara had lost everything, and she wouldn't be able to share with anyone the reasons how or why. What could she possibly tell John's family? Months had passed since their disappearance. Were photographs of them shared around the internet or on the evening news, pleading for information? Her parents probably hadn't given up their search of them, even after all that time.

'And you,' she asked Daniel, 'what will you do? Will you go home to your parents?'

'It's just my dad,' he said, sadly.

Daniel had never spoken about his family. There was a

shared respect for the past. It was painful to talk about that which they might never see again. And some memories were sacred. They had no place in the forest.

'Will I tell you something?' he said, whispering now, but Mina could still hear him.

'Of course,' Ciara replied.

'That day, when I left on my bike, I was leaving. My home, that is. I just wanted to ride as fast and as far as I could and see where my life took me.' He chuckled to himself. 'It didn't take me very far. But it's far enough from my dad. I'm never going back there. So, I suppose I don't have anywhere to go, but that's okay. I'll figure it out.'

'You'll come with me,' she said, reaching over to touch his hand. 'I'll be glad of the company.'

Empty cans were scattered around her. The soup was just another stain on a jumper that was green once upon a time. None of them were in the shape of their lives, but Ciara seemed to shun the very thought of exercise. The trek south could be too much for her. But Mina knew she was stronger than those kind eyes let on. They had all witnessed that side of her.

Daniel was a different case. He was fitter; probably the strongest amongst them. But it wasn't his body that would slow them down. The boy's fears were out of control. It made him unpredictable.

And then there was Madeline – the eldest and weakest but only in the physical sense. If any one of them could make the journey, it was her. She didn't join them on the floor where they dined within an arm's reach of another helping. Instead, she brought her food back to the desk and ate alone.

They were an unlikely outfit. Their strengths and weaknesses spread thin between them, but Mina had to believe that together they could do it. Otherwise, what was the point in trying? She couldn't imagine the loss of any one of them. They were the weird family that lived in the woods, dysfunctional and damaged, but always too stubborn to die.

'Mina,' Daniel whispered, calling for her attention, 'do you really think that there's a boat?'

Madeline hadn't heard him, or if she had then she didn't react. Huddled in her shawl with her back turned to them, she kept on scratching away at the can with her long fingers, chewing slowly, like she always did.

'Kilmartin went to a lot of trouble setting this place up,' Mina replied. 'What would be the point of risking everything to study these things if he didn't have an escape plan? He knew that nothing works here and he found a way around it. The fact that we have light is nothing short of a miracle.'

'What do you mean?' Ciara put in.

'Think about it,' she said, leaning forward. 'Cars don't work. Danny's bike broke down. If there's any way out of here, then it has to be by boat. So long as the river runs fast enough, we'll make it.'

'And if it doesn't?' Daniel asked, his worries multiplying by the second.

'I don't know,' Mina replied, sitting back. 'We'll all go skinny-dipping and scare the watchers away.'

'What if someone has already found this place?' Ciara whispered nervously. 'They would have seen the video and they would know about the boat.' She hugged her body as if suddenly cold. 'What if the boat is already gone? We would never make it back here on time.'

'We will be lucky to make it to the boat at all,' Madeline said, turning in her chair. 'I don't know how large this forest is, but I guarantee you that the river is a full day's journey. And no, Ciara, no one has set foot in this place since Kilmartin. Look around you! Nothing has been disturbed. No food other than what he himself ate is missing. The man was spotlessly clean. It's a shame that the same cannot be said about you.'

'Fuck this place,' Mina shot back, coming to Ciara's defence. 'Feel free to pick up the mess if it makes you happy, Madeline. In the morning we're out of here and we're not coming back.'

Madeline seemed not to hear, or else she was simply so uninterested in Mina's response that it didn't even register. She collected the compass from the table and held it flat on her hand. Her long neck arched over it as she paced around in a circle, making sure that it was functioning correctly. The woman would stop and she would frown, and then she would repeat the process again and again.

'It's working,' she said eventually, speaking more to herself than to anybody else.

A sudden thud echoed through the hatch above. One of the watchers must have jumped down from the ceiling, throwing all its force at it, and probably breaking itself in the process. Everyone flinched. Everyone except Madeline who still stared, hypnotised, at the compass.

'I hope, Mina,' she said, 'you're not planning on taking that bird of yours with you.'

Mina looked at the yellow one, still smiling, and still

waiting for its dinner. There were five of them making the journey, and all five of them would make it.

'Don't you worry about the bird,' she replied. 'Remember what I told you. When I leave this place, he's coming with me.'

Just as Mina expected, Madeline said nothing.

20

They had rushed inside like a plague of locusts, wrestling one another to fall first upon their feast, their untold talons scarifying this building of brittle, plastered blocks. The coop's light didn't deter them. They scrambled beneath it without hesitation, smashing the open door aside. Their waxen skin shimmered like wet marble. Their muscles contorted like worms, glistening in sweat and spittle. They all fought towards the hatch, piling their naked flesh atop of it, tearing at each other, their teeth whetted and salivating. The chaos did not abate. All night they indulged this frenzy. The steel may have dampened their ungodly screams to those buried beneath, but they were never so loud and their rage never so wild.

With her eyes closed Mina listened to the horror above, trying to count how many were up there, fighting over who got to kill her first. She had joined Ciara on the bed and sat with her back against the wall, one bare foot dangling over the floor. She might have slept. She couldn't remember. If she had then she had dreamt only of the watchers and of this coffin that was now their home.

Underground, there was no knowing what time it was. This made the anticipation all the worse. They could be summoned at any second. Unprepared despite expectancy. The stars – like embers in the ether – would be quenched. All that black would bleach to light, and the sun would chase the watchers back into their dens.

21

A sliver of light framed the floor when Mina lifted the hatch. The silence hinted at the watchers' retreat. The darkness of the coop confirmed it. Their frustration was commemorated on every inch of concrete, in a room mauled and hewn out of shape. Fluids born from their breath and bodies dripped down the glass like sweat. Blood, too, was sprayed in patches, from when their anger had turned inward. Everywhere there was disease and infection – a poison you could taste in the air; black and alive. Mina guessed that this was what Madeline knew was coming. This was why they couldn't wait another day.

'The light's off,' Ciara whispered, voicing what everyone already knew.

Morning's light had yet to perforate the forest. The night's inky black still pooled around the corners. With the lid open, and the glow of the safe house slipping up into the chill air, the thought of staying below had never been so appealing.

The birdcage was light enough to carry for now. Mina's

sojourn in the forest had weakened her; deprived of light and food, there were days when even the short walk to the spring had left her exhausted. She remembered how her body had ached that day when her car broke down, and the shoulder pain that never really healed. She was so determined not to leave the yellow one behind. But what if Madeline was right?

'You ready for this?' she whispered to the bird; both shivering against the cold.

'Good to go,' Daniel said, rubbing his hands together furiously, not entirely sure who Mina was talking to.

'Wait,' Madeline snapped, her large hands held the compass, pivoting her body to mimic its magnetic needle.

'It is working, isn't it?' Mina asked.

'Yes. Yes, of course it's working. South is in that direction,' she said, pointing towards the wall to the right of the mirror, where their bed used to be.

'Well?' Mina pressed.

'Well, *what*, Mina?'

'Let's get fucking moving,' she said, hoisting the cage up into her arms.

Through the broken door and down the corridor they walked in darkness. Mina heard Daniel retch. He was gasping into cupped hands, his fears rising like acid in the back of his throat. The taste in the air was vile. Madeline went about releasing the chains and bolts. Their bodies piled up against one another, all eager to breathe fresh air. When the door was unlocked it yawned open ever so slowly like some grand reveal, teasing them. Every speck of faint light and particle of that crisp, raw air carried with it some illusory sense of promise.

One by one, they stepped out like prisoners released, unsure as to how the woodland had changed in their absence. The cold was startling. It stiffened their bodies and fogged their breaths. Teeth rattled aloud like castanets. Mina was stood behind the rest, staring at her feet and the toes that squelched into black soil. They had numbed to the point that the pain seemed to belong to someone else. They weren't her feet. Mina's feet could never be that filthy.

'Mina,' Madeline whispered, so loud that she might as well have shouted, 'where are your shoes?'

'The watchers took them,' she said, 'that night when...' She knew better than to open old wounds. 'I lost my socks, too.'

'And you just thought that you would walk barefoot to the boat?' she snapped.

'I didn't think,' Mina replied, feeling genuinely stupid, but what other choice had she?

'Well,' Madeline said, 'if you can't keep up, then that's your problem.'

'It's not Mina's problem,' Ciara said. 'We're all in this *together*, and we're getting out of here *together*.'

'Well, let's go then,' Madeline replied, already turning to walk away. 'You can all die *together*, if ye so please.'

There was a time when Mina thought the woman was content to live out her years in exile, never considering for a merciful moment that escape was possible. Looking at her now, as she stormed ahead through that wilderness of horror, there was no stopping her. For one so frail, she moved with a haste that surprised them all, her long gangly strides hidden beneath the blanket that she was never seen without.

Daniel glanced over his shoulder. Mina thought for an addled second that he had forgotten something. But no, the boy in him – the one that Madeline had brutalised so effortlessly – wanted to run home. The safe house was warm and its steel impenetrable. She followed his eyes north, where they searched for the coop that was now nowhere to be seen. It was too late. The opportunity had passed. The forest had swallowed it out of sight. So dense were its untold trees and so sprawling the brake that he may never have found it again. There was one option remaining – south. And only Madeline knew the way. The compass was hers to hold and nobody else's.

With her feet soaking into a soil that was cold but comforting, both brittle and soft between her toes, Mina had never been so perceptive to textures nor so disturbed by their each and every imposition. The blanket that cocooned her body drew the damp from above and below. It made her sweaty, but never warm. The frost was far from content to settle by her toes. It had gripped her ankles, before swelling like a rising tide to the height of her knees, and then it seized her thighs like a vice carved from steaming ice. She ignored the pain as best she could, until eventually she felt nothing. Legs ploughed forward like dead, wooden stilts, and even these early minutes in a journey of unknown hours dragged on like a cruel joke. Her fingers were locked through the cage's bars and the bird was quiet. For all Mina knew, the yellow one was slowly dying. Maybe she was too, but she just couldn't feel it.

Madeline had led the way, charging through great covens of brambles and ferns, all snagging and sticking, slowing their pace to a crawl. She abided by the compass's needle, resolved to travel as the crow flies in a land that the clever crow knew to avoid.

'Madeline,' Mina said, as she stood behind her, with Ciara and then Daniel taking up the rear, 'we can't keep going straight.'

However much time had already elapsed, they had made little ground. The sun was higher, Mina knew that much. Here and there it tore through in javelins of light. There was no horizon – no open ground or river. There was an endless parade of trees. If this was indeed their path, then they were the first to break it. There were no fissures to slip through and no gaps to guide them home.

'What would you have me do, Mina?' Madeline said, turning to face her, seeming taller than ever before.

'We'll fan out and find the fastest way through,' she replied. 'There *are* four of us, Madeline. We can help, you know?'

'With your bare feet, can you?' she said. 'Can you really help?' Her frustration unleashed.

'You can have my shoes, if you want, Mina?' Daniel said.

Everyone stopped. He was already unlacing them before Mina reached over to grab his shoulder.

'I'm not wearing those old things,' she said, smiling, and almost crying from the cold. 'Let's all just find a way through this. We've gotten this far, haven't we?'

Mina *liked* these people. Their flaws were as obvious as their situation was grim, but she cared for them. She loved them. And as opposed as she was – as she had always been – to these bonds, these ties that stretch and strangle you, she wanted them to get through this. These weren't the kind of people that you walk away from without saying goodbye. Not anymore.

'Okay,' Madeline said, looking around her, reassessing everyone's role and worth, like a manager burdened with a team of amateurs. 'Let's all spread out.'

With their lives aligned south they worked to find the quickest passage. Their efforts strengthened by fear and hope. The former tracked their every step. The latter lay ahead of them, but always out of sight, hidden within a maze made up entirely of dead ends.

One would make a breach in the thicket and together they would funnel through, tearing up great chunks of briars, searching for the next, calling to each other whenever they found some means to penetrate the next unforgiving tract. They swept the forest, searching for tomorrow. The days used to come so easily. Now Mina had to work for them.

'Over here,' Daniel called out.

The boy had seldom spoken since *that* night. The sound of his voice, and the fact that he thought it necessary to use it, caught everyone's attention.

'What is it, Danny?' Ciara asked; Mina couldn't see her fiery red head anywhere, but she sounded close by.

'It's a path, I think,' he replied.

Sunken into the mud, and hastily arranged, were a number of tiles. Slate shards coarsely cut by hand, with no distinguishable shape. The brambles had thrown their spindly selves over them. This wasn't nature's doing. Someone had been here before.

'All paths lead somewhere,' Mina said, running a toe along the slate, thinking of her mum's mantra that had seen her through life's every misadventure.

'Move out of the way,' Madeline ordered as she stormed forward, swinging at the briars. Daniel shrank back behind them, eager to relinquish his discovery. He was content to follow Madeline's lead from a distance. Ciara joined in, beating back whatever stood in their way, though her strikes lacked the same speed and violence. Mina followed close behind, her grubby, bare feet avoiding the thorns and sharp things that now littered the way.

A thatch of gluey branches clung to Mina's shoulder like a distraught child. She pulled it aside only for it to throw its neediness onto Daniel. Everywhere – as they drudged over the black tiles – thorns and thistles whipped at them from all angles. Keeping an eye on the ground was impossible. This, of course, wasn't a problem for those wearing shoes.

Mina's yelp nearly sent Daniel tumbling over. All sensation in her toes and feet had been forgotten until that moment, when the thorn shot up through the skin. She held on to his shoulder for support, hopping on one foot whilst Madeline cast her that look of abject disapproval. How dare she hurt herself and slow them down? Mina clenched her teeth through the pain. She could see it in her foot – the thin black needle that still protruded out, just enough to pinch between her fingernails.

When she got home, she would have to disinfect it. This was the first thought that crossed her mind and one that gave her cause to smile, even during the pain as the thorn passed out through the skin. For too long her home had been a place in her past, like the rose-tinted memories of a childhood summer.

Mina had it all planned out. She would run a hot bath.

That bottle of wine – the *Sancerre* that she received for her birthday and had somehow saved for an occasion worthy of its price tag – would be opened and every mouthful cherished. Mina's taste buds had wilted, and no doubt her tolerance for such pleasures had waned to nothing. She would be drunk after a glass. Even the smell of it would probably make her dizzy. And the thought of this – that old, familiar drunkenness – thrilled her enough to bypass the pain. She flicked the thorn away and rubbed some feeling into her foot.

'Are you okay?' Daniel asked, holding her hand into his shoulder.

'Never better, Danny,' she replied. 'I'll put something on it when I get home.'

Mina visualised her bathroom – where wine and hot, bubbly water awaited her – and all of those suspended little jobs and doings. Her bath towel still hung over the door. The mirror was speckled with soap stains after she had washed her hands in a flurry. Always late and always rushing. She hadn't cleaned the floor since the weekend before she left. Long black hairs had gathered like tumbleweed behind the door and clung like cracks to the porcelain sink.

Only one person could have disturbed it – Jennifer. She had been given a spare key in case Mina lost hers. Maybe she had come looking for her. She rang so often and so rarely would Mina answer. But they always touched base eventually. As persistent as her sister was, she might have just given up. Mina could imagine Jennifer sidling into bed beside her husband, ranting as she did about her no-good sister – the one who drank and smoked too much, and never answered her phone. What would Mina tell her when she got home? Would Jennifer even have the patience to listen to her lies?

Madeline stopped suddenly and Mina almost crashed into the back of her. The path *had* led somewhere. They stood before a clearing. A bald patch in the woodland. Nothing natural broke the soil, but in its centre stood that which snapped the air from their lungs.

A stone doorway was sunken into the earth. Around its frame was carved a pattern of spirals and weathered symbols, corroded by age and the elements, but still visible beneath the sun that now soared high in the sky above. Its entrance was blocked by a colossal boulder, and packed tight with earth so that not even a wisp of air could escape from within.

'What is it?' Ciara whispered.

Mina was aware of Daniel's head peering over her shoulder, using her body as a shield. It looked as though the soil had been built up around it. Centuries of hard rain had blasted it clean. The ominous etchings, and the sheer size of the portal alone were enough to hasten the boy's breathing, and that's all Mina could hear as she stared at the oddity before them.

'This is where they buried them,' Madeline said, taking a step forward. 'They banished the watchers under the earth and sealed the doorway shut.'

Mina looked to her in puzzlement. The woman had never mentioned any doorway to them in the past. She didn't even appear surprised by its discovery. But then, Madeline's expressions were limited strictly to disinterest and displeasure. And she hoarded secrets like an avid collector.

'How can you be so sure?' Mina asked her.

'Because these things were never meant to escape,' she replied, running her hands along the engravings. 'But they found a way. They weren't going to stay hidden forever. Just long enough for the world to forget that they were real.'

All that she had told them was true. Like Kilmartin before her, Madeline had come to that place looking for them – these fairies of folklore; never lending a thought to the horror that their existence would bring, like a seafaring explorer searching for the edge of the world and finding it.

'Come on,' she said, 'let's keep moving. We don't have much time.'

22

Faces were nicked and scratched. Hands were rusted with blood, and all fingernails were black-lined or broken. They had torn through the woodland's leafy walls since dawn and still the end was nowhere in sight. Panic was setting in hard. Not even a fool's hope could ignore it. Their palms were mottled, and burned from the thistles' touch. Skin was rough as old gloves; their leather chapped and faded. Here and there the sun flashed between the trees, but it never lingered long enough to dispel the cold. The shadows were too quick.

They had reaped fresh wounds and their bodies had tired, but nothing else seemed to change. They traversed the same noiseless prison where everything worked against them. Mina felt as though they had been travelling in the same circles. She dreaded the possibility that they would fall upon the coop, and that all their efforts would be for nothing.

Madeline still clutched the compass. Their lives were in her hands. The woman hadn't spoken for what felt like hours. Nobody had. Only the yellow one was brave enough to make a sound. It perched in its cage like a backseat driver, chirping and giving out every time Mina lost her footing.

She couldn't have attempted the journey alone as John had done. And Mina knew that these were the thoughts that haunted Ciara's every step; the last moments of the one she loved – the foundation of all her memories, and the one she spoke to when everyone else was quiet. How far could he have gotten? Without a compass and with no path to guide him, he never stood a chance. He would have heard the watchers' approach. He would have known the end was coming long before they found him.

Between the branches, the sky was beginning to bleed. The sun would soar no higher. It could only go one way now. The moon was waiting in the wings to take over. The winter days were short. And if they didn't reach the boat before sundown, then their night would be even shorter.

The light would turn on soon. Mina pictured the coop, with the watchers' feculence tarred across its floor, the glow of the safe house reaching like a stem to the ceiling, and the window – not yet a mirror – with that wretched view that she would never forget; those familiar trees, the lesions through their bark, and the scratches in the glass that glistened white in the morning frost. She could still smell the dust and the concrete, and she could taste the staleness of its air.

The watchers would rush back inside. Even after the prior night's failings, they would never give up. Mina realised now that they should have closed the hatch after them. It might have bought them more time. But these things were hunters. They were trackers. The path they had cut through the forest was anything but subtle. The watchers would fly through the trees, chasing their scent, and they wouldn't rest until they tasted it.

'Madeline, what time is it?' Mina gasped.

'It's after five o'clock,' she replied, in that voice of hers that seemed oblivious to what she'd just said. 'We're running out of time. The last of the light will be gone before six.'

Was there ever any chance of reclaiming their old lives? Kilmartin's recording wasn't dated. Granted, the technology that adorned his little bomb shelter was relatively current but there was no knowing when he conducted his research there. The promised boat could have turned to rot by now. They tread on the narrowest tightrope of hope, or was it desperation? Perhaps they were one and the same.

Another possibility crossed into Mina's mind. What if Madeline knew that they were a doomed party? Making decisions for them without prior discussion was by no means beyond the woman. Maybe death was a kindness. One last, short scream instead of a long, drawn-out cry for help that wasn't coming.

Madeline's pace never faltered. Her shawled body forced through whatever stood in her way, shouldering and trampling, swinging at the surrounding barbs like the last knight on a battlefield, overwhelmed but defiant in the face of sure defeat. The forest belonged to her. It had been the woman's home for so long. It was her past and present but not her future. She owed it nothing. Mina had caught her glancing back at them more than once. And though the woman's face was too embittered by experience to ever express her concerns, Mina knew what she must have been thinking. They were too slow. They weren't going to make it. The sands of the hourglass were piling high, burying them alive.

A crucible of adversaries guarded their path; enlisted for their branches, their leaves, and most of all their thorns. Every opening was fought for, offering no reward, only the repeated, torturous obligation to face their next foe. And the forest's champions had waited centuries to prove their worth. As the hours passed, Mina had tired from the fight. She couldn't remember the last word she had spoken or to whom. If impressed to speak, she wouldn't have known what to say. *Run! We need to go faster!* She knew they were each trying their best, but it was becoming more and more obvious that their best simply wasn't good enough. A darkness was falling like a curtain closing over their lives, concluding the tragedy of their final act to riotous, taloned applause.

Mina had just squeezed her way through a screen of glossy leaves, hugging the yellow one's cage with both arms, when she saw Madeline stood stock-still in front of her, inhabiting the half-light like a phantom trapped for all eternity, waiting to be saved, and yet cursed only for disappointment.

'What's wrong?' Mina gasped, her bare feet stepping silently behind her, toes black as the soil rising between them.

Madeline craned her head to one side. She was listening, but not to Mina. 'It's nothing,' she replied, staring ahead. 'It's just another pit. No different from the others.'

It was the widest opening that Mina had encountered, and she had uncovered her fair share. The earth around it had been cleared by the watchers' nightly surfacing. A sense of death snaked around its edges. Deep gashes lined its clay, and the stench was unsettling even at a distance. The fastest way was straight ahead, so close to the pit that the eye could meet the darkness within, where naked bodies were coiled to pounce, salivating as the sun sank lower, their sweaty skin simmering like a fever.

'We don't have time for this,' Madeline said, looking Mina in the eyes directly, never more serious than in that moment. 'We can't slow down, do you understand? They're coming, Mina. And when they do there's nowhere you can hide that they won't find you. Throw the boy over it if that's what it takes. We can't afford to waste any more time.'

With that she was gone, storming ahead just as Ciara had finally caught up, panting and holding a hand to her side where the pain had warped her into a curtsey.

'What was that about?' she asked, breathless, running the sweat through her hair. 'Are we nearly there?'

'We have to move,' Mina replied sharply. 'That's the fastest way.' Here she pointed towards the murky hole in the earth that Madeline had already crossed without a care.

Daniel emerged from a shock of leaves, like a wanderer falling through a low-lying fog. His cheeks and forehead were bloody with cuts. The boy had heart, there was no denying that, but would it carry him past the pit? Mina knew how they affected him like a phobia he couldn't reason with.

'Danny,' she said, taking his hand in hers, 'we don't have time to think about this.'

'What are you talking about?' he asked, squinting at her through the sweat. 'We don't have time to think about what, Mina?'

Ciara grabbed his other hand. 'Do you trust me, Danny?'

'More than anyone in the world,' he replied, smiling down at their fingers entwined.

Testament to Daniel's word, he didn't dig his heels or hesitate. Mina and Ciara escorted him forward and he acquiesced, gripping both of their hands as the pit loomed closer, always strongest when people believed in him. If the sight of it had triggered any alarms, their company on either side of him were enough to silence them. As they neared the burrow they broke into a hasty queue, slipping single file beside it. Ciara pressed Daniel ahead of her before the darkness could lure his courage into its depths. Mina was following close behind them, but she stopped, just like she promised herself she wouldn't. Ciara was too busy throwing an arm over Daniel's shoulder to notice. *They're leaner and they're longer.* But what do they look like? She edged closer to the pit where the shadows swirled like the blackest fog, suffocating its secrets out of sight. The others hadn't noticed Mina lowering onto her haunches, ignoring those sore muscles that ached at her to stop. She stared into the abyss, seeing nothing and hearing not a sound.

'What are you doing?' Ciara called back to her. 'Mina, we have to...'

'Just one minute,' she interjected, eyes transfixed by her own imaginings. 'I just...'

The shock of the scream came as a blast, knocking Mina onto her back. The yellow one screeched and ricocheted against its bars. The sound seemed to shake the very earth; echoing, lingering, and festering long after it was released like a nightmare that refused to be forgotten. It travelled up the tunnel's throat like a gust of wind, breaking the surface and shaking the branches above, spreading terror like a murmuration of winged devils. Mina scrabbled away from the pit, her feet slipping, digging ruts in the soil as Ciara seized under her arms and dragged her to safety. That shriek felt near to her as that first night by the window. But back then, its intent had been to startle her, to reduce their latest prisoner to tears. This somehow sounded worse than that; crueller, angrier, more terrorising than before. They weren't the watchers' pets anymore. The days of being toyed with were over. Their intention was clear as that voice still ringing through Mina's ears – death, and the unspeakable pain that precedes it.

If one of them had seen her, then their position was known to all those tearing at their nocturnal chains to chase them. What had she done? How could she have been so reckless. Had the sound of their footsteps alerted the watchers' ears to listen? But they had never ventured so far from the safety of the coop. The parrot's cry might have covered their tracks. A bird had flown close to its death, that's all. Every possibility remained that the watchers would return to the safe house first, buying them more time and a few extra moments of life before all hell broke loose upon them.

Together they ran, following the wreckage of Madeline's efforts. Mina stared skyward at the slivers of ebbing light, like dim fractures in the ceiling of their prison. She could feel the darkness growing around them, creeping out from the lowest leaf and spreading under boughs like black fungus. Madeline turned as they approached her. Mina got the impression that she was taking a head count, her eyes snapping over them but resting on Daniel a little longer.

Whether she was surprised to see him, or relieved, her face gave nothing away.

'Night is coming much faster than you know,' she said. 'We should have reached the open by now. Spread out. Find the quickest way through. Call to me if you lose your bearings. Go, now!' she shouted, so loud as to betray the fear that she hid so well.

Even the yellow one understood their urgency, screaming at them like an overzealous mascot as Mina used its cage as a battering ram to break the undergrowth. She would apologise if they made it.

'This way,' Daniel's voice shouted from somewhere unseen. 'There's a clear run through here.'

In every direction that Mina turned, it all looked the same. Nature's undead things had veiled their course with delusive copycats, tricking them into losing their way. Daniel's discovery drew everyone to his side where they raced through a rare gutter of open earth, too clear for nature's chaotic design; one perhaps carved by the watchers themselves. A fine mist lined the way, seeping up from the caverns below like ghostly spies tracking their movements. It was always this way before the coop's light came on.

'Are we going to make it?' Ciara cried, and her tearful desperation made Mina reach out to comfort her, but no words came in that moment.

Nobody voiced their acknowledgement. They just ran, tripping and floundering, holding anyone up whose legs had spent their last. Ciara had fallen behind, but Mina could hear her panting, so tired at that stage that she loved her all the more for not giving up. Trials such as they had endured would break the body and mind of the strongest, most able-bodied. And when they'd abandoned the coop, they were, none of them, at their best.

'We will,' Mina called back to her, hoping to spur her on. 'Ciara, we're going to make it.' But the lie sounded so unconvincing that she regretted it immediately.

Could they have covered more ground? Mina's shoulder ached as though her arm had popped out of its socket. She had been so stubborn, like a petulant child acting out. Madeline knew the bird would slow them down and yet Mina hadn't listened. The yellow one could have flown high above the trees to safety, its feathers shining golden in the sunlight. They didn't all have to die in that place. Mina decided there and then, if the watchers found them, her last act on this earth would be to release the fifth member of their party – the one that never complained and smiled when all those around it had forgotten how.

Ciara's sudden shriek almost tripped Mina up. The mind can frame a million horrors in an instant. She had been taken; dragged underground as the watchers' first meal before sundown. Or else an injury had befallen her, one so tragic as to bring her journey to an end. Could Mina and Daniel carry her if that were the case? Would Madeline leave them behind? She had threatened to do so if they slowed her down. But no, she stopped like the rest of them, gripping her compass in frustration as they all turned to face whatever had brought their flight to a standstill.

Ciara was wincing on the earth, her weak arms straining to lift her up. A root had snagged her foot, sending her crashing forward. The shock of it no doubt derailed her more than the fall itself. Beneath the forest floor were a hundred hands, and their race south had been too desperate and blind to mark the pits they could reach from.

'We have to move!' Madeline screamed.

Mina dropped to her knees, holding Ciara like a doll. 'It's okay,' she gasped, running her fingers through her hair. 'You can do this.'

Daniel joined in, helping Ciara to her feet. She hobbled for a step, but she could walk. 'I know,' she said, shaking now, those dazzling green eyes as vivid and hopeful as ever. 'We're going to make it.'

Mina held her face, her cold fingers caressing those soft cheeks that had shrunk since they met. Ciara's honesty was incorruptible. The truth was the only card she presented to the world, and Mina sided with Ciara's optimism like a stray cat that had finally found a home.

'We're nearly there,' Madeline called back to them.

'How can you tell?' Mina asked, as the thought of the end jolted some feeling back into her bones.

'Can't you hear it?' she whispered. 'Can't you hear the water?'

'I can't hear anything,' she replied.

'Come on, quickly,' the woman snapped back. 'The river is close.'

Was Madeline lying to them, dangling their freedom like a carrot on a string? Mina strove to hear any sound other than their bodies breaking forward. But was it getting brighter? Their eyes had attuned to the dim, scraggy shade of the woodland. Now there was light in the distance, and between the trees she saw the first splinters of sky.

Their course through the woodland had been a full day's labour. They had fought for every southerly step. If the forest had had its way, its ivy would have cocooned their bodies; making them as much a part of its hellish decay as it would always be a part of them. But the treeline was in sight, and it spurred them on with an energy that ached. The soft breeze reached out to them. Its scent of petals and herbs whelmed the spoil of damp and dying wood. It was some heavenly hand pulling them from the darkness and into the light, where grasses grew tall beneath the blood-red sun.

Mina collapsed from the woodland. One last tacky strand of weed released its grip on her, and she was free. Her hands fell on grass that was soft and cool to the touch. The yellow one's cage toppled over and he clawed at the satin tufts that slipped through its bars. They had reached open ground. The vastness of the landscape – the forgotten colours and sheer sense of awe kept Mina on her knees, dumbstruck by the beauty of it all. She beheld a world more magnificent than she had remembered.

The grasses led down a hill. They moved in soothing waves in the wind, singing the softest song. Decay had seeped through the forest floor, but here there were luscious greens of life as far as the eye could see. The sun burned like a fireball crashing over the horizon, its flames flashing through powdered clouds, dissipating in colours that Mina could taste and smell, and with her arms outstretched she fancied she could feel them. The distant Connemara hills gleamed in the dying light. The blades of grass slipped between Mina's toes and swayed like silk across her open palm.

The river wasn't far. Now she could hear it like a low lullaby. From where they stood, Mina could see its water trickling through the shallow, and flowing proud in the deep, shimmering like a bed of crystals beneath the sun. It was shored by slabs of stone and great scatterings of pebbles, as though nature – the artist – had placed each one with care. But she couldn't see the boat.

Mina heard Ciara and Daniel breaking through the trees behind her. The ecstasy of the open sky stole the last air from their lungs. Their voices carried no words, only the garbled disbelief that they had made it. But their moment was short-lived. They had arrived just as the sun's last flake of light was being doused. Night was falling, and with it came the watchers' screams. Like a doomsday siren, their voices howled in their hundreds.

'Quickly,' Madeline shouted, 'they're coming.'

The watchers were agile. They were faster. Long limbs now glanced between branches. Naked shapes, slick with sweat, torpedoed through lightless tunnels. Nature's wilderness succumbed to the chase; never hindering, never slowing them down. The watchers would find the trail immediately. There would be no hesitation, no communication between them that couldn't be screamed into the night's sky.

The rush of bodies broke around the stone portal, white waves of flesh rippling beneath the moonlight. The sound of splintering wood filled the air like the cracking of a thousand whips spurring them on. They flashed between trees, these shadows that snarled and screamed. In the darkness they could see. No step was misplaced. Every claw of earth launched them onward. Nothing would stop them. Nothing could.

Mina stood, fingers tensed around the yellow one's cage, staring into the forest's lightless depths where their voices surged like a tempest. Branches seemed to claw towards her as though the damnable place was alive, its fingers seeking to drag her back into its gut.

Ciara grabbed her arm, twisting Mina around and breaking the woodland's spell over her. 'Come on,' she shouted but she was hardly heard over the pandemonium.

Every second counted. Without the sun as their guardian, each action that followed would save or cease their lives. Kilmartin was organised. His misguided venture wouldn't have lasted a single night had he not planned every diminutive detail. If this was his escape plan, then the boat couldn't be far. They ran to the riverside. Madeline's pace left them all floundering behind her. She was knee-deep in water before Ciara's legs had remembered how to run.

'Where is it?' she shouted, twirling in circles and sploshing water around her. 'It has to be here!'

'Over here!' Daniel called out.

The boy was heaving the tarpaulin out of place. Kilmartin hadn't just thrown a cover over the boat, as Mina had expected. A hollow had been dug into the earth, the exact length and width to slot in the vessel and hide it out of sight. Mina came to Daniel's side and threw her arms around him. She would never have found it. She knew that much for sure.

'We have to get it into the water,' she shouted.

Ciara, out of breath and holding her sides in place, was the last to arrive but she went straight to work. She wiped the clammy hairs from her face and threw Mina that smile that meant everything – *we're going to make it*.

The pit was sodden. When Mina gripped the boat's frame she could feel the softness of its wood, where the water had soaked in, rotting its edges. Kilmartin's one miscalculation – he had buried it too close to the river. It would still float. They just had to get beyond the watchers' reach. Once they were safe, then the boat could sink like a stone and Mina wouldn't care.

It was a wooden skiff, painted battleship grey but tarred black where the water had bruised through, and it measured maybe fifteen feet, if Mina had to guess. The boat wasn't quite what she had imagined. Her artist's eye had conceived a streamlined speedboat with racing stripes and an engine that would roar them into the sunset. The reality was a little less sensational. But it would fit all four of them and the bird. Mina dropped the cage into the boat, and the yellow one shrieked and sang like a captain bellowing orders to its crew. It was surprisingly light to lift between the four of them, as though Kilmartin had modified it to suit the needs of one man. A pair of oars had been placed side by side beneath it like two ceremonial swords. Fortunately, these were aluminium, and had persevered through the flood. Had they been carved from wood they would have crumbled in Daniel's hands as he jumped into the hollow and threw them up onto the grass for Mina. Every exertion was a challenge for them, such was their fatigue. But this was the end, and Mina couldn't believe it was happening.

'Keep your focus!' Madeline said to them. 'We're not out of here yet.'

Together they slid the boat through the high grass, pushing all their weight into it, exhausting what strength remained. Mina's bare feet couldn't find their grip and she nearly slipped down face first. The boat crunched and cracked over the loose stones before sploshing into the water, soaking them in seconds. The river's flow was cold enough to numb their skin that spectral shade of blue, startling their nerves and sinew into action.

The watchers' screams were intensifying, rolling through the night's sky like thunder. Mina tried to hold the boat steady as Ciara struggled to clamber up and into it, flailing like a fish splashing silver. When Mina looked to Madeline, she found the woman's gaze fixated on her, as if she had been watching her the entire time, waiting for their eyes to meet.

'What, Madeline?' she panted. 'What are you doing? Get in!'

'The boy,' was all she said, almost sadly. 'The boy isn't here.'

Where was Daniel? In the commotion of hurtling the boat down to the river, Mina had lost sight of him. Was he not pushing it with them? Her last memory was of him clawing his way out of the pit after having passed her the oars. She started to wade back towards the riverside; the moonlight sparkling like polished steel on its black water, straining her vision to focus where the night was darkest, where the forest grew from the hilltop like a shrine to all her fears and nightmares.

'Don't do it, Mina,' Madeline said. 'You're too late.'

It was never *too late*. They were a family, and nobody was getting left behind. That's how they had gotten this far, and that's how they would get home. Mina's feet splashed onto the pebbled shore, detached from feeling and reason, aware only of her unhinged need to get Daniel on that boat.

'There, Mina,' Ciara called out from behind her, 'towards the forest.'

Mina saw him, stained with the lightest wash of moonlight. Daniel was approaching the treeline with slow, uncertain steps as though it were whispering to him, seducing the boy back into its hellscape. Could she make it to him before the watchers broke out into the open? Such was the report of their voices, Mina was surprised they hadn't poured into the night's air already.

'Danny,' she called out, scrambling up the hill as he edged further away from her. 'What are you...'

Then she saw it; that which had stolen Daniel away from them, tripping him at the final hurdle. She fell to her knees, planting both hands into the grass like bulbs, close enough now that she could hear him speaking. Mina stared in stunned disbelief at the one standing amidst the trees, motionless as a portrait.

'Come on,' Daniel was saying to him, 'please, hurry. She needs you!'

The man's pale face and shoulders swelled from the shadows like a phantom. His jaw and cheekbones were solid, and the brow heavy. Shadows leaked over eyes that glinted with a lifeless glaze. There was no expression, just that sinister vacancy that kept the lips pursed and narrow.

'Come on, John,' Daniel shouted, reaching out his hand towards him. 'They're coming! We have to go!'

'Daniel,' Mina said, lifting to her feet and staggering a step backwards. 'That's not John.'

That voice from the pit; the darkness Mina had disturbed. Had it followed them from there, arriving before the others? Daniel retracted his hand slowly, balling it up into an unsteady fist, and looked back at Mina. It was that second of realisation – the regret, the fear, and the sad acceptance of the end – that would haunt Mina forever. She had sketched Daniel's face so many times, studying its every kink and nuance. But this was the culmination of all his fears into a single look, centred strongest in those eyes that met Mina's with a love that was heart-breaking. She retreated backwards, silently pleading with Daniel to run to her, but still that thing was watching him, pinning him in place.

'Run, Mina,' he whispered. 'Don't look back.'

He was invincible when they believed in him. But he had strayed too far from Mina's reach, and into the watcher's unblinking gaze. He had never looked so young nor so terrified. All the while, the screams grew closer. They were out of time. She couldn't wait for him.

'I'm sorry,' she whispered before leaving the boy behind.

Mina raced through the cool grasses to the beat of a thundering heart. She could see the boat. Ciara had the yellow one's cage held on her lap, and in front of her was Madeline, oars locked in their sockets, her long arms already taking them south. But Mina knew that Madeline was too strong – too determined – to break away so slowly. She was waiting for her, watching and listening, counting down however many seconds remained until Mina was deemed a lost cause; just like Daniel, and John before him.

She was sorry for not standing up for him all those times that Madeline beat him down. She was sorry that she hadn't told him how special he was, so kind and strong. And, most of all, she was sorry that she had failed to save him. He had gone back for Ciara's sake; thinking of others, risking his life for their happiness. And they didn't even realise that he was missing.

Mina needed to know if he was coming. She would run to him, hold him, and carry him if she had the strength. But when she glanced back to the forest, Daniel was where she had left him, and the watcher had stepped into the open, towering over him on its spindly legs, skeletal in the moonlight, its long arms arched out by its sides, taloned fingers spread wide. The creature's body was grotesque in its proportions, and yet that face – now slanted to one side with its eyes entranced – was still John's. For so long the boy had been watched behind the glass – safe and oblivious to its eerie fascination – and now he was within its grasp.

The boat had drifted deeper into the river like deadwood kicked from the shore. Madeline couldn't wait much longer. She was stalling, tempering her urge to drive the oars through the wash. Both she and Ciara looked to be shouting, their arms thrashing about the stars, guiding her home, but their voices were lost to the watchers'. Mina splashed forward, crashing into the deep, catching only sharp glimpses of Madeline leaning forward from the boat, reaching for her as it swayed back and forth so violently as to almost capsize. That icy water spilled into Mina's lungs, choking, distorting her senses. A weightless weakness overcame her. Legs couldn't kick hard enough. Arms were stretched out only to linger lifeless in the water, too tired to return to her. But Madeline seized her like a hawk, dragging her to the surface, floundering and helpless.

Mina retched, vomiting water onto the soft wood that cradled her, and Madeline grabbed the oars like sacred weapons, her knuckles bleaching white, all strength summoned to see their journey through. They looked back to where Daniel stood alone, dwarfed by those who crept into the moonlight, those monsters in masquerade. More of them had reached the open. Mina counted five spindly bodies, pacing around the boy, as though goading him to flee. Predators dallying with the weakest of the herd, ogling his soft flesh and every trembling part of him. The moon was never so bright; like a fearful eye it shone upon them, revealing the faces that stared down at Daniel from their lofty shoulders, snapping at the night like starving animals.

It was the single most terrifying sight that Mina had in her life beheld, the kind that leaves malleable minds deformed. These things were aware of the horror they wielded. They brandished their worst to splinter the boy's heart before breaking his body. Daniel collapsed to his knees, gazing up at the ring of faces all mimicking his own, each one warped into an abhorrent reflection resembling both boy and monster. Some wore features that were chillingly convincing, others grotesquely deformed. They circled him like giants, as more of them manifested from the woodland, their pale skin skulking in the black. There must have been twenty of the fiends swarming around him. Daniel hid his head in his hands, waiting for the inevitable, for the claws and teeth seen only in nightmares until that moment.

'What are they doing?' Ciara wept as the oars creaked and groaned in Madeline's hands.

'They've waited a long time for this,' Madeline replied. 'They're going to make it last.'

'Oh, Danny,' she cried; all her cracks torn apart anew, exposing her tired heart.

The forest's ragged treetops stretched under the sky like ramparts, its branches swaying and cracking as more bodies tore into the open, fattening the crowd of their kind, all gathered around Daniel – their prize; one priceless enough to distract their attention. Some scattered down the hill in fleshly waves, slicing through the tall grass, rallying back like a kettle of vultures. Some sprinted around the gathering on all fours like enormous insects. The distance and the dark conspired to keep Mina from identifying the masks they now wore. Had they assumed the face of another? Was Daniel now surrounded by *their* faces, the only ones in the world who cared about him; those who now held some chance of escape because of his sacrifice.

The watchers' screams intensified as their circle closed around him. Daniel lowered his hands, resigned to the end. Mina watched as his head tilted back, looking up at the creatures staring down at him. Their ancient breath engulfing him in its sickness. She hoped his thoughts had flown elsewhere; anywhere but under their heaving shadows, talons flexing, the starlight winking in all those black eyes.

Mina remembered John's cries for help, drawn from him with surgical precision; torturing, damaging, but only killing when there was nothing left of him to save but Ciara's memories.

'Don't look,' Madeline whispered. 'The boy wouldn't have wanted you to see this.'

Mina turned her back on the woodland, her body coiled like a creature under threat, convulsing uncontrollably as she fought the urge to throw up. It was too much. She couldn't accept the horror of what was happening. It felt as though only the smallest, weakest part of her was in that boat. Whatever strength she had left, and all that happiness that could have been, was by Daniel's side. Mina held her cold hands to her ears. Madeline's silhouette worked the oars like a mechanical engine, and behind her, Ciara hugged the yellow one's cage, her head at rest atop it, weeping.

Every ancient voice suddenly screamed as one. An unhallowed cacophony so intense that it did more than bore through Mina's eardrums, it flooded into her skull. It caved in her throat so that she strained to steal any air. It seized every receptive part of her and attacked it without mercy, igniting a fear so blinding that it burned. But Daniel's pain was over.

Mina didn't want to imagine the horror that lay behind her. She had witnessed how the watchers moved. She had seen the nightmarish shape of their bodies. Standing tall, they were still and sinister as a snake waiting to strike. But when they ran – on all fours with those monstrous arms pulling them forward – their speed was inescapable. Were they already coming for them? Mina looked to Madeline, too terrified to find out for herself.

'Are we going to make it?' she asked, but even she could hardly make sense of her words.

'Take the oars, Mina,' Madeline said, ignoring the question.

Mina could hardly keep her head up. But Daniel hadn't died for nothing. And she mustered the strength to prove it. Through her grief and exhaustion, she took Madeline's position in the centre of the boat and rowed as hard as she could, eyes tensed shut, suffering through the pain. Ciara had tried to help, but Mina was having none of it. With the river's flow as her ally, the boat soon picked up momentum, and with every groan that Mina made they were edging further and further away.

'Keep going, Mina,' Madeline said, gazing at the treeline as it shrank into the distance.

'Are they still chasing us?' Ciara asked from the far end of the boat, cringing from the unrelenting chaos that still sounded so close to them.

'We'll know any moment now,' Madeline replied, but only Mina heard her.

The river dipped and the current quickened. Mina rowed with all her strength, but she had little left to give. The natural rush of the water was taking them south, and it was doing so without her backing. Soon all they could see were the tops of the tallest, oldest trees, like ghostly spectators all gathered to see them off. And then there was only sky, and stars dashed like glitter across it.

They all watched the horizon. Mina still tried to work the oars, but the water felt viscous now, her arms too limp to make a difference. Even if the watchers caught them, they would die knowing that they couldn't have done any more. The moonlight rippled through the river in silver strands as every second brought them closer to home. All the while those distant voices grew fainter.

With their pets lost, the watchers would have ransacked the building. Kilmartin's bunker – so neurotically organised – would have filled with their bodies, their stench, and their savagery. They would have destroyed everything, eradicating all evidence that he was ever there. But Mina's sadness and all that lost time, that would live on until she took it to the grave with her. She would never shake the sight of herself, night after night, reflected in that mirror, with their eyes watching her from the dark – the same room where Kilmartin had stood, dizzy on curiosity and lethal ambition, where he had watched them mimic his dead wife's face, twisting it and making it theirs. Maybe they knew the effect that it would have on him. Maybe it's for the best that the damned thing lay in ruins. It was a bad place, and it was home only to bad memories.

Kilmartin didn't say it, but could it be that the water was the key? What if the watchers had sniffed like hounds around the burrow where the oars had lain like doomed lovers? Maybe they had followed the boat's trench through the earth, only to lose the trail there. Whatever the reason, Mina didn't care. She listened out for any sound to the north, but there was nothing. No screams. No gallop of bodies. There was only the tired creak of their boat amidst the silence, and Ciara's tears intermingled with the river's flow.

For months, Mina had been denied the stars and the cold calm of a winter's night. Because of the coop's nocturnal state, it never really seemed like night-time. It was an unnatural place of flat surfaces and tired reflections, where time bore no relevancy and the moon was never seen. It might as well have not existed. Now and again, Ciara would jolt up, and the boat would shake uneasily. Maybe they were safe, and what they thought they heard were but echoes of the horror that was.

Mina listened to the water's calming burble, homing all her thoughts and unease in on that one sound. She felt every motion. The cold air brushed her cheeks with the lightest touch, and her rosy nose sniffled, not from the dust of the coop's concrete as was always the case, but from the raw, open country. Her toes curled against the damp wood and she shivered under her blanket. The water had seeped through its every thread. Heavy clouds had moved in, obscuring the moon and snuffing out most of the stars. Even the water ran black. The eyes struggled in the absence of light. They had adapted to those long nights in the coop. And now, looking at the lands around her, Mina couldn't discern a single detail that wasn't her mind's invention. The watchers could be running silently along the riverside, and she would have been none the wiser.

She could hear Ciara quivering from the cold, sharing in the unspoken pain that played not only on their fears, but also on their bodies. *Not like this,* she thought. They had survived too much to succumb to the elements. These were Mina's *friends* who she genuinely cared about. She thought of calling out to them. But she couldn't draw the words from her lips. Mina couldn't bear the thought of losing another. To call out and to receive no response – that was now her greatest fear. She kept the parrot's cage tucked inside her shawl, hoping that what little heat her body still held might keep it alive. She prayed that it was sleeping, for it didn't make a sound. Madeline seemed unaffected. She still stared back into the darkness like a scarecrow watching over them. Mina couldn't gauge what the woman was thinking. With her eyes placid and bright beneath the stars, she almost looked sad. Mina hated when she referred to the coop as their home. But for Madeline, maybe that's what it had become.

In time, the night's depths – where the land and sky divide – began to pale. Weak at first, like a daub of white in a black pool. It spread slowly but steadily, merging upwards, diluting the darkness with light. The surrounding lands came into sight as though they journeyed towards the new day, leaving the night and its nocturnal creatures behind them. Mina found it all so familiar. This was the same unremarkable terrain that had led her to the woodland when she had cursed the very sight of it. But now, with the dawn breaking, she saw it differently.

Wild grasses of green and fiery amber flared up from the earth. The sunlight washed over the distant hills where soft contours of stone shimmered like fresh snow. Nothing was dead or dying. Not anymore. Even the air was alive, infused with the morning's bouquet of unfolding petals, and herbs softening from their first touch of warmth.

'Hey,' Mina whispered, to which Ciara stirred wearily beside her, 'wake up!'

'Where are we?' she asked; her voice hoarse and half asleep.

'I'll be fucked if I know,' she replied, 'but we're a long way from the coop – that's for sure.'

'There's a bridge ahead,' Madeline said, squinting into the distance.

The woman spoke as she always did, with no inflection of feeling. She was sat, huddled in her blanket, those tight lips set straight when those around her were smiling. A bridge meant that there was a road, and that was all they needed – a path to lead them home. Whereas Ciara strove to arouse some feeling in her bones, Madeline was already perched high like a heron. So thin was her hair that it trailed like cobwebs in the breeze. The sunlight exposed her every crease and blemish. The woman hadn't slept. She had watched over them all through the night. Ever their guardian, and ever their Madeline.

The bridge was built of mismatched rocks, held together

by their own weight and whitewashed after a long life of Irish weather. Mina couldn't understand how it hadn't fallen apart. She could only guess that someone more recently – with some cement and a trowel – had reinforced their ancestors' labour.

'Mina,' Madeline said, 'you can take us onto the land now. I think we've journeyed on this river for quite long enough.'

Mina rubbed some feeling back into her fingers before she returned them to the oars. Her palms still stung where they had worn away the skin. But she was secretly proud of her wounds. They were proof that she had played her part. After a few failed attempts she worked out how to control the boat's course. And as they neared the shore, Ciara reached out to the chubby tufts of grass and drew it in.

Mina was first to clamber up the embankment. Her sudden, clumsy motions awoke the yellow one. And as Ciara passed its cage over to her it fanned its feathers like golden petals unfolding in the sunshine. A road led away from the bridge, stretching off into the horizon as far as the eye could see. But the eye saw nothing. There was no end in sight.

'What was it you said?' Ciara asked her. '*All paths lead somewhere.*'

To simply walk as far as where the road drifted out of sight could take hours, and they were each exhausted. Madeline joined them on the road. This was what they had wanted – some link to civilisation. But all they could see was more of the same – the vast emptiness of Connemara, too many miles from home. They didn't even know what direction led there.

'We can't walk that,' Mina said. 'I can barely stand.'

Madeline frowned, and looked her up and down as though searching for some physical sign of tiredness. Mina's stomach was empty, and she could feel the blood pulsing around her skull like a crown of thorns. She heard pebbles scratching beneath Ciara's shoes as she lowered herself onto the road to lie on her back; every movement mired in discomfort. They weren't walking anywhere.

'We can just wait,' Ciara said, staring up at the sky. 'Someone is bound to find us eventually.'

'Yes,' Madeline replied, after a long, thoughtful silence. 'Look at the road. Its centre is coarser than its sides.'

'Okay,' Ciara said, sitting up and shrugging her shoulders at Mina. 'What?'

'Vehicles come this way,' Madeline explained, 'probably every day. You're right. We can wait.'

'Oh,' Ciara said, smiling like a child who had just passed an exam, 'okay.'

And so, with little other choice, they waited. A few swarthy clouds had teased a downpour but the shadows kept their distance. On the ground, ducked low enough to dodge the breeze, Mina turned her face to the sun like a spring daffodil. It was the warmest she'd been since December. Ciara was panned out like a body washed up on dry land, listening to the tinkle of the yellow one's cage as it danced again on its perch. Eventually, even Madeline sat on the chalky road. Unlike the others, however, she watched the distance; her patience brass-bound and unyielding. Mina kept glancing to where she imagined Daniel would have been, most likely constellating around Ciara's orbit. What she wouldn't have given to hear his voice, and to know that he was there, looking out for them. Not a boy, but a man.

'Listen,' Madeline said eventually, tilting her neck. 'Do you hear that?'

Mina sat up and rubbed her eyes. Again, she couldn't tell if she had slept or not, nor did she know how much time had elapsed since they had abandoned the boat. She couldn't hear a sound.

'There,' Madeline said, 'something's coming.'

It was a bus or maybe one of those larger air-conditioned coaches that brought tourists on sightseeing trips around the west. Whatever it was, Mina couldn't take her eyes off that black speck in the distance.

'We're going to be okay,' she said, placing her hand on Madeline's shoulder, squeezing it gently.

The woman flinched and shifted quickly away, gleaning only discomfort from Mina's touch. Even now, after all they had been through, Madeline still couldn't muster a smile.

Heaven knows what the bus driver thought. They must have looked like trolls that had crawled out from beneath the bridge. Mina stood in the centre of the road, barefoot and filthy, her blanket held wide like wings with a golden conure between her legs. And she wasn't moving.

FEBRUARY

23

Life after the woodland was never going to be the same. Mina was sat by her window, watching the street below, like a home recording of happier times. The cushion on the ledge had been tossed to the floor. Her bones had conformed to the coop's concrete, and comfort just wasn't comfortable anymore. Mina's black coffee was cold. Only a sip had been taken, and even that was swallowed through a grimace. It was too bitter. Nothing like she remembered. The same could have been said for a lot of things.

Mina observed couples walking, hands held, all toothy smiles as they shared in the diehard optimism of new love. Children were play-fighting over small change; skinny, harmless things with too much energy. There were straight-faced men and women in suits striding with a profound purpose that was *almost* convincing. Given the hour, they were most likely going for lunch; wraps and rolls from the delicatessen. Two women sat outside the café across the road, sipping cappuccinos in massive bowl-sized mugs. Their coffees were nowhere near as hot as the gossip. One spoke incessantly. The other nodded her head, absorbing every word, occasionally gasping when it all became too much.

Mina was back in the world again, but she didn't feel a part of it. Traipsing through the trees to collect water from the spring seemed a whole lot easier than crossing the road to buy a proper cup of coffee. Her window was on the third floor. Only the birds could reach it. But she still felt so vulnerable. Its glass was too thin.

It wasn't long after midday. The sun blazed in a sky of unbroken blue and shimmered across cold slates and chimney pots; that hidden place where pigeons and seagulls consort away from prying eyes. Mina was hypersensitive to every sound – luggage wheels rapping on cobbled stone, car doors slamming, bicycle brakes screeching, and, of course, the voices. Every laugh and shout caused her to flinch as though some invisible, cruel hand was constantly pinching her. There were only two people that she felt safe with, and they had left her, alone, sitting beside a window that would never keep the monsters out.

She would never forget the sheer stupefaction on the driver's face. The mere sight of them would have encouraged most to switch up a gear. He had one of those tightly cropped white beards that always made Mina think of Father Christmas, and after he fumbled to remove his sunglasses, she saw that he had the kindest eyes. They shone silver in the sun. Maybe common sense had told him to drive on. But he wasn't the kind to leave anybody on the side of the road; even them, in all their squalid glory. The bus slowed to a halt and let out a gassy hiss before its door slid open.

'Jesus,' he had said, looking Mina up and down, his confusion tarrying for a moment on the parrot. 'What's happened to you, dear?'

He was the first one to ask that unanswerable question. Mina would have loved nothing more than to tell him the truth, to spread the horror a little thinner. That would have certainly kept him alert during the journey. Or perhaps he would have driven her straight to the loony bin. Instead of glass and concrete she'd be imprisoned in a room of padded white walls, where shrinks would sit with her every morning, between her first prescriptive cup of pills and a makeshift continental breakfast. They would nod their heads and encourage her to tell them what happened, all the while their safety pencils would scrawl out the word CRAZY, underlining it whenever she mentioned the fairies that kept them as pets.

A memory flashed across her mind like a strike of lightning. Mina saw again those things standing around Daniel, their circle closing like a mouth devouring him. She lifted the cage up into her arms and steadied her breathing.

'Where are you headed?' she managed to say, as if his destination mattered.

'Back to Galway,' he replied. 'I think this crowd in the back have taken more than enough photos for one day.' Here he winked towards the coachload of tourists, all now staring at Mina, barely resisting the urge to reach for their cameras. 'You're welcome to hop on, if you want? There are some bottles of water by the bin there, and I've some crisps on the seat behind me. You're free to help yourselves. I hope you don't mind me saying, but you look more than a little famished.'

They clambered up and into the front seats, and there they sat, in uneasy silence as though they didn't belong amongst other people. Voices buzzed behind them like a hive of bees. Mina couldn't bring herself to look back at them. She knew they were watching her. And being watched was something she had never grown comfortable with. The door closed, and the hum of the engine returned. Mina turned her face to the window. She swallowed back the tears as the river disappeared into the distance. Somewhere – half on the bank and half in the water – was Kilmartin's boat. It was unlikely that anyone would find it before the rot spread. But if they did, Mina hoped they had the good mind not to row it upstream. She knew from personal experience that some people are just that unlucky.

'You've had a tough time of it, I'd say,' the driver said to her, their eyes meeting in the rear-view mirror.

'I've had better,' she replied, letting her body sink into the seat, 'but it's over now.' She gazed out towards the distant hills bathed in sunlight, sparkling like spilled sugar, and after two or three blinks she fell asleep.

It was night-time when Mina awoke. Streetlamps flashed overhead, rhythmically bathing her body in peels of orange and staining her eyes with restless speckles. Cars or vans or other buses drove by. She couldn't see them and couldn't tell what they were; these mechanical monsters that patrolled the city streets. They startled her forward in her seat, enlivening familiar fears in a now unfamiliar world. The colours and lights all bled together. She felt a swelling ache behind her eyes just trying to process it all. Everything outside was disorderly and loud. Bodies rushed along the pavement, an arm's reach from vehicles that roared impatiently forward, stealing any space they could. A car's horn blasted through the air. Mina could hardly contain the scream it roused.

None of them knew where to look or what to do. Ciara had her face buried in her hands, hiding from the myriad sights and sounds that engulfed them like a warzone. No doubt had Daniel been with them, he would have held her in his arms, keeping Ciara safe. Mina could imagine him mesmerised by it all, his mouth lolling open with the streetlights dancing in his pale eyes. They were, as always, divided by glass. Madeline scrutinised everything, horrified by the discord of it all – the gaudy colours and the immutable din. She wore her frown like a woodland souvenir and hadn't spoken for the entire journey, not even to criticise. The woman held her shawl tight against her chest, seeming older and frailer than Mina remembered.

When the bus arrived at the coach station, not one of them made any attempt to move. The concrete was back, but it was smooth and clean. It kept them safe from the maddening crowds and muted the sounds that spoiled the air. There was glass, too, and behind it the lights of the station's lobby, where strangers dallied in loose clusters. Some carried the tiredness of a journey's end, others the fresh excitement of a trip just beginning. Mina recognised it all, but the memories didn't seem like her own. They felt as though they had been stolen from a movie or stage performance; a fictious world populated by actors where only she knew what was real and what wasn't. She had stepped out from the curtain and seen the monsters that had, all the while, been watching them.

The tourists trickled down the short steps of the bus, silently and neatly. Some glanced back at Mina. Others were careful not to turn their heads for fear of making eye contact. A young girl waved at the parrot before being dragged onward by her mother. She had Spanish eyes and black curly hair and wore pink wellington boots that squeaked. Mina instinctively studied their faces from the corner of her eye, but not for those reasons that inspired her sketches once upon a time. She looked for any expression, some tangible proof that they were human. Such fears, she whispered to herself, were irrational. But one of the many lessons that the forest had taught her was that her fears don't care.

Mina ran her fingers down the cold glass. The significance of its transparency was ingrained in her psyche. But whenever she looked away, a thin reflection watched her in the periphery of her vision, as though she was haunted by her past self – the one still sitting on the floor of the coop, waiting to be saved.

The driver closed the door after the last passenger had stepped off. He rubbed his hand through his snowy beard, working his gums as if sucking on a strong mint, and looked at the oddities that he had picked up, settling eventually on Mina as their representative. As though the woman with the caged bird seemed the sanest one amongst them.

'Do you want me to call someone?' he asked. 'I don't know if you've any family who might be looking for you. I can call the guards or maybe the hospital? It's whatever you want.'

Mina looked to her companions for an answer, uneasy in the role as spokesperson. Madeline's lips were sealed. No surprises there. Never had the woman appeared so unsure of herself. All that she knew and learned had gotten her this far. But now these skills were worthless when faced with a lobby full of new faces and the steady rumble of their voices. Ciara sat with her arms crossed tight as though she might fall apart if she ever released them. She stared agog at the driver as though she hadn't understood a word he had spoken.

'I don't live far,' Mina replied, coughing to clear her throat, 'just on Mainguard Street.'

'And are you all staying together?' the driver asked.

Mina hadn't thought this far ahead. They were, quite simply, together. There was never any choice in the matter. Eventually they would each go their separate ways, but the horrors they shared were still too strong to be divided.

'Yes,' she said, firmly, 'they're staying with me.'

The driver nodded understandingly and returned to his seat. He slipped back on his belt, and the door squeaked closed. Another loud sibilance came from beneath them, right before the engine's warm drone drowned out all other sounds.

'I'll get you as close as I can,' he shouted back to them. 'We can't have you walking through the town looking like you do.'

The sights of the city were as Mina had remembered. As she had every day imagined them to be. She caught glimpses of faces by glowing shopfronts, pockmarked with shadows, and some she thought she recognised. Maybe she had drawn them or passed them on the same street so many times that they had earned some place in her memory. Was this how it must feel to die and return as a ghost? To see how the world moved on without you, only to find that it never even realised you were gone.

The bus slowed to a stop. Its indicators clicked like a metronome over the low grumble of the engine. Mina could see her street; a mirage that stayed solid. There was a queue of taxis patiently lining the rank. Some of the drivers' faces were visible by the light from their phones. She turned away sharply. Her fears manifesting in beads of sweat. It was John's face that haunted her the most. She knew it couldn't have been him, and yet it had looked so human. Could the watchers wear all their faces with such ease? Mina imagined a hundred versions of herself standing amidst the trees, all staring skyward at the cracks of moonlight dancing in their dead eyes.

The take-away on the corner, with its wide windows, was bright as the coop. Those four words – *stay in the light* – were all that Mina's mind could see, above the fireplace, in that room where she had sat so many times, wondering if she would ever make it home. She watched the oblivious diners, chewing on food that she had forgotten the taste of. It was bizarre to think that she could casually stride in and buy a warm meal. No bird traps. No foraging. Did people ever realise how lucky they were? Her hand felt around the pocket of her jeans and touched the hard shape of her keys. To think she had nearly tossed them away that day when Madeline had found them.

'Are you going to be okay?' the driver asked.

'We'll be okay,' Mina smiled tiredly, looking at the others. She wanted to embarrass the man with torrents of gratitude but she couldn't find the words. Talking to someone outside of their closed little circle felt strange.

The door made a short screech, and the city sounds slipped into earshot.

'Go on,' the man said, smiling back. 'Whatever hell you've all been through, it's over now.'

'Thank you,' was all Mina said, and never had she so sincerely meant it.

The floor of the bus carried a light carpet, like worn felt, that her toes had enjoyed. It made the pavement outside feel all the colder. They stood together on the street, looking like tourists who had travelled from a very, *very* poor country.

'Nearly there,' Mina whispered to the golden one, who looked both thrilled and terrorised by everything that was happening.

The bus didn't pull away immediately. The door to Mina's apartment building was only thirty or so feet away; cobalt blue and scratched to white where one of her neighbours always missed the keyhole after a night out. What if her key didn't fit? It had been in her pocket for so long that one of her protruding bones might have warped it out of shape. She took a deep breath, and felt her ribs rising. *Please work*, she thought. Her wrist turned. She leant her weight against the door and pushed it open. As the others funnelled in after her, Mina could hear the bus driving off.

The automatic lights blinked awake before the door clicked behind them. Mina heard Madeline's nostrils sniffing behind her. The stone-tiled stairs and entranceway must have been mopped that morning, as the whole place stank of bleach. Mina had forgotten what *clean* smelt like. Her home was only three floors' worth of stairs away, and they met each one with care and silence, listening out of habit for any sound not of their making – a habit founded on fear. Even the bird respected it.

'Home sweet home,' Mina said as she slotted the key into her apartment's door.

The storage heaters had squandered electricity every night, and the boiler would have heated the water, too. It was so warm; so perfectly suffocating. To think of all those days Mina had huddled by the stream, dousing her body in liquid ice, her heartbeat racing against the cold. *Forget about it, Meens. We're home now.* She switched on the light and stopped in the doorway of her kitchen come living room; a single space burdened with a dual purpose.

Mina didn't know if she wanted to laugh or cry. So, she did both. This little room – this most ordinary, insignificant little room – framed a million memories before her eyes. Moments, once deemed as dispensable, were recognised and revalued.

Christmas-themed junk mail was piled in the basket on her kitchen table; fold-out flyers for supermarkets and cheap envelopes embellished with bells and holly. An old box of matches lay atop its crest. Beside it ran a trail of dry tobacco, spillage from a hasty roll. She used to leave traces of it everywhere she went. One of the two chairs was pulled out, with her favourite burgundy scarf draped over its back. *I could have done with that over Christmas.* The clothes horse by the window was bare save for a single sock that looked like it had shrunk in the sunlight. The dirty plates were in the sink. The half-full bottle of wine still perched on top of the fridge. Had she known the winter that lay ahead of her, she wouldn't have left a drop behind. A faint feeling of dust was everywhere. The room was a time capsule. Jennifer had not come looking for her. No one had.

Madeline strode straight over to the window. God bless any poor people who might have looked up and seen her. She watched the street as though everything was new to her. Gone were the trees and their concrete cell, and that one view into nothingness. Madeline still watched the world through glass. But there was finally something to see – the world they had so longed to return to, unchanged from Mina's memories and yet different in every way imaginable.

Daniel should have been there with them, probably entwined into a shock of nerves and unease as though he had landed back at a stranger's house party and was too shy to speak to anyone. It didn't seem possible that she wouldn't see him again. Mina had overheard his conversation with Ciara that last night beneath the coop, but never had the chance to speak to him about it. Daniel had no family to miss him. His father – that cruel bastard – would never know how brave his son had become; a better man than he could have ever been.

Madeline's eyes darted around the room as if following an insect. Mina guessed that the normality of their surroundings had left her bewildered. She was struggling to adjust, too. They seemed to stand around out of politeness, waiting for someone else to experience happiness first. In the coop, when the light was on, it was routine to do nothing, to breathe and wait. Doing nothing was something they had each mastered.

Ciara ambled awkwardly around the room, examining it like a prospective buyer, taking into account the curtains, the flooring, and the layout of the furniture. Aspects that even Mina had never lent much thought to. But her attention kept straying to the two windows facing onto the street, and then back to the door. It carried none of Kilmartin's reinforced locks or chains should something come scratching at it.

The night wouldn't be theirs again for a long time. And even then, regardless of what beauty they found in the moonlight, they would never feel safe knowing what walked beneath it.

'Welcome to your new home,' Mina announced to the yellow one, placing the cage on the kitchen counter. It beamed at her as though it secretly understood. The little bird had been with her every step of the way, and their journey was finally over.

The overhead light was too reminiscent of the coop, and so Mina plugged in the old-fashioned lamp that came with the lease. Frayed tassels hung sadly from its lampshade, faded to an insipid yellow. Its glow was kinder on the eyes, and it made the room feel a little more like home – the *real* home. It seemed much bigger and far more colourful than Mina remembered.

'It's not very fancy,' she said, standing like a stranger in her own sitting room, 'but you're welcome to stay with me for as long as you like.'

'Thank you, Mina,' Madeline said; the first words she had spoken since they boarded the bus.

They had made it, just the three of them. There was no John. No Danny. If their escape from the forest was cause for celebration, then they had more reasons to grieve. And Ciara, more than Mina and more than Madeline, had left so much behind her. Mina had gotten the chance to say goodbye to her mum, and still she regretted all those things she hadn't said. Ciara never had that comfort.

'I know what you both need,' Mina announced, eager to distract Ciara, to postpone the mourning of the life that the watchers had taken from her.

'What's that?' Ciara sniffed, sweeping a single tear slowly from her eye.

'Some proper home-cooked food,' Mina said, already pacing onto the kitchen tiles. 'I'm sure I've something here that we can eat. Just don't expect any birds or fucking berries, okay?'

'Okay!' Ciara laughed, eyes still sparkling. Her face was never so beautiful than in those moments when she smiled.

The freezer's contents were cracked from their icy tomb. If it was edible, it was cooked. Mina knelt beside the oven, watching the food brown like a breaking news report. Ciara was soon busy stirring soup and baked beans with a wooden spoon in each hand. Madeline's attention finally strayed from the window as Mina placed some plates down on the table, like a dog that heard the clink of its bowl. Amidst a cloud of steam, the food was devoured. No one seemed to care how hot it was. The hotness was probably the best part of it.

Mina dragged the spare mattress from the wall of her studio and let it drop onto the floor, sending sheets of paper swirling through the room. Her nostrils tingled from the eruption of long-undisturbed dust, but the sneeze never came. The blank canvas still occupied the easel, dabbed only in lint and wasted potential. Her artistic enterprise had yet to find its feet. *Soon*, she thought.

They slept in the living room that night. Between the mattress and the couch there was enough space for them all. The heaters had withheld ample warmth to last the night, and the dim glow of the lamp was practically darkness compared to what they were used to.

There was never any question in Mina's mind about staying together. She told herself that she was doing it for Ciara. She, especially, needed the company. But Mina needed her just as much. Madeline had returned to the window, dissociating herself from them as she always did. The woman looked so disappointed in the half-light of the wall's recess. Mina sat on the mattress, with Ciara and the yellow one beside her, leaving the couch for Madeline should she have wanted it.

'What am I going to tell my parents?' Ciara asked. 'And John's? I've been missing since the summertime and they're...'

'You'll tell them nothing,' Madeline interjected, 'just as we agreed.'

Easier for some, Mina thought. Out of the three of them, Ciara was the only one who probably had family missing her.

'But they'll have so many questions,' Ciara said. 'I'm not such a good liar, Madeline. What if they don't believe me?'

'Even if you did tell them the truth,' Mina put in before Madeline could answer, 'they would never believe you. We've nothing to prove that we were even there.'

'That's not entirely true,' Ciara said nervously, rooting into her pocket. 'I do have *this*.'

In the soft light Mina couldn't quite make out what she was holding. It looked like a black matchbox with a wire dangling out of it. She had certainly never seen it before that moment.

'What's that?' she asked, leaning in for a closer look.

'I found it in the forest,' Ciara explained. 'I think it's a camera, but I'm not sure. Maybe it has some memory in it. For all we know it could be hooked up to a PC and we could show everyone that the watchers exist. Then they'd believe us!'

Madeline's head turned in a flash, frowning at the device as though its presence alone was a threat to them; a bomb that could detonate in Ciara's hand, sending their world up in smoke.

'You have to destroy that,' she said, with noticeable venom to her voice.

'We'll see,' Ciara replied, slipping it awkwardly back into the tight pocket of her jeans. 'It's just a little keepsake, Madeline, and I'm fairly sure it's broken.'

Madeline's gaze lingered on Ciara. Only Mina saw the look in her eyes. The woman wasn't in charge anymore. Those days were behind them. Big deal if Ciara wanted to hold on to the thing? Kilmartin said that he had destroyed all his research in the safe house. And it was highly unlikely that the broken camera lens held anything more than scratches.

'Don't worry,' Mina said. 'I'll go to the university, and I'll deal with whatever remains of Kilmartin's research. There'll be no evidence that the watchers or that woodland ever existed, and nothing to lead anyone there. It's over. Can't we just get our lives back, please?'

Madeline didn't reply. Maybe Mina had averted an argument. But as calmly as the woman conducted herself, both hands were clenched to keep them steady, and her eyes burned like amber stones in the streetlight. Just when Mina thought they had unravelled all the woodland's mysteries, she looked at Madeline – at the last conundrum, the one she might never solve. The woman had saved her life. She had taught her how to survive. Could Mina do the same for her?

The time had come for everyone to get some rest; everyone, that is, except for Madeline, who stayed stubbornly at the window, monitoring the street below.

'Aren't you going to get some sleep?' Mina asked her.

'I'll sleep soon,' she replied without even turning her head.

Ciara was the first. Curled up like a kitten on the mattress, she dozed off the moment she rested her head. Mina listened for a while to the soothing sound of her breathing, and soon she couldn't stifle her yawns, nor could she keep her tired eyes from closing. The warmth and the novel sense of safety were like a sedative, and her body gave in without a fight.

When Mina awoke, fresh daylight was streaming through the window, and Madeline was gone. No note was left behind explaining why.

'Where could she have gone?' Ciara asked, sitting on the couch with the birdcage on her knees, keeping the yellow one entertained.

'I've no idea,' Mina replied, peering outside in the off chance that Madeline was sipping a coffee in the café across the street. 'I don't even know where she lived before the coop.'

The more Mina thought about it, the less she knew about the woman. What possible reason could have drawn her outside? And after all they had shared together, how could she vanish without saying goodbye? That used to be Mina's trick. She knew that Madeline wasn't ready to face the world. After a single night, hidden away like escaped convicts, none of them were. The woman needed help – the expensive psychological sort.

'Should we try to find her?' Ciara asked.

'She knows where I live,' Mina replied. It was the way she imagined Madeline would have reacted. 'If she needs us, she'll come back.'

Madeline never shared with them what possibilities her future held or what relics of her old life remained. There was no telling where she had gone, or why she had left. If their company was so dispensable, then she could have fled the coop alone and left them behind. Or maybe, Mina thought, Madeline needed them – to negotiate the forest, to row the boat, or to be cast overboard should the watchers have ever caught them. But that was to assume the worst of the woman and Mina had done that for long enough. As cold as Madeline was, there was still some warmth in her. The woman's actions, not her words, had proven that.

'We'll have to wait and see if she comes back,' Ciara said, sadly. 'I never thought I'd miss her. I hope she's okay, out there on her own. It must be very scary for her.'

Ciara's worries came as no surprise. She had every reason in the world to despise the woman, but she didn't. Perhaps she had finally come to realise that had Madeline opened the door that night, she would not be standing where she was now. None of them would be.

Madeline could take care of herself. Mina had no doubts about that. But something still bothered her. It was the way the woman had stared at Ciara when she produced the camera from her pocket. Madeline's eyes had never seemed so dark, nor had a frail, famished woman ever looked so dangerous.

'She'll be okay,' Mina said, 'you have to focus on taking care of yourself now.'

Their lives in the coop had been indistinguishable. They shared the same routines and responsibilities; no better or worse than the other. There was no wealth. There were no privileges to ease the day-to-day chore of staying alive. But now their disparities were finally revealing themselves. So focused had Mina been on getting home, she never stopped to wonder who would be waiting for her, if anyone. Jennifer was the only one. Mina thought back to that last voicemail, right before her car broke down. *I'm not going to call you again, okay? I'll leave it up to you.* She knew how stubborn her sister could be when she set her mind to it. Nobody had missed her. And there was no one to welcome her home. For these reasons and more, she hugged Ciara hard enough to make her squeak.

Their parting was inevitable. They had postponed it for as long as they could, dallying around the kitchen, treating the room as they might the coop, never really saying much. The silence between them wasn't uncomfortable. It was simply their way together. Company, rather than conversation, was the key to their harmony.

Mina had offered her the use of the shower. There was certainly plenty of hot water going spare. But Ciara's heart was set on her own bathroom. She had spoken so excitedly about the size of the tub, and of the scented soaps and salts that John had given her. Mina smiled and mirrored her sprightliness, but she secretly feared for the girl's heart. She was returning to an empty house.

'Are you going to be all right?' Mina asked.

'Come stay with me,' she replied as though she hadn't heard the question. 'We'll find our feet together. And, if I'm being honest, I don't relish the thought of being alone when it gets dark. I know it's silly and we're...'

'It's not silly,' Mina interrupted, holding Ciara's shoulder. 'It's going to take us a long time, okay? But we have each other. And I'm not too thrilled about being alone tonight either,' she added with a smile. 'Apparently monsters really do exist now.'

She embraced Mina in a hug, and they held each other, both aware of the other's tears. It still didn't seem real. Before she left, Ciara wrote down her address and phone number, and a few directions in case the taxi driver should get lost. Her hand had all but forgotten how to handle a pen, and after a short scribble she had to massage the pain from her palm.

'Sorry about the writing.' She laughed. 'I swear I didn't use to write like this.'

'I'll come to you as soon as I can,' Mina replied. 'There are just a few things I have to take care of first, and I want to be here in case Madeline comes back.' It was unlikely, but she owed the woman that much. 'For all we know she's gone to collect some water from the river because she's forgotten how the tap works,' Mina added, immediately regretting her facetiousness.

'I'll see you soon,' Ciara said, before she closed the door after her. Mina slipped the lock in place.

She braved another taste of her coffee, wincing as it

slipped down her throat. That was enough of that. She looked at the wine bottle on top of the fridge. All its notes would have been sharpened to vinegar by now. She would buy the *Rupicolo* that she loved. Not the garden-variety one, but the overpriced reserve that she had ogled like forbidden fruit but never reached for. If her taste buds had forgotten their affection for red wine, Mina would make them remember.

The longest, most highly anticipated shower of Mina's life awaited her. She would fawn over her wardrobe of laundered clothes, turning a blind eye to anything black or brown – the colours that had fallen over her life like a filter. The old rags would be black-bagged and tossed in the bin. Given the chance she would have loved to burn them. All the filth and foul memories would sprout in clouds of black smoke like purged demons.

Then, Mina would follow through on her promise. Kilmartin had been a lecturer in the university. Nothing else was known about the man, except that he had a wife once. Although Mina didn't know when he had held this tenure, he must have operated out of an office. He would have had documents – research and records – pertaining to the coop's construction, and the oddities that would be his subjects and his ruin. And she would destroy them all.

24

'What do you think?' Mina asked, with one hand on her hip and her best leg forward.

The cage was set on the table, wiped clean after the prior night. Every elusive motion made the yellow one's feathers phosphoresce in the afternoon sun like precious metal. The little guy's expression was one of absolute confusion. Its head tilted from side to side, like an art critic scrabbling for an opinion.

'You probably don't recognise me,' Mina explained, retracting the leg. 'I'm dressing incognito. You know, going undercover.'

The bird was seen to nod its head understandingly. It watched as Mina pulled out a chair and sat down beside it, her legs weak at the thought of going outside. She crossed her arms on the table and buried her head in them. She couldn't act like everything was fine. Her eyes lifted to the yellow one, still smiling, supporting her every step of the way like her silent, feathered therapist.

'I can't do this,' she whispered. 'I just can't, can I?'

The walk to the university should take her no more than fifteen minutes. If she went the scenic route, along by the canal, there was a chance that she could make it there undetected. It was far too soon for small talk, or eye contact for that matter. Galway had all the intimacy of a gated community. Everyone knew someone who knew someone else, and introductions between residents were practically obsolete. She had learned to swallow back her fear every time she stepped out of the coop. But this was different. The yellow one let out a chirp.

'Okay,' she said, sitting back straight. 'You're right, I can do this.'

The navy trench coat had been bought on a whim during the spring sales. It had deep pockets, tailor-made for a stubby sketchbook and had a certain *French spy chic* to it. Mina had thought it was black in the shop, and only realised her mistake after she had brought it home. A red price tag still dangled from one of its buttons, and it looked black whenever she held it away from the sunlight. It had been worn a grand total of zero times.

She clutched it in both hands and held it close, still trembling, 'Get it together, Meens. Just get dressed and we'll take it from there.'

In the darkest recesses of the wardrobe she unearthed her black fedora with the wide brim. Next, her broken nails were hidden inside dark woollen gloves. Mina's eyes still looked as sore as they felt. Her biggest sunglasses – the bug-eyed, red-framed ones – were perched on her nose to keep them hidden. Every addition felt like another clunky piece of armour. A fit of laughter and tears overcame her when her feet slid into her old pair of black *Converse*, worn and faded, with the inevitable tear in each shoe at the bend. Her toes had been washed and scrubbed until the last of the forest's filth swirled down the shower drain like a black hole imploding. Her fingers tied a little knot on each shoe, remembering what Mina's mind had forgotten. *Dressed!*

'I did it,' she called out to the parrot in the kitchen.

Facing the mirror took a few failed attempts. It was ridiculous, of course. Mina was aware of that. It was just a mirror. There was nothing behind it anymore, but Madeline's lessons had been drilled into her so deep that it would take some time to extract them.

The daylight laid bare every imperfection; every freckle of dirt that wouldn't wash. It hollowed in around her cheeks, making the bones pop like a fleshless skull. *Here we go again,* Mina thought, *picking out all the ugliness.* Her brown eyes were still there, somewhere, between the flagging lids and the bags beneath them. The teeth had yellowed. Especially around the gums, which looked worryingly blanched. Her lips felt chapped. Even after a wad of lip balm they didn't feel like a part of her. More like something she could tear off like a wax strip. She had aged, but she had survived, and it had certainly made her face that bit more interesting. Finally, maybe one worthy of sketching.

Mina poked her sunglasses back into place. They were either far too large or else her head had shrunk, as they kept sliding forward from her nose. She made a mental note not to look down. Otherwise, they would fly off her face, spoiling all anonymity. After her extended sentence in the woodland, there was the chance that everyone she once knew had forgotten about her. But then again, maybe they hadn't. The hat and glasses were staying either way. This was it – time to venture out into the world and do as she had promised.

'Okay,' she said to the bird, staring it in the eye, but seeing instead only the forest, the coop, and whatever monstrosities skulked in the shadows of her mind. 'I can do this, right? Of course, I can.'

Kilmartin's research had to be disposed of, and not because it was the man's dying wish. After what he had done – leading all those sacrificial labourers to their doom – he deserved what he got. His records were, quite simply, too dangerous. If they contained the location of the woodland, which was highly likely, then others might seek it out. More would die because she had failed to act. And Mina's head was a muddled mess already without adding guilt into the mix.

She grabbed her house keys from the hall table and lifted her sunglasses just high enough to peep at the address that Ciara had left behind. The girl's writing was ludicrous but legible, just about. *An Diadan* was possibly the house's name. The phone number would take a little longer to decipher.

'Mind the house while I'm gone,' she called out to the yellow one and let the door slam behind her.

With her head down and keeping a pace that belied her aching bones, Mina reached the university's campus without ever catching her breath, and without encountering anyone. Its lawns and tennis courts were deserted. The elderly trees around them were bare; their bark thick and stained. She scanned them for any ominous scratches. The subconscious act of doing so sent a chill down her neck. Was it always going to be this way? Had *scared* become her new default setting? *Get your shit together, Meens*. The hum of traffic dampened after veering off the road, until she could hear the soft squeak of her shoes on the tarmac. Soon the library slipped into sight and she slackened her stride. Sunlight danced on the glass, making mirrors of its windows in a way that made her lips twitch. Everything tried to remind her of all that she wanted to forget.

'Nearly there,' she whispered, taking a moment to steady herself. 'I should have brought the parrot. He's always good in these situations.'

There was an unmistakable loneliness about the place. Any voices heard were weak and distant. Bodies were coming and going, but they were so few. Those who crossed her path wore the most mirthless expressions. Exam season was obviously approaching. So accustomed had Mina become to the dead silence of the forest, that her ears perked at the slightest sound. A crow pranced across the grass, and she was aware of its every delicate step. If she focused, she could still hear the traffic on the road. She glanced around the campus, taking in the bushes that hemmed in the lawn and those thorny old friends of hers from the forest that now sprouted out from the trimmed hedges. Her eyes picked out and counted their coloured berries in seconds. She imagined Madeline nodding her approval.

There used to be four or five table-benches on the concourse, near the library entrance. As damp as they were, with their moulded wood and creaking seats, Mina used to sit and sketch for hours. Galway's latest influx of faces gathered there every September when the campus was blanketed in crunchy leaves. Two lost pleasures were habitually by her side – a coffee and a trampled pile of cigarette butts. Her artistic fuel once upon a time. Life was so simple back then. Mina just didn't know it.

The library's receptionist was a twenty-something bearded chap whose breath spoke of a hard night, and an obviously more difficult day after. His jaded eyes strained against the room's halogen ceiling. Even the carpet's geometric pattern was enough to jeopardise his sanity. As much as Mina had missed alcohol, she hadn't missed that feeling.

'What does he lecture in?' he asked, coughing into his hand to clear his throat.

The man's cheeks were plump and flushed. His youth was camouflaged behind that bristly, coffee-coloured beard. Glossy ginger hairs burnished its chin and moustache. The eyebrows were wild like two fuzzy caterpillars, and he had the air of an old soul trapped in a young body.

'I have no idea,' Mina replied, disappointed for not seeing this hurdle coming.

The receptionist licked his dry lips and let out a tired sigh. The air around him stank like a brewery. He had never heard of Professor Kilmartin and lacked the energy to act even remotely interested. After a quick succession of taps on his keyboard he sat back and considered the monitor, working his jaw like a cow chewing the cud, all the cogs in his brain turning to make sense of the simplest task.

'Professor Kilmartin is, or he was, a lecturer in history, or so it says here,' he said, screwing up his eyes to look at Mina through the fog of last night's whiskey. 'It says here that he wrote some papers on folklore and...' again he barked to shake whatever was caught in his throat '...stuff on myths and legends, by the looks of it.'

'Is there any research or work that he left behind unfinished?' she asked.

The man's eyes were seen to scroll down the monitor. He ran his hand through his shaggy hair and wiped something imaginary from his eye.

'Ah, yeah,' he said, looking a touch confused, 'it says here that a box of his papers are stored down in the basement. They're not listed as being anything particular. What was it that you were after?'

'Everything,' Mina replied, leaning forward, her elbows set on the counter.

'*Everything?*' the man repeated. 'Okay, well, you can't take out his papers, but you can look at them in the reading room. All the primary sources and stuff are delivered up there. When do you need them?'

'How soon can you get them for me?' she said.

'I mean,' he replied, 'I could probably get them for you now, if it's important.'

'I'd really appreciate it,' she said, smiling long after the words were spoken.

'Okay.' He sighed. 'If you want to wait for me in the reading room, I can drop them in to you.'

There was never any request for identification. The receptionist staggered away from his desk, probably still piecing together his memories from the night before. It made sense that history was the professor's area of expertise. That was how Madeline had come to find the woodland. It was possible that she had examined the same papers. For all Mina knew, the woman had known of Kilmartin before they gathered around to watch his last recording. Madeline's face was a book full of blank pages. There was never any telling what she was thinking or what she knew.

In the reading room Mina was met by the smile of a strikingly small woman. She was seated behind a desk facing four long tables, flanked on one side by a wall of windows that Mina was careful not to look towards. Having a nervous breakdown in such a quiet room was more than likely frowned upon. The woman was possibly in her early thirties but had the stature and jejune features of a child. Her blonde hair trailed like wheat below her shoulders, and her sky-blue eyes were so big and beautiful that they made her perky nose and lips seem all the smaller. She was like a doll propped in a chair, with ceramic skin and the tiniest nub of a chin fresh from a mould. Her clasped hands rested on a desk that was meticulously organised and polished to a mirror's sheen. Her pens were aligned side by side next to a tower of folders. The fingers were thin and elegant, and their nails shone with a gloss that made Mina conscious of what hid inside her gloves.

'I'm just waiting for some papers to arrive,' Mina whispered, leaning low to meet the woman's eye level.

'Okay,' she replied, in a voice so meek that Mina couldn't imagine her ever speaking louder than a whisper. 'You can take a seat wherever you want.'

Mina did as she was told. The room smelt of old paper and leather, and a faint haze of dust haunted the air. Despite the ample daylight, it awoke that claustrophobic feeling of Kilmartin's bunker. It must have been the smell. Strange to think that the man had probably sat in this very room. Maybe even at the same table. Fat book spines lined the length of the wall, behind two steel cabinets. The grey plastic bulk of a microfiche reader lurked in the corner. The woman at the desk was reading, utterly at peace amidst the silence, and still smiling with those dainty lips.

'Excuse me,' Mina called out in a shrill whisper.

The book was carefully closed and placed down so that its length was parallel to her pens. The doll smiled and nodded its head, acknowledging Mina without disrupting the peace.

'Did you know Professor Kilmartin when he was a lecturer here?' Mina asked.

'I did,' she replied. 'I think his work is fascinating. I used to sit in on his lectures whenever I had the chance.'

'When did he leave the college?'

'Oh, let me think,' the doll said, her eyes straying towards the ceiling, 'He took his sabbatical maybe three years ago. I thought he was only going to be gone for a year, but he still hasn't returned to us. It's a shame. I used to love listening to all those fairy stories.'

The bearded receptionist had to work the reading room's door handle with his knee, as both arms were cradling the cardboard box. Rolls of paper and stiff folders poked out of it like a bouquet of drab flowers. The doll watched him unblinkingly as he used his back to close the door after him.

'Now then,' he said, out of breath as he placed the box down on the table, 'that's everything.'

He stood stiffly for a moment with both hands pressing into his lower back, as if the task of retrieving the research from the basement had been a trial like no other; worthy of applause, or maybe some ibuprofen to ease his headache.

'Okay,' he said, glancing awkwardly over at the blonde doll at the desk, 'well, if you need anything else just let me know.'

'I will, thank you,' Mina replied.

'Right, okay,' he said, stuffing one of his hands into a pocket as he turned to leave. 'Cool. I'll see you later.'

The doll beamed at the man until the door eased closed behind him, and then returned to her book, dabbing two fingers on her tongue before turning a page. Never had a paperback looked so huge in those tiny hands.

Mina laid out the contents of the box on the table. This was all that remained of Kilmartin's academic legacy. After he failed to return, they must have cleared out his office and bundled his papers into storage. It had sat on a shelf in the university's basement ever since, waiting to be discovered or, as would be the case, destroyed.

There were folders bulging fat with paper, all dog-eared and grubby from fingerprints. Some were the professor's own research. Others were scholarly papers with vast tracts of text highlighted in pink and yellow blocks. It would take Mina months to trawl through it all. But that was never her course. The box would burn in minutes, and the facts therein would leave this world as smoke.

Three rolls of paper were bound in elastic bands like broken telescopes. Mina snapped them free and spread them out on the table. They were maps; all black and white except where Kilmartin had marked in red the location of the woodland. There it was, posturing as something normal – hell, as she knew it. Her hands tightened around the map, and she had to fight the urge to tear it to shreds. To the south she saw the river. The professor had scrawled an X beside it. There was no way to pinpoint how close the coop was to it. Mina started leafing through the other charts but stopped herself. *Don't, Meens.* She pushed them aside before her eyes could make sense of them. She didn't want to know where it was.

The texts were all studies in folklore and Irish mythology, as Mina had expected. They treated the myths as stories because, of course, that's what they were. These books would be pardoned from the flames. The maps wouldn't be so lucky.

One book stood out from the others. Its crimson leather binding was spongy, and its corners had faded. This was Kilmartin's journal. This was what Mina had been searching for. Its pages were handwritten in a scrawl as cryptic as Ciara's address. Page after page of what must have been the man's thoughts and theories; the making of an obsession that would inevitably destroy him. Mina froze when she leafed as far as *that* page. The professor was no artist, but his sketches packed a punch. There it was – Mina's home, her prison, and her sanctuary. Kilmartin had drawn a rough design of the coop and the steel chamber buried beneath it. She flinched from the very sight of it, nearly letting the journal slip from her fingers. This was where it all began. Mina recognised its every inch. Despite the sketch's simplicity, she could feel again its cold concrete. She could taste it on her lips. Her eyes squinted involuntarily; a nervous twitch triggered by memories of that fluorescent light whose buzzing she could still hear in some distant corner of her mind.

As Mina turned to the next page, a photograph slipped out and landed on the table. Her knees weakened at the sight of it. She sat with one hand over her mouth, detaining the scream that yearned to escape.

Mina recognised Kilmartin, clean-shaven and smiling, seated at a candlelit restaurant table, the camera's flash caught in the window behind him. He bore little semblance to his recording. He was young, and he was at peace. His left hand pinched the stem of a wine glass. Sitting across from him, looking directly into the lens, was Madeline.

Her hair shone like sun-kissed sand. The woman's smile was one of coy reluctance. She was beautiful and she was bashful, and she was happy. Her skin was taut and smooth. She had leaned in to pose with her thin, elegant arms in view, and her hands were not as Mina remembered them. They were neat and manicured. Her silver necklace was worn over a simple black dress, and she appeared shorter than was possible. The Madeline that Mina knew touched on six foot. She was this towering fount of bitterness and misery. The woman in the photograph couldn't be *her* Madeline.

Mina struggled to her feet and approached the doll at the desk. Simply standing was a challenge. She wasn't sure if she would even be able to talk.

'Do you know who this woman is?' she asked, sounding close to tears, her jaw tensed.

The woman took the photograph. Her smile stood fast, but a palpable sadness fell over her eyes.

'That's Professor Kilmartin's wife,' she said. 'They look so happy together, don't they?'

'How did she...?' Mina couldn't get the words out.

'She passed away from cancer. I think it must be five years ago now.'

'What was her name?'

The doll handed Mina back the photograph. *Please,* she thought, *don't say it. Don't say it.*

'Madeline,' she replied. 'Her name was Madeline.'

25

The door to Mina's apartment had been smashed open. Ruptures split at the point of impact, around the lock and handle, where a single devastating blow had rendered it *open*. Its pine wood within the cracks looked like exposed bone. She could hear the yellow one. It sounded distraught – twittering and flapping against its cage; the way it reacted whenever Madeline was close by. Maybe the bird always knew, and just lacked the words to warn them. With a gentle push the door swung in. The floor was a hash of splinters and chipped paint. It was possible that whoever spooked the parrot was still in there, somewhere.

'Hello?' she called out.

The bird, upon hearing her voice, fell silent and tucked its wings. Mina leaned in, listening. One minute passed, and then another. A pigeon cooed in an overhead gutter, but inside there was nothing. Either the apartment was empty or whoever was inside wanted it to seem that way.

'Madeline?' Mina shouted. 'Are you in there?'

After she left the university Mina had sat by the Corrib River, on a low, stony ledge, staring blindly into its flow, plagued by visions of two Madelines. There was the real Madeline – the smiling woman who had dined by candlelight, the one who had been dead for five years. And there was the *other*.

On the Long Walk – a narrow road aligned like a pier by the water's swell – life went on. A couple had sat further down from her, whispering like two spies sharing secrets. A man strode past, walking a rough-haired terrier whose little legs took ten steps for every one of his. A pair of ducks clung together, letting the flow guide them towards the bay like two lovers eloping.

Something Madeline once said to her kept repeating over and over, so that now her cold lips mouthed it without her even realising. *They're leaner and they're longer. They're leaner and they're longer.* The Madeline that Mina knew was tall. Her arms were skeletally thin, and those hands were monstrous. All protruding veins and gnarled fingers. They just looked wrong. Mina had never seen the woman's body. Madeline had always kept it hidden beneath that blanket, never revealing more than an extended arm, and only when necessary.

'Get your fucking head together,' Mina had whispered to herself; scrunching her eyes closed. '*This is crazy.*'

She would have known. If Madeline wasn't human, then she would have known, wouldn't she? They had spent every night together. They had shared meals at the same table. They had held hands, for Christ's sake. Mina always thought that she was strange, her face so devoid of nuance and expression. But that was Madeline. That's the way the woman was! Mina still thought of her as a *woman*, but what if she was wrong?

Kilmartin's wife had been dead for five years. Isn't that what the doll had said? All that remained of her were photographs. But the man had shown one of these to the watchers. In order to understand how the changelings altered their appearance he had encouraged them to practise on her image. There is no knowing what he told them. All that Madeline knew – the history, the myths, and the lies that Mina had believed – she could have learned them from him, creating a backstory that none of them would ever question.

Mina dragged the brim of her hat down over her ears, trying to block out these thoughts like an alarm bell she couldn't ignore. Where did Madeline go all those days when she disappeared? The woman hardly ate. She never even seemed to close her eyes. The alarm was getting louder.

What Mina wouldn't have given for a friend; someone to patiently sit beside her, and just listen. She wasn't seeing sense – that's all it was. Despair and sorrow had been her peers for too long. She had succumbed to their point of view and their cynicism. Of course she would sooner call Madeline a monster than assume that the worst of the horror was over. *But it wasn't.* The facts couldn't be ignored.

The professor thought he was losing it. The isolation and the stress of his endeavour had bested him. He feared that he was no longer alone during the peaceful hours, when the sun chased the watchers back into their dens. But it couldn't be called paranoia if it were true. Mina thought back to what the man had said: *I know they can't come above ground during the day, but what if they can? What if even one of them has found a way?*

Mina stepped over the threshold, tiptoeing through the hallway and into the kitchen. Her foot swept the wooden slivers towards the skirting boards. Nothing had been stolen or damaged. Not that she supposed for a moment that her home had been burglarised.

It had to have been Madeline. The thought of Ciara forcing entry was absurd. And besides, why would she have come back? If Mina hadn't spent so long by the riverside she would have been at home when the door crashed in. Maybe Madeline had rapped those knuckles like wrecking balls against its wood, seeking shelter – a safe place from the surrounding city. But Mina suspected otherwise. She had come looking for her because Mina knew the truth.

The camera that Ciara found was no more than a gloomy memento, like a lock of hair from a lost lover – the heart-breaking variety. But her notion that it might still store some footage had elicited from Madeline a choler that she had tried to conceal. The very sight of it seemed to raise her hackles. They had agreed to never speak of their experiences to anyone. What if Madeline didn't trust them to do so?

Mina couldn't stop the questions coming, and yet she failed to flower a single answer. A million *what ifs* had grown around her like weeds, taking over, choking all else into submission. She pondered the purpose behind the masquerade. Madeline was a chameleon mastering a new colour. Alone her oddness could be identified, but in the company of others it would be less apparent. Is that why she had kept them alive?

Mina had walked to the university with her head down,

eyes set on her shoes. She might as well have been wearing blinkers. Madeline could have pursued her in plain sight, and she would have been none the wiser. She needed someone to tamper with Kilmartin's research, to erase the evidence. And Mina had done just that.

She had slipped the man's diary into her handbag. There was an old-fashioned CCTV camera above the door, staring directly at her, and so the misdeed was carried out under the table, where neither the doll nor the unblinking eye could see. The maps were folded as quietly and discreetly until they could fold no more. Kilmartin's research had not been disturbed since his disappearance. It was highly unlikely that anyone would come looking for it now.

What were Madeline's intentions once the papers had been destroyed? Mina had to contact Ciara. She had jotted down her phone number before she left. If Mina could harass a neighbour for the loan of a phone, she could call her. Luckily, wherever *An Diadan* was, Ciara was safe.

It was in the hallway, by the draught of her broken door, Mina realised that something *was* missing. The piece of paper where Ciara had jotted down her address and its directions was gone. Madeline had taken it.

26

Ciara

Ciara was drawn to the hot coals. She sat on the marble hearth, mesmerised by the cracks of red burning in the black. In the forest, where Madeline tended to the fire like it was a sick child, branches and twigs had kept the flames alive, but they never gave off a warmth like this. Ciara gave it one final stab, flaring sparks like golden sea spray, and returned the brass poker to its holder. She looked to the mantel. It held a line of photo frames of varying styles and sizes, like a timeline of her life with John before they set out on *that* Sunday drive. She considered them with a smile that belied her sadness, envying the woman who stood beside her husband. The room had floors of light maple, with an oval rug – soft like hotel carpet – in front of the fire. She had left the lamps off. The wallpaper's pattern was subtle enough to be lost in the evening light.

She would close the curtains soon. The sight of the windows made her uncomfortable. Ciara's house was isolated. The once manicured lawn had grown wild, and the surrounding flower beds were graves of rotted stems and shrubs. Over the wall were fields of nothing, and in the very distance – far, but not far enough – she could see a few trees in the dying light. There wasn't another house around for miles.

The coop's light would be coming on soon. She tried to imagine how it looked. Was its glass still in place? Had all those tins been torn into sharp little shreds? Ciara held her hands over the coals to stave off that cold feeling she got whenever she thought about it. She should close the curtains soon. There was no telling what could be out there, looking in.

Ciara had idled outside her home long after the taxi pulled away, leaving her alone for what felt like the first time in her life. She suffered an uneasy disconnect with the memories laid before her. It was as though she and John were still in there – the ghosts of what could have been, sharing in a happiness that she would never find again. She had no clue as to what day it was, but it felt like Sunday. The spare key was where he had hidden it, under the flowerpot to the right of the front door, untouched since his hand had held it.

'You promised to get me home,' she whispered, rubbing the dampness deeper into her eyes. 'Well, I'm home. *We're* home.'

The stillness was harrowing. Ciara drifted from room to room, too afraid to touch anything lest it dissolve, and she should awaken back under the coop's light. Someone had been there since they left. She remembered that Sunday so vividly. The couch's cushions had been rearranged. The television remote wasn't where she had thrown it. The dish rack had been cleared. Was this really *her* home? It must have been her parents' doing. Or what if the Gardaí had sent someone to investigate their vanishing? While she and John were trapped in that forest, someone had come looking for them, studying her home like a crime scene, treading their dirty boots across her floor and touching things that didn't belong to them.

She had taken the phone from its station, still unsure as to what she would tell her parents, but she needed to hear their voices as much as they needed to know that their daughter was alive. Familiarity drew her to her corner of the couch; the last place she had sat. The child in her still hoped that her life would magically reset. John's head would peer around the doorway, offering to take her on some wonderful adventure to spice up their weekend. She would run into his arms and tell him that they most certainly were not. Ciara placed the phone down and eyed it like a bomb that she should have known better than to touch. She wasn't ready. There was peace there, in the silence, with John. And she wasn't willing to disturb it just yet.

Ciara took a long bath, misleading her thoughts with the pleasures she had promised herself. For over an hour she lay immersed in bubbling soap, woozy from fragrances that her nose had forgotten. Now and again the house would creak, and her eyes would snap open. No matter where her mind wandered, the watchers were there, standing around Danny atop that hill. How had they been so blind as to lose him? And why did he run back to the forest? Mina never told her what she had seen.

Her pyjama bottoms had warmed by the fire, and her woollen hoody hung open over her T-shirt. Her body didn't feel like her own. Her clean skin and its floral scent had to belong to someone else. Ciara looked towards the window, and to the darkness beyond it. Night had fallen. Without the coop's light to mark the end of the day, she hadn't noticed. She paced over and snapped the curtains closed. Never had so swift an act been so satisfying. She went about switching on the two tall lamps in opposing corners of the room. It was starting to seem a little more like home. Something that Danny never knew. What she wouldn't have given to have him with her now. Even during those weeks when she had shunned him – hating him for taking Madeline's side – he still offered her his food when he didn't have half enough to share. Whenever she left the coop, she suspected that he plumped up her blankets to make them comfier for her. He was always so kind, and so afraid. She was the one he came to if something was worrying him, and Daniel's worries followed him like a loyal dog, scratching at his legs when they didn't get enough attention.

On their last night, in the safe house, Mina had drifted off to sleep as Madeline sat at the desk, the hunch of her back concealing whatever she was doing. Danny had nudged in close to her, like brother and sister, sharing whispers in their room, trying not to disturb the adults. She always felt safer when he was beside her.

'What do you make of all that stuff about the watchers changing the way they look?' he had asked her, staring anxiously at Madeline in case she had heard him. 'I know that we never actually saw them, but do you believe all that?'

'I don't know,' she replied, shifting in against him and leaning her mouth to his ear. 'Maybe it's for the best that we try to forget about it. We have a long day tomorrow, Danny.

We're going home.' Here she gently elbowed him in the side. 'I bet you thought we'd never be saying that.'

'But what about the next person whose car breaks down here? Even if they find the coop, what use will it be to them now? How will they know what to do?'

'I don't know,' Ciara said, solemnly. 'At least we had Madeline to take care of us. I know we haven't always liked her way of doing things, but we're still alive, aren't we?'

'Do you know all those days when she would disappear?' Daniel asked. 'Where did she go?'

'I always thought she was showing you how to work the traps?'

'No,' he replied, speaking even lower now. 'I heard her telling you that a few times, but I wasn't with her. I don't know. I just always thought it was strange. I mean, why would she lie about it?'

'That's our Madeline.' She smiled, patting Danny on the thigh.

'Where do you think she really went?'

'I don't know,' Ciara replied.

'There was one day,' Daniel whispered, awkwardly kneading his hands together, 'when I was out preparing the traps. You know, looking for a good tree that I could climb. It was so quiet. I mean, there wasn't a sound, and I was listening, trust me.'

'It's always so quiet here,' Ciara put in, 'and cold.'

'Well, anyway, I turned around and there was Madeline, standing right there behind me. And I swear she wasn't there a second earlier. There's no way that she could have crept up on me that quickly and without me hearing her.'

'What are you saying, Danny?'

'It was like, I don't know,' he said, agitated now. 'It was like she just appeared. And there were burrows around there. Big ones. I saw them myself. What if Madeline goes underground?'

'Danny...'

'I know, I know,' he cut in, 'it's mad. It was just so bizarre. It wasn't like she had sneaked up on me. She was suddenly there, as surprised to see me as I was to see her. Not that you can ever really tell with Madeline, I suppose. Her face never seems to change.'

'Just the eyebrows,' Ciara added with a smile.

'Yeah,' he replied, 'and only to frown at us whenever we do something stupid, like talking or breathing.'

Ciara missed Danny so much. She'd never thought to tell the boy how much she loved him. No Danny. No John. Was life ever meant to be this cruel? Ciara looked to the mantel. The man that she loved was gone, and those memories were all that remained, interspersed with the horrors that she hoped someday to forget. If only he had stayed with her instead of seeking help. But any change to the past would have sent tremors through to the present. Would Daniel have snatched Madeline's key? If they never discovered Kilmartin's bunker, his message would have never been heard. They could still be sitting in the coop, none the wiser as to what secrets lay buried beneath it.

Why had Madeline left them during the night? Ciara was surprised by how much she missed her. In her own weird way, she had taken care of them; sweet as she was sour. Only you couldn't taste the sweetness. She had to be strict. Ciara had come to understand that. The rules were there to keep them alive. And as nasty as she could be, Ciara knew that she would never do them any actual harm. Every family has their oddball. It doesn't mean they aren't loved.

The two corner lamps suddenly lost power, leaving only the fire to fend off the shadows. The coop's nocturnal light had denied them such profound darkness. It was thick, as though Ciara could feel it in her lungs. It seemed to swarm around her, primed to swallow her up should the flames falter for a second.

'It's okay,' she whispered, more so to John than herself. 'It's probably just the fuse box.'

John had educated her in the ways of rectifying such a problem. It was actually quite simple, and yet when she had flicked the switches up to restore light, he had given her a high five like a master proud of his apprentice. Ciara didn't need any light to find her way, but in the darkness of the hallway she saw only black trees and even darker eyes. She listened, waiting for a scream that never came.

'We're home,' she mouthed as she hugged her body tighter. 'There's nothing to be afraid of here.'

Memories of John guided the shuffle of her slippers to the utility room beside the kitchen, where she knew he had left a torch for this exact predicament. It was the electrician's fault, apparently, and had been the only issue in their otherwise perfect home. She groped around for the torch, patting her hands over the corner shelf until she felt it. The pokiest room in the house was flooded in white light, making the prevailing darkness beyond its open door seem even more ominous. Ciara shone the torchlight over the fuse box, already reaching to pinch its switches. But they were all set in the correct positions that John had showed her.

'Any other ideas?' she whispered to him. 'Because that's all I got.'

Ciara returned to the sitting room where the flaming coals kept her company. She could feel the unease rising within her. As sore as the coop's light had been on her eyes, at least she always felt safe when it was on. Coming home alone was a bad idea. Where was Mina? Didn't she say she would come stay with her? Ciara sat on the edge of the couch, fanning the torchlight around the room, scattering the darkness into its corners, never letting it settle. She picked up the phone, deciding that now was the right time to call her parents. She stabbed its every button with her thumb, but the tone stayed the same. Hadn't John once told her that the electricity and the phone weren't connected to one another? How else would he have phoned his cowboy electrician that night when they lost power?

A bright light fanned across the curtain. Ciara listened as the front gate groaned open, and quick footsteps were heard sploshing through the chippings on the driveway. She shrank deeper into the couch. Somebody was out there, behind the glass. There was *always* something behind the glass.

'Ciara,' Mina's voice called out, 'it's me! Let me in!'

'Oh, thank God,' she muttered, holding her hand to her heart.

Such was her excitement that she almost fell out of her slippers as she lifted off the couch. As Ciara passed into the hallway the doorbell started to ring rapidly. Why did Mina have to make so much noise?

'I'm coming,' Ciara called out, skidding across the floor. Everything was going to be okay. Mina would know how to get the power back on. Or maybe she had brought Madeline with her. She was even sharper when it came to fixing things. Her smile fell as soon as the door opened; when she noticed the panic on Mina's face. She had the parrot in its cage on the front step. She really did take the yellow one everywhere she went.

'You're okay!' she said to Ciara, breathless, looking her up and down.

'Of course, I am. Mina, what's happened?'

The headlights panned across the wall and Mina turned back towards the taxi. It had already reversed on the road and was beginning to drive away. The parrot began to screech from all the commotion; a sound Ciara had secretly missed, like the familiar voice of an old friend.

'No, no, no,' Mina shouted, waving at the oblivious driver. 'Come back.'

'Mina,' Ciara said, waiting for her to calm down, 'what's wrong?'

'It's fine,' she replied, stepping inside with the cage. 'We can just call for another one. Are all of the doors locked?'

Ciara nodded. She had never seen Mina like this before, even during the worst of the woodland's horror. They *were* safe, weren't they? All she knew was that they certainly weren't calling for another taxi.

'You're *sure* that everything is locked?' Mina restated, holding Ciara by her shoulders.

'Yes,' she replied, feeling suddenly less certain. 'I locked all the doors before I took a bath.'

Mina rested her back against the door and looked around her. 'Why are all the lights off?' she asked, squinting against the torchlight.

'The power just went out,' Ciara replied. 'Tell me what's wrong, Mina?'

'It's Madeline,' she said.

'What about her?' Ciara asked. 'Did she come back?'

27

Mina

The taxi had rumbled down country roads so narrow that the driver had input Ciara's address a second time, doubting his all-knowing GPS. Its arrow didn't change, neither did the man's disbelief. The distance remained, with no lights ahead but the stars. Theirs was the only road on the screen; a testament to how far they had drifted from the shores of civilisation.

It all felt eerily familiar – the parrot on the back seat, the engine's hypnotic hum, the sheer absence of everything outside of the headlights. Mina couldn't keep from fidgeting. She had expected the car to die at any moment.

When eventually they reached Ciara's house and she saw it all in darkness, Mina assumed the worst. She panicked, thinking she was too late. She threw her money at the driver, snatched her parrot from the back seat and ran without even closing the door behind her. Of course he drove off. She would have done the same.

Ciara had led Mina into the sitting room, where the coals

still smouldered. She treated her like a patient, remarking how ghostly pale her face looked beside the fire. Ciara probably assumed that the loneliness had bested her, so inured had they become to each other's company. The truth was that Mina hadn't spoken because she didn't know where to begin. It almost felt cruel to tell her – to spoil their ending – but she needed to know.

Mina sat on the coffee table facing the fire while Ciara went around the house, lighting candles. She could hear her plodding up and down the stairs, pausing here and there, striking matches to wicks. The coals ticked quietly in their bed. The parrot was beside her, entranced by the amber glow glinting across its cage.

'You tried to tell me, didn't you?' Mina whispered to it.

Eventually Ciara returned, all smiles and energy, her slippers skating across the floor. She set two tea lights on the table and squeezed Mina's shoulder. The power cut didn't seem to faze her anymore. It almost seemed like a novelty to her now that she had company, a chance to huddle together by the fire. That would soon change.

'I need to tell you something,' Mina said, calmly as she could. 'It's about Madeline. You're not going to want to believe it, but you have to.'

'Did something happen to her?' Ciara asked, holding a hand to her lips with worry.

'No, it's nothing like that. I just need you to listen to me for a moment, okay?'

She sat on the floor in front of Mina like a child being read a bedtime story, her smile steadily dissolving as she listened, until only terror and disbelief remained. Mina told her everything, and Ciara listened without once interrupting.

Of that she was grateful. She didn't have the answers to her questions. All she had were fears and facts. As unimaginable as it was, somehow it made sense. *Madeline wasn't one of them*. She was something else. For months they had lived side by side with something else.

Ciara believed all that Mina had told her. That much was evident from the way she shivered beside the coals, sniffing as though she had caught the truth like an illness.

'Are all of the doors and windows locked?' Mina asked her again, only now the answer carried some consequence.

'Yes,' she whispered. 'Everything is locked.'

'When did the power go out?'

'Not long ago,' Ciara replied, 'maybe ten minutes before you arrived. Why? You don't think that Madeline...' The thought was enough to cut her short. 'We're safe in here,' she said as she reached for the brass poker on the hearth.

'What are you planning on doing with that?' Mina asked.

'I'm not sure.' Ciara shrugged, holding it like a toy sword. 'Do *you* want it?' she offered, holding it towards her.

Mina fanned it away. If only Ciara had seen her front door. Nothing could keep Madeline out. The coop had been designed to withstand her kind. Its glass was fortified. A bullet probably wouldn't break it. The door was heavy and lined with locks, and its walls were thick. Ciara's home was like any other. Every room had its windows, and all of them could shatter with no more than a snap of Madeline's fingers.

Mina's memories were of a woman. Despite her tenacity, she was malnourished and vulnerable, just like the rest of them. Madeline was forever tugging that blanket around her cold shoulders. Her joints creaked and cracked. The woman's skin was brindled with stains and blemishes, and her hair clung to her shoulders like wet silk. She was tall but she was weak, and in those moments when Mina would catch her staring at her own reflection in the glass, she even looked sad. She even looked human.

But what monstrous body had she hidden out of sight? How tall did she stand when that shawl was dropped from her shoulders? And could those long fingers spring claws?

Ciara gripped the poker in both hands, flexing her fingers around it. Did she honestly think that they stood a chance at stopping what was coming? Mina didn't have the heart to tell her. She would find out soon enough.

'Did you hear that?' Ciara's shrill voice whispered.

'Hear *what*?' Mina asked.

'Shush!' she replied, raising a finger, both eyes fixed on the curtains. 'There's someone outside. I just heard them step on the gravel. Didn't you hear it?' she asked. 'I swear I heard something.'

Mina hadn't heard anything. But this was Ciara's home. She knew its nuances – its spaces and sounds – and now wasn't the time to doubt the girl.

'She's here,' Mina whispered. 'Come on, quickly, upstairs.'

Ciara couldn't pry her attention away from the curtains. The glass behind them was thin, the kind that shakes in a storm. Even she could smash it. The horrible realisation dawned on her in the darkness – they weren't safe. Madeline was out there, somewhere. A watcher *had* followed them home.

The yellow one beamed at Mina as she stood up, roused by the prospect of being moved elsewhere, such was the theme to its day. But she couldn't take him with her. Not this time. The bird always screeched whenever Madeline approached it. They might as well ring a bell to announce where they were hiding.

'Keep an eye out for her,' Mina said softly, touching the bars of its cage. 'I'll be back soon.'

She gestured towards the torch that Ciara had picked up and shook her head. *No*, she was shouting without saying a word. *Don't you dare turn that on!*

During their escape from the forest, Madeline had demonstrated the keenness of her senses. She was the first to hear the river's distant flow, even before they had reached open land. She had heard the bus before it broke the horizon. No sound within the house would elude her, and no light would go unnoticed.

'Follow me,' Ciara whispered, and together they stole out of the room, much to the dismay of the yellow one watching them from the coffee table.

A jarred candle by the front door lit the way. Its cinnamon scent sang of the Christmas they had missed. Hot port in cold hands, and sparkling trees above every shop front. Atop the stairs, another wicked flame could be seen on the landing table. If the silence hadn't been so sacred, Mina would have praised Ciara for lighting so many. Without the candlelight they would both be bumbling around in the dark.

Ciara led the way. Her slippers touched each step with fitting care, as though their wood could crumble from the slightest press. Slow and steady was the order. Mina followed close behind. One step was followed by another. They counted maybe fifteen to the top. It was midway – on the seventh stair – that the most harrowing creak sounded. They both flinched and ceased their climb. The maple wood of that single step cried out in protest from the weight of Ciara's foot. She might as well have stepped on a cat's tail.

'Keep going,' Mina whispered, shooing Ciara upward, half-expecting the front door to blast in behind them.

Atop the stairs, Ciara steered them to the left. The high ceiling and wooden floors seemed to heighten the silence. Through their open mouths they breathed so lightly that they barely breathed at all. To the right was the candle on the landing table, its wax liquefied and warm. Shadows and shapes quivered across the walls like an oily, restless stream.

With the light behind them, they crept onward, towards the corridor's end, where the door to Ciara's bedroom was ajar, and through it – brooding ominously in the sky – Mina saw the moon. It was bright enough to distinguish a double bed amidst the dark, and the chest of drawers beside it, aligned by the window. They entered on the tips of their toes. Mina closed the door after them, stealing one last glance at the candle standing guard at the top of the stairs.

Ciara approached the window and peered outside. When Mina noticed her touting their whereabouts, she stormed over and whipped the curtains shut. She felt like snatching the poker from her hand and beating her over the head with it.

'What the fuck, Ciara!' she screeched in a high-pitched whisper. 'Keep away from the window.'

With the curtains closed, the dark was never so menacing. Their breathing – panicked and short – was too loud. The fear of making a sound made silence impossible. Their eyes searched hopelessly for a break in the black. But their blindness was absolute. Mina fumbled around for Ciara's hand. She seemed so far away, but then every step into the unknown was immeasurable. She pulled her towards her, fastening her fingers around her hoody, and together they sat on the edge of the bed, listening.

Time's meaning and purpose were forfeit. The second and the minute ceased to elapse, and there was instead the immovable present. There was no knowing how long they sat there, sweaty hands held, searching for some sound to betray what was to come. Could Madeline be reasoned with? Should Mina call out to her now, to plead with her for mercy? Then they heard her.

It was torturous to listen to – that rapid succession of scrapes and scratches, of a body scaling the side of the house. So quick was the action, so effortless. She had passed close by the window to Ciara's bedroom. For a heart-sinking second Mina thought she was angling her body towards it, that in the darkness she would find them, smashing inwards amidst a hail of glassy shards. But instead, she climbed higher.

Footsteps thudded across the slate roof. How could she be this heavy? And how could she be so strong? A shriek filled the sky; bone-chillingly identical to the watchers' cry. It was the same voice that Mina had heard so long ago, when her car had broken down, before she ran into Madeline's arms for safety.

'Oh God,' Ciara cried, to which Mina squeezed her hand tight.

Was Madeline really like those *things*, or did she yearn

to be human? Mina had seen her recoil from the watchers' stench. No matter what vile body churned beneath her disguise, maybe she no longer considered herself one of them – an exile and a changeling. What other possible reason could she have had for living amongst them as a human being?

The bird in the room below started to screech, the way it often did when Madeline was nearby. The cage could be heard lifting and tapping down on the coffee table. The poor thing was frantic. Mina willed it to quieten down, for its own sake. She knew now that she had done the right thing. If she had brought it with them, Madeline would know exactly where they were.

When the watchers besieged the coop, Mina had prayed for morning. The daylight had been their saviour and their guardian. But Madeline was the creature that gave the late professor cause to doubt his mind. Removed from the nocturnal shackles that bound her kind, she was free to face the sun. The morning wouldn't save them this time.

There was a sudden slam against the slates. Ciara bit down on her knuckles to keep the scream contained. Some tiles trickled down the roof, dancing like musical bones all the way to the gutter. Then there was an almighty smash of feet on the gravelled driveway below. Pebbles scattered like shrapnel, skipping off stone and glass. Whatever guise Madeline had assumed, she now scuttled towards the sitting room window. Was she listening with an ear pressed to the pane?

The bird fell quiet. Maybe it could sense that she was out there, as the fly feels the silver thread tingle from unseen legs. Upstairs, both bodies were as stone. Only the blood within them moved. The wooden floor had already proven itself untrustworthy. A single unlucky step – one creak, however delicate – would alert Madeline to their whereabouts.

Madeline would have seen the taxi's headlights from miles away and heard it even sooner. Mina wondered if she had finally smiled at the sight of her running to the front door; the only two people in the world who knew what she was, together, with nowhere to run.

The window shattered, spraying the room with grains of glass. Mina could only listen, imagining the scene below. The curtain hooks popped from their sockets and Madeline touched the floor, her neck twisting towards that which had snared her senses – the bird that stared defiantly from behind the bars of its cage. The glass was slow to settle, tinkling atop the wood like chimes. By the fire's ebbing glow, Madeline breathed in the scent of her prey; one she knew so well, one she had nurtured and protected. It was strongest by the coffee table, and led into the hallway, towards the stairs, where candlelight flickered from the draught of the open window frame.

Mina listened with mounting horror to the glass crunch beneath Madeline's feet. Sounds travelled unchecked through Ciara's home. It was possible that she already knew where they were. Although they strove for silence, Madeline's hearing was acute. It was a hunter's trait; inherent and honed.

She was coming. Escaping via the stairs wasn't an option. Mina eased herself off the bed, and gently drew the curtain aside. *Was there any other way?* The drop from the window was too high. All below was unforgiving stone. Ahead, the moonlight cast its cold sheen over the open country. Even if both of them landed like limber felines, with all bones intact, where could they possibly run to? Madeline would always catch them.

Ciara's nervous fingers touched the torch that she had left on the bed, resisting the urge to turn it on. Would it have made any difference at that stage? Madeline had them cornered. They concentrated on her footsteps across the maple floor, picturing her movements. She had entered the hallway downstairs, where the cinnamon candle burned in its jar. Was its scent fresh to her senses? Had she paused to breathe it in?

Mina and Ciara stared at each other in the moonlight of the room. Mina with a finger over her lips, safeguarding the silence, and Ciara with her mouth open, anticipating and dreading in equal measure whatever sound was to come next. Was she still there? There was no crackle of glass. There was only torment in the silence. The grim promise of the inevitable. *Don't come up,* Mina thought. *Don't come up.* Then she heard the creak of *that* step on the stairs. Madeline was already halfway there.

Ciara swung around to face the door. Her sweaty hands were shaking as they clutched the warm brass of the fire poker. Whatever was she going to do with it? This was a fight that they could never hope to win. Mina took the torch from the bed. There was no point in hiding in the dark anymore. Madeline was out there, at the far end of the corridor. Whatever her intentions towards them, Mina needed to see how she really looked. What was she without that mask?

'Stand back,' she said, stepping forward, tightening her fingers around the door handle.

'Are you sure about this?' Ciara asked, moving up behind her.

'Just let me talk to her. Maybe it doesn't have to be like this.'

Mina eased the door open, little by little, ready to slam it shut at any moment. For what it was worth, its laminate timber might buy them a few seconds. Standing in the hallway she saw Madeline's tall, blanketed silhouette, framed by candlelight; stoic, and staring from the darkness, as though she'd been waiting for her.

'Mina,' she said in her usual impassive voice, as if they were still sat side by side in the coop, 'I haven't seen you this scared since the night we met. It doesn't suit you.'

Mina had expected to be met with a monster – the kind that races up walls, all claws and snarled teeth. But it was just Madeline. Strands of hair hung like fine mist from her skull, and though her face was lost to the dark, it was always the same. It was the skeleton within the cloth that Mina couldn't imagine. She had seen them at a distance, that night they had made their escape, with only the moonlight to betray the truth behind their horrific form. Could Madeline really be like them?

'I see you've taken over responsibility of caring for Ciara,' she added. 'I suppose someone had to.'

Ciara nudged in behind Mina, her breathing fast and heavy. *Stay,* she thought. *Stay where you are.* What the hell was she doing?

'I do hope you don't intend on using that,' Madeline said. 'Yes, *I can see you.* I'm surprised you have survived this long without me.'

As Mina suspected, she could see despite the darkness.

Nocturnal creatures have all the luck. The advantages were hers to hold. Cornered and blind, it was a wonder that Madeline hadn't killed them already.

'You don't have to do this,' Mina said. 'We won't tell anyone. I promise.'

'Maybe *you* won't. You were always the strongest of the three. To be honest, Mina, I thought you knew. The way you used to watch me, always studying my face as though I had let it change quite by accident.'

'I knew you were lying about something,' Mina said, pressing her weight into Ciara to keep her steady. 'But everybody tells lies, Madeline. Maybe the professor *taught* you how.'

'He taught me so much,' she replied, her words evincing the softest sorrow.

Her pensiveness came to Mina as some surprise. She had never contemplated how Kilmartin and Madeline had interacted. Regardless of who was watching who, how close could they have come with a wall of reinforced glass between them?

'I watched those men toil away,' she continued, 'carving their path through the forest. Their machines all fell silent, and so they worked the animals to the bone. At first, I thought they brought war to us. Unprovoked contest after such a prolonged spell of peace. But no, I was mistaken. They knew nothing of what was beneath them. All those eyes in the dark, divided by a few feet of soil, listening to the havoc above, waiting. Not only were we banished, Mina. We were also forgotten.

'I watched Kilmartin crawl into his cell as the dusk darkened in the sky. More men came each day, like offerings.

Fearless, innocent lambs primed for the slaughter. And the professor met them with a smile. He shook each of their hands. He thanked them for travelling so far. They worked deeper, digging ugly scars through the earth – *our* earth – until he called on them to stop. The pit was dug, and the container was buried. Cement was poured on deep. Walls were built. Glass was locked in place. I knew when their labour had finished because the peace returned. The last men were abandoned to the night. Some of them hammered on the hatch, thinking that their employer was hiding from his debt owed to them. They soon learned what it was he hid from.

'We learned fast, he told us. Like infants, we absorbed everything. He taught us how to change. He gave us back that which we had forgotten. But it didn't change *them*. They loathed the very sight of him. He was their prisoner, and their plaything. And they would never let him leave.'

'You speak like you're not one of them,' Mina interrupted.

'That's because *I'm not*,' Madeline snapped back. 'The daylight doesn't burn my skin. I don't spend my days buried underground. Can you possibly fathom how long I walked that place alone?'

'So, you didn't kill the professor?'

'I played no part in his death,' she replied. 'I urged them to spare him. He still had so much to teach us. But it made no difference. By the end, Kilmartin craved death more than anything else. Escape was impossible. His injuries were too severe. And the means in which they bedevilled the man – distorting his love's likeness – it broke him utterly, and completely.

'I watched him every day, Mina, but I didn't approach

him. Not once. I could imitate only two faces – that of his wife, and his own. The poor man was fearful enough during the night without losing his days.

'It was Kilmartin who wrote on the wall, the same day he stood by the middle frame, waiting for the night, watching the forest around him darken for the last time. He had committed to his death long before the deed was done. *Stay in the light.* I believe he wrote that for me. He knew I was watching him. And so, I did just that. I lived as he did, above ground, in the home that he built for me.'

Madeline let that thought linger. The coop was hers – a gift from its architect. She had always treated them like unwelcome guests. Now they knew why. Though Mina saw it as a prison, it was Madeline's home; the only one she'd ever known.

'You knew about the safe house all along,' Mina said. 'You're the one who sealed it.'

'The professor taught me how to be human,' she replied. 'Why should I suffer under the earth like the others? It was his wish that I live in the light, Mina. I buried my memories of him in that tomb. Safe until the day you discovered it, when you awoke the machines and showed me his last request.'

Madeline hadn't seen the professor's recording until they had all stood around her in the safe house. She was from a different time, oblivious to the technologies that Kilmartin had left behind him. No wonder she buried the room. It was evidence of everything she was not; a constant reminder that she wasn't human.

'You went to the university today, Mina,' she stated as fact. 'I trust that the professor's research has been destroyed?'

'You followed me?'

'Answer the question, Mina?' she pressed impatiently.

That's why Madeline had come for them – to eradicate all artefact and memory of the watchers' existence. And this was the only reason they were still alive.

'If Kilmartin's papers were gone,' she replied, 'then we'd be the last loose end, wouldn't we?'

No response. The candlelight burned behind Madeline's silhouette, and she moved not an inch.

'I knew you were smarter than the others,' she said eventually. 'Always searching for answers to questions you couldn't understand, and constantly scheming in that book of yours. I thought you were going to present a problem for me.'

'Then why didn't you do it?' Mina asked.

'Why didn't I do *what*, Mina?'

'Kill me,' she replied. 'It's not as though you didn't have your chances.'

During those bleak months when they had suffered side by side, Madeline could have taken any of their lives. But she never raised a hand against them. Their shortcomings evoked in her only a sense of disappointment, not violence. Madeline had trained them how to survive, like pets, and Mina knew that without her guidance they would never have escaped that place.

'You took care of us, Madeline,' she said when no response came. 'You're the reason we're still alive.'

The black silhouette didn't move, and yet Mina heard bones splitting, like cracks racing through thin ice. Only when it ceased did Mina realise where it had come from. She turned on the torch, gripping it in both hands to keep it steady, and shone it towards Madeline's face. But it wasn't Madeline's face anymore.

Her skin shone – creamy and unblemished – in the torchlight. The face was the perfect heart shape. It always seemed so ordinary in the mirror. Pedestrian, like an extra in a movie. The eyes looked as sad as ever, and that was without the eyeliner. The lips still didn't work. No surprises there. Smiling for Mina had always been difficult. For Madeline it was impossible. Had it not been for the limp hair that trailed by her ears, the imitation could have passed for perfection.

'I needed to study you,' Madeline said in a voice that was indistinguishable from Mina's.

She was chilled to the spot. The white light from the torch fluttered across the walls. Mina's hands couldn't keep it focused. The face that she had deemed worthless to the artist had been stolen. Compared to the mask that Madeline had worn for months on end it appeared, in that instant, beautiful. She wanted it back, appreciating it only now that another had taken it from her.

'Don't worry,' Madeline said. 'I have no interest in being *you*, Mina. I can change any aspect of your face that I so please.'

Mina's legs nearly gave way. It was all too much. Fear, anger, and sadness had been stirred together so violently that she wasn't sure how she felt anymore. She was just drained and defeated. The voice, the appearance – Mina was talking to a mirror image of herself, but her copycat didn't speak as she did. Madeline would always be Madeline, no matter what face she wore or what voice she spoke in.

'I was content to stay in the forest,' she said. 'My home

was there. And during the day there was peace. But when I saw Kilmartin's recording, and heard his last wish, then I knew what had to be done. So, I'll ask you again, Mina, and this time you would be wise to answer me. Has his research been destroyed?'

Ciara's breathing was growing more laboured behind Mina's shoulder. She could hear her knuckles cracking as she wound them around the poker. Mina pressed her hands against either side of the doorframe, blocking her in. Whatever she was planning, it wasn't a good idea.

'And what happens to us?' Mina asked. 'What if I told you that all of his maps and writings were gone? Would you...'

Ciara suddenly barged her way into the corridor, colliding Mina against the wall and slipping the torch from her fingers. Its light died to the sound of batteries skidding across the wooden floor. Ciara's sudden charge had caught her by surprise, and she was out of her reach before Mina realised what she was doing.

She had never witnessed this side of her. In lieu of the kindliness that defined Ciara's every thought and action, there was only grief and anger; two devils that Mina had encountered before. It was the loss of John and Daniel, and the realisation that Madeline could have saved them, but instead did nothing. She could have sought out John and brought him back to her. She could have raced to Daniel and pleaded with her kind to let the boy live. Everything that Madeline had done to blend in with humankind proved her undeserving of the species, and Ciara wouldn't rest until this watcher shared her pain.

Before the light of a single flame, Ciara raised the poker

above her shoulder. A few quick, blind steps had brought Madeline within her reach, and she was primed to strike. But the bray of her voice was cut short. Her weapon fell clattering to the floor as Madeline's long arm extended, and her hand seized Ciara by the throat. The shawl slipped from her shoulders. Delineated by the candlelight, Mina watched as her silhouette lengthened, unfolded into its true form, and she pinned Ciara against the wall, leaving her feet flailing.

'Madeline!' Mina screamed. 'Don't hurt her!'

Ciara choked and spluttered, trying to pry Madeline's fingers open. One arm – sinewy and stretched – held her aloft. Her strength was monstrous. It was as though Ciara weighed nothing.

'Please, Madeline,' Mina said, taking a step forward, 'don't hurt her.'

She jerked Ciara even higher, her limbs seemingly able to stretch on command. It was too dark to discern Madeline's face. But her profile against the candlelight was unrecognisable. There was little to no trace of a nose protruding. The jaw almost seemed to expand, if only to contain the teeth that sprouted like nails from her mouth.

'You don't have to be one of them,' Mina shouted.

Madeline's head turned to face Mina. Ciara's legs hung, dangling above the floor. The life was being choked out of her. The hellish body that bound her was unmoving.

'Please,' Mina said, moving even closer, her arms held aside in surrender. 'Just let her go.'

Ciara's feet had kicked off the wall as she fought hopelessly to free herself. But she was fading, turning limp as she gasped for air but found only Madeline's gnarled fingers locked around her throat.

'It's done,' Mina shouted, fearing for Ciara's life. 'I burned Kilmartin's papers. They're all gone! And you have my word, we won't tell anyone! You don't have to kill her. Please, Madeline! I don't have anybody else! *We* don't have anybody else!'

Madeline threw Ciara to the floor. Her head and shoulders bore the brunt of the impact, and in the ill light of the hallway she came to lie like a pile of bones; unconscious or dead, she wasn't moving. Madeline's attention now turned to Mina. She strode towards her, stopping so close that their faces were inches apart, eyes locked, though only one could see in the absence of light. Madeline's spine was arched. Her arms, like a mantis, flanked Mina on either side; elongating through the shadows to the sickly sound of splitting bone. *Please, make it quick,* Mina thought as she heard Madeline's claws grow from her bony, branchlike fingers.

'You're just as scared as we are,' Mina said, tears now streaming down her cheeks. 'None of us belonged in that place, Madeline. I know you think that the coop was your home but it wasn't. *This* is a home! And if Kilmartin cared for you at all he wouldn't want you there, always angry and alone.'

The cracking of Madeline's bones loudened. Were her arms stretching around her like a spider draws in the fly. The darkness was a gift. Mina didn't want to see what Madeline had become.

'You should never have left us,' she continued. 'We're in this together. Isn't that what we said?'

The darkness receded slightly as Madeline's arms shrank back. Mina expected, with each passing second, to die; to feel that hand fasten around her neck, or the swift slice of a claw through skin. She thought of Ciara's wooden floor. Would the blood pool around her, or would it reach the stairway and wash like a waterfall all the way to the front door?

'If you're going to kill me,' Mina said, breathing through the tears, 'then hurry up and fucking do it. *Or* you can stop being one of *them* and go back to being one of *us*.'

Madeline jumped back with such force that the whole house seemed to quake. The candle's flame was extinguished, its hot wax splashing on the table, leaving the corridor in darkness. The sight of her silhouette had fleeced Mina of faculty. But knowing what stood before her and being unable to see it was somehow even more mentally destructive. Madeline's presence was exposed only by the delicate crepitation of her bones. Mina edged away, until both hands felt the doorframe.

'Is Ciara okay?' she asked.

'She's alive,' was Madeline's reply, sounding like her human self again.

Madeline could have snapped her neck if she so pleased. Then why hadn't she?

'What happens to us now?' Mina said.

In that dark, suspended moment she waited for an answer. As complex as it may have seemed, it was a simple case of life or death; compassion or cruelty – human traits that Madeline could only mimic.

'Keep your promise,' she said.

'We will,' Mina replied.

She listened as Madeline descended the stairs. One step creaked halfway down. Her feet crunched over broken glass. The door's single lock opened, and she was gone.

MARCH

28

Life was similar in some aspects to what Mina remembered. Sights and sounds mostly. Some memories felt redundant now, as though they belonged to somebody else. *That* Mina was the reflection in the glass. And *that* Mina wasn't the one who made it home. The woman who walked into the forest and the one who fell out its south side were two different people.

Mina's first steps were tenuous and uncertain, like a child learning to walk. She fell so many times. She had hidden away for days on end, enslaved by that crawling suspicion that the watchers' eyes still followed her every move. But these days became weeks, and little by little she found her footing, steadying herself on Ciara for support, reclaiming the life that the forest had taken from her. Mina's mum had wanted her to be happy, and she was the only one watching over her now.

A spring shower had splashed the table clean around midday. There were no hand-rolled cigarettes slotted head down, with their legacy of ash staining the ceramic.

Not even a few crooked butts. Mina hadn't revisited that particular habit. The forest had taken so much. It could keep her cigarettes. Her sister would have to focus the criticisms on her drinking and supposedly deluded career choices. She remembered the street so well, where she used to sit and sketch, always searching for the beauty in other people but never seeing it in herself.

The sun hit her like a spotlight. She fumbled in her jacket pocket for her sunglasses. Their lenses were grazed from falling off her face whenever she looked down. Not once did she manage to catch them. Mina couldn't keep her foot from twitching. The horrors of the woodland were parasitic. She could feel them crawling through her thoughts even now, in the daytime, as she forced her mind to stamp them out. But they never went away. Every day they would reassemble anew, and every day she would try again.

The coop's mirror always occupied some corner of her mind. And the reflection of her past self would always be there, watching her. Mina's fears weren't nocturnal, and they certainly hadn't stayed behind in the forest. Try as she might to fit in, to sit outside the pub like everyone else, each day was a struggle. The eyes still wandered, led by that enduring curiosity to watch the world around her, but those faces that once inspired her hands to sketch only caused them to tremble. Even now, the din of the voices gathered like a storm on the street; violent and expanding. She would glance and she would look away, and that was enough for now. But still her fingers itched to hold a pencil again. The parasite hadn't chewed into that part of her brain yet.

Like actors waiting off stage for their mark, the city strollers returned when the clouds spread apart in long loosely knitted sheets. Ruts of rainwater glistened between the cobbles, snaring the sunlight and blinding those walking west. Mina's eyes fell somewhere around her shoes as she pressed her sunglasses onto her nose for the umpteenth time. She crossed her legs tight to steady her feet.

Layers, Mina's mother once told her, *are the key to spring dressing.* She had thrown a denim jacket over her purple hoody. The nest atop her head had been pruned. It had to go. Mina's options were limited, but the pixie cut suited her. The woman who operated on her head like a world-class surgeon was of the opinion that Mina had the perfect face for it.

The pub's wicker chairs dried fast in a breeze. What with their rickety legs and the causewayed street, they rocked back and forth when the real wind picked up. The tables were no better. Mina had seen too many glasses slide off and smash to the ground; followed, always, by mortifying applause. It would only be a matter of minutes before people sat down for coffees and pints, seizing the clemency that could abandon them at any moment. For Mina, the open sky was the greatest novelty. The absence of black branches overhead gave her good reason to keep her chin up.

'Well,' she whispered to herself, forcing her eyes to look around her, 'this isn't so bad now, is it?'

A cluster of tourists – all ponchos and rain jackets – had gathered in the centre of the street, where a decidedly German-looking chap with fair hair and a square face as serious as a cinder block regurgitated historical titbits that he had probably memorised on the flight over. His audience huddled around him like sheep to a shepherd, blocking the local few who had places to be.

Mina had yet to take a sip of her wine. She eyed it like a former lover, caressing its stem, resisting its advances. Coffee, black and bitter, was what she came for. But Peter wouldn't hear of it. He had met her arrival with stunned disbelief; both hands seizing the bar for support as that tawny, shark smile spread over his face. And Peter was sober. Some things obviously *had* changed in Mina's absence. Their hug lasted long enough for her to be hopelessly immersed in the mustiness of his wax jacket.

Where had she been? It wasn't too removed from the truth to say that she had been away. What else could she tell him? Peter threw his head back with laughter when Mina offered to buy the bird. Judging by his reaction, he had to think for a moment to fathom what she was talking about.

'Jesus, Mina.' He laughed. 'You can keep him. I'm sure Tim's forgotten all about that by now. You never found the buyer's home? Didn't I give you a map, or did I not?'

'That's a longer story than you'd think,' she answered honestly.

'There's nothing out that side of the world,' he replied. 'A few sheep, I suppose. I'm glad you're back to us.' He grinned, roping his arm around her shoulder. 'Let me get you a drink.'

She didn't blame Peter for what had happened to her. It was nobody's fault. Bad things happen every day, and Mina would just have to learn to live with it. She was one of the lucky ones. She had been given a second chance at life.

The pub was exactly as Mina remembered. She couldn't contain her smile when the door sprang closed behind her. The din of cars and chattering schoolboys was silenced; refused at the door. In their stead was the low hum of music and mellow conversation. Smoky light slipped through the panelled windows, and the air was flavoured with coffee beans and steam from the soup cauldron simmering on the counter. The same bodies hunched over the same pints, having the same conversations that Mina could join and abandon as she pleased. Not yet. But hopefully soon. She just needed time.

The window's alcove in Mina's apartment – where she used to sit like a cloistered monk wilfully divorced from the dangers below – was bequeathed to the yellow one. The pigeons now flocked to its sill, stealing sideways glances at Galway's latest exotic addition. Its new cage was twice the size of the old one, with dispensers for food and water that Mina kept filled to the brim. No more berries. No more nuts. The little guy ate the expensive parrot food; the stuff that smelled absolutely horrendous.

Mina had left home without her sketchbook that day. Even though she still couldn't focus on anything creative – like a needle skipping off a record – its absence made her anxious, like a warrior without her shield. Her hands still toyed with a phantom pencil but gone were the days of searching the street for those *perfect* faces. Mina was wary to study them too closely. She knew the tell-tale signs to look for, and her eyes were sharp as ever.

How many of them, she wondered, still believed in *fairies*? Even the most incredulous adults were kids once upon a time. The word alone conjured up sparkling notions of winged *Tinker Bells*, inspiring joy and wonder wherever their magic took them. How would they react if Mina told them the truth? She would be defined by a single, socially incriminating idea. No, for the sake of a simpler life it was best not to play the girl who thought that fairies were evil, although the role had come so naturally to her.

The tables were aligned by the wall of the pub. Its blue paint shimmered with an ocean's gloss beneath a sky that was being unusually kind for the month of March. Every chair, with no single exception, faced towards the street. Behind her sunglasses – shelved between people on both sides – Mina felt invisible. She almost felt safe. Even her feet had calmed down.

The other chair at Mina's table was empty. There was a time when she would have certainly thrown a scarf or some similar deterrent on it, just in the off chance that, God forbid, someone might make a move to sit down beside her. But not on this day. Mina was determined, however reluctant, to stay outdoors. The yellow one was perfectly happy on his own, and the sky held a crystal ocean. She had to put herself out there. That's what her mum would have wanted.

Every face that caught Mina's eye made her wish she had brought that sketchbook – the fresh hardback one she had picked up way back in December. Was she finally ready to draw again? All those crisp untouched pages were calling to her. She examined both sides of a beermat. It was far too busy to draw on. Her fingers were starting to fidget. Every artistic bone in her hand ached to put the nightmares down on paper, to purge them from her thoughts the only way she knew how. Her mind's eye was pinned and forced to suffer an endless cycle of memories. The more she tried to block them out, the faster they flashed through her head, explosions of blood and glass.

Her toes squirmed in her boots at the thought of that inky,

gritty sludge that leaked like sewerage through the earth. She could taste the cement as though it had dispersed an invisible powder that had settled forever on her tongue. No manner of brushing could scrape it off. Bright lights made her nervous. The dark nights were worse. Sketching the coop wouldn't be difficult. Charcoal on white paper could capture all its colours. But then she always thought of Madeline, and the promise she had made to her. There would be no evidence of what they went through, not even a doodle.

She met with Ciara every week, sequestering the spare bedroom from a gang of teddy bears that John had given her. There was talk of selling her house. But Mina knew that the good memories far outweighed the bad ones, and Ciara would guard those until the end. She was still the only person she felt genuinely comfortable with. There was no pressure to talk or to act like someone else; she could just be herself. And Ciara didn't judge her when she arrived at the door each time with a bottle of wine. Their experiences and the secrets they shared would keep them from ever straying apart. And they spoke of John and Daniel often. The wounds would never heal, of course. But whereas the mention of their names once brought tears, they now made them both smile. They handpicked their fondest memories from the past and buried the bad ones as best they could. Neither of them had seen Madeline since that night. They each had their notions as to where she might be. Ciara thought that she would have returned to the woodland, to restore the home that Kilmartin built for her. But Mina doubted that. They just hoped that wherever she was, she was happy and had finally found her place in the world.

The sun soared as though some otherworldly hand had

turned the heat up to ten. It blistered in a sky so clear that it was actually hot against Mina's cheeks. She closed her eyes, savouring each second. She had forgotten how it felt – the sun, happiness, safety. The more that people around her remarked on how wonderful it was the more convincing it became, and almost believable, that summer had skipped over spring. But the days were short. The shade would spread across the street, from the pub to the jeweller's, swallowing up the cobbles in its cold. Some thought it wise to leave their homes in short-sleeved tops. Regret would race up their bare arms as gooseflesh, making all those sunny smiles chatter.

Jennifer had answered her phone with the cool nonchalance that Mina had expected. If her sister had been worried about her, then she refused to let her voice express it. She dreaded that call. Jennifer was the only close family she had left, and yet there had never been any palpable closeness between them. Not even as children. Her mum always joked about how different they were. But now that she was gone, the joke just wasn't funny anymore.

'I tried calling you at Christmas,' Jennifer had said. 'I thought maybe there was one day in the year that you might want to talk to your sister.'

'I wanted to,' Mina replied, fighting back a flash-flood of tears. 'Honestly, you've no idea how much I wanted to. But I just couldn't. I was…' she hesitated, conceding to the lie '…in a strange place.'

'That's not even an excuse,' she snapped back. 'That's just you, always doing your own thing and to hell with the rest of us. I promised Mum that I'd look out for you – did you know that?'

'Is that why you call me? Because Mum asked you to.'

'Why else would I bother?' she said. 'Do you think I don't have my own life, Mina, without trying to fix yours? Jesus, you're so self-absorbed.'

Never had a scolding awoken such a dizzying sense of déjà vu. Every missed call had planted another seed of guilt in Mina's heart, and she had let them grow, thinking – or perhaps hoping – that her sister hounded her out of love. Mina needed fixing more than ever, but Jennifer wasn't the one to seal up the cracks. She never was. That was the last time they had spoken.

Someone stepped in front of the sun, draining the day of light, and lingered across from Mina's table. She didn't turn her head. It was best not to invite conversation. Maybe after her glass of wine she would consider it, but that wasn't likely. It was still too soon. But even a staid exchange about the weather would be enough to convince Mina that she had made the effort. She still felt like a caterpillar crawling amidst the social butterflies, trying to fit in.

'Is this seat taken?' a man asked.

Mina's face was still set towards the street, not wanting to meet him face on. She guessed from the voice that he was maybe sixty years old. Irish, but not local, with a light rasp to his words; his throat and lungs were probably piecing themselves back together after a lifetime of hard cigarettes.

'It's all yours,' she said, fixing her glasses in place lest her defences should slide off her nose.

The brakes of a bicycle moaned loud enough to turn every head in the vicinity. Mina jumped forward in her seat but played it off as a twitch from the cold, rubbing her hands frantically together to convince anyone who might have seen her. Even those ensconced in newspapers and paperbacks lifted their eyes. The cyclist seemed oblivious to the bodies that washed on either side of him like shoals of fish. He rested his arms on the handlebars and stood, one foot on a pedal, the other on the ground, casually chatting to some friends; all small talk and big smiles. The blockage on the street was instantaneous, like food caught in a windpipe. The slighter ones weaved and slipped through. Most stopped in their tracks; an epidemic of impatience spreading amongst them. Mina could see it across all their faces, a frivolous distemper that made her smile. To think that this was the worst thing that had happened to them that day.

Every head bobbing amidst that sea of shoulders was making headway in some direction, and it was this direction alone that held their interest. All, that is, with exception of one. She was taller than the rest. Mina recognised her immediately. The face's proportions were as perfect as she remembered, just as she had drawn them. The skin was sleek as plastic. It was *the android*, and she was staring directly at Mina; expressionless, and altogether indifferent to the comings and goings around her. Mina gripped the arms of her chair for anchorage, as the sight of her induced a sudden, fearful weakness. It was as though Mina was the only other person on the street that day, so focused was the woman's attention upon her.

'Madeline?' she whispered as she lifted the sunglasses from her nose.

Mina's sore eyes reeled against their sudden exposure, and when they regained focus the woman was gone. Evening's early shadows had begun to peel down the wall.

Though still under the sun's guardianship, Mina pulled her hood over her head, suddenly cold, her jaw clenched, fingers fidgeting. Every face now seemed insidiously sinister, all posing some veiled design against her. Mina's unease must have shown.

'Are you okay?' the man seated at the table asked her.

Mina turned sharply. He wasn't as old as she had earlier speculated from his voice. The face put him in his early fifties, and despite its seriousness, it was quite handsome; rugged features ripped out of a comic book, but now lined and loose from a life's adventuring. He wore a long, big-fitting coat; charcoal grey, a shade or two lighter than his hair.

'Yes,' she replied as she stood, hands shaking as they placed the sunglasses back on her nose, legs weak. 'I'm fine, thank you.'

Mina was not ready for this. These weren't the shallow waters that she and Ciara had discussed – their soft reintroduction to society. This was the deep end. Mina wasn't *fine, thank you*. She was drowning. And on that street, beleaguered by dizzying waves of faces and bodies, the dark waters were rising.

Mina's first thought was to get out of there – to run home, to lock her door, to hide. She stepped awkwardly over the man's long legs and walked with her head down, averting her eyes from anyone who might be looking at her, for they could each of them be Madeline. The sunglasses slipped from her nose and cracked off the ground. One of the lenses popped out and skimmed across the cobbles. She kept moving.

'Let me get that for you,' the man called after her.

'No,' Mina said, waving him away, flustered, 'please, just leave them.'

For months she had studied Madeline, trying to read what she was thinking. *The android's* face evinced the same qualities – the intensity of the eyes, those inert features so dispassionate that they insinuated no definable emotion. But Mina had seen this woman before. Madeline must have mirrored her appearance. There was no other explanation.

It has to be her, she repeated to herself in muttered panic. *It has to be her.* Had Madeline been watching Mina without her knowing? She stopped and turned, tempted in the confusion of that second to run back and find her. Madeline might have sought Mina out for help. They had all kept their mouths shut. There was no reason to be afraid.

'No, Meens,' she said, catching her breath. 'Go home and call Ciara.'

But she hesitated. Some part of her wanted to talk to Madeline. She couldn't keep running from the past. So, Mina stood, scanning the crowd for that face, just like she used to. People were milling around the street, going about their own business, paying no heed to Mina's. And then she saw her. Standing at the end of the street from where she had just come, taking no measures to conceal her interest in Mina, was *the android*. It was the expression – or the lack of one – that could only be Madeline's.

The shadows cast their black limbs down from roofs of moss-ceiled slate, where gulls and crows kept their distance, watching with wary eyes the one who didn't belong. Bereaved of sunlight, the street was now deathly cool. Smells and flavours are said to spark old memories.

For Mina it was the cold, the darkness, and that fear she knew all too well.

She had tried to bury it deep in the back of her mind. But the friable soils of her subconscious broke easily, and the memories wouldn't rest. They would always claw to the surface. Peace would never come unless Mina seized it for herself, and so she took the first step forward, her gaze set on the mask that was, to all but the birds, so terribly convincing.

'I see you, Madeline,' she said, the words shivering between her lips.

There were people everywhere. Madeline would never break character with so many witnesses. Mina was safe in the company of her own kind, though their number had lessened. What could she possibly have wanted? And why appear now after so long?

'Okay, Meens. It's just a talk. She needs your help, that's all.'

Mina stopped. Another had come to stand shoulder to shoulder with *the android*. She had dark hair styled short by her ears, with a face uniform and pretty. No feature was too weak or prominent, but she was tall. Both women stared at Mina with the same chilling vacancy.

She felt a hand grip her shoulder. Mina turned, startled and flushed with fear, and was met by the man who had sat across from her earlier. He was taller than she had first thought.

'Mina,' he said. 'You can't stay here.'

'Who are you?' she asked, swiping his hand away.

But she knew. Despite the masculine tenor of the voice,

there was no mistaking who it was. It was in the eyes, and those myriad nuances that betrayed no hint of emotion.

'Madeline?' Mina said in disbelief.

'I was wrong. I thought I was the only one.'

'What do you mean?' she asked, backing away.

'You're not safe here anymore. They're everywhere, Mina. They've been watching you.'

STAY IN THE LIGHT

A.M. SHINE

The nightmare is only just beginning...

After her terrifying experience at the hands of the Watchers, Mina has escaped to a cottage on the west coast of Ireland. She obsessively researches the Watchers, desperate to find any way to prolong the safety of humankind.

When Mina encounters a stranger near her home, she fears the worst – for she knows the figure is not what it seems. She soon discovers her elderly landlords have disappeared. But someone – something – is inhabiting their home...

Mina knows the Watchers' power is growing. She flees for her life... but when she reports her fears to the police, she finds her sanity questioned.

Mina must convince staff at the psychiatric hospital where she is taken that her stories of malevolent beings are not fantasy but fact – but that will soon be the least of her troubles...

A chilling modern twist on the Gothic horror novel, perfect for fans of Kealan Patrick Burke, T. Kingfisher and classic horror.

Reviews for A.M. Shine

'One of our great authors, particularly in the literary horror genre.' **RTE1**

'A dark, claustrophobic read.' **T. Kingfisher**

'An intimate glimpse into the fraying edges of each character's psyche.' **Booklist**

'Horror fiction is teeming with great boogiemen and *The Creeper* ranks with the very best of them.' **Horror DNA**